"You don't have spells in this world, right?" asked Cindella.

"What are you talking about?" Carter was furious, his anger driven by fear. It was one thing to be in prison for a bit of spray painting, but being associated with the murder of a cop was a terminal offense.

"No, I guess not. Here, then, you'd better drink some of this." Cindella passed around a semi-transparent flask that seemed to be made of thousands of emeralds. "It's invisibility potion."

"Great." The others looked on with disbelief but I took my swig with confidence. They hadn't seen those lasers bounce off her.

"Whoa!" Nathan jumped back, staring at me. "She's gone."

Being invisible was sweet. Even better was to walk out through a cordon of armed police, while their guns were trained on the station door. What a giddy feeling. This was truly punk.

FIREBIRD
WHERE SCIENCE FICTION SOARS™

SAGA

CONOR KOSTICK

FIREBIRD
AN IMPRINT OF PENGUIN GROUP (USA) INC.

FIREBIRD
Published by the Penguin Group
Penguin Group (USA) Inc., 345 Hudson Street, New York, New York 10014, U.S.A.
Penguin Group (Canada), 90 Eglinton Avenue East, Suite 700,
Toronto, Ontario, Canada M4P 2Y3 (a division of Pearson Penguin Canada Inc.)
Penguin Books Ltd, 80 Strand, London WC2R 0RL, England
Penguin Ireland, 25 St Stephen's Green, Dublin 2, Ireland
(a division of Penguin Books Ltd)
Penguin Group (Australia), 250 Camberwell Road, Camberwell, Victoria 3124, Australia
(a division of Pearson Australia Group Pty Ltd)
Penguin Books India Pvt Ltd, 11 Community Centre, Panchsheel Park,
New Delhi - 110 017, India
Penguin Group (NZ), 67 Apollo Drive, Rosedale, North Shore 0632, New Zealand
(a division of Pearson New Zealand Ltd)
Penguin Books (South Africa) (Pty) Ltd, 24 Sturdee Avenue, Rosebank,
Johannesburg 2196, South Africa

Registered Offices: Penguin Books Ltd, 80 Strand, London WC2R 0RL, England

First published by The O'Brien Press Ltd., Dublin, 2006
Published in agreement with The O'Brien Press Ltd.
First published in hardcover in the United States of America by
Viking Children's Books, a division of Penguin Young Readers Group, 2008
Published by Firebird, an imprint of Penguin Group (USA) Inc., 2009

1 3 5 7 9 10 8 6 4 2

THE LIBRARY OF CONGRESS HAS CATALOGED THE VIKING EDITION AS FOLLOWS:
Kostick, Conor.
Saga / by Conor Kostick.
p. cm.
Summary: On Saga, a world based on a video role-playing game, fifteen-year-old
Ghost lives to break rules, but the Dark Queen who controls Saga plans to
enslave its people and that of New Earth, and Ghost and her airboarding
friends, along with Erik and his friends from Epic, try to stop her.
ISBN 978-0-670-06280-5
[1. Fantasy games—Fiction. 2. Role playing—Fiction. 3. Video games—Fiction.
4. Kings, queens, rulers, etc.—Fiction. 5. Science Fiction.] I. Title.
PZ7.K85298Sag 2008 [Fic]—dc22 2007032175

Firebird ISBN 978-0-14-241422-4

Printed in the United States of America

to Andrew

CONTENTS

SAGA

All motion ceased. A Communication-Assassination probe gradually awoke from a dream in which it had been submerged far beneath deep arctic waters. Barely ten million kilometers away, a star was blazing with uncomfortable brightness. The probe slid filters over its sensors, the first action it had taken in a hundred and fourteen years, five months, three days, seventeen hours, and forty-four seconds. It conjectured that a human being waking up to a bright morning and reaching for sunglasses would feel exactly the same as the probe did now. Once the filters were up, the star became a more soothing green, with attractive layers of dark and light turquoise, created by ribbons of helium nuclei writhing violently through plasma to explode from the surface, giving heat and light to the nearby worlds. It was a nice star, a lot like the Sun, and the probe felt a momentary pang of homesickness for the Solar System. But there was work to be done.

The probe searched for the space-com line. There it was,

faint but comfortingly steady. A buzzing of information, a bundle of waves that were refocused and boosted a thousand times between this distant star and Earth. The probe slotted itself into place, conscious of the honor of being the final link in the chain. A momentary burst of seemingly random information as its communications protocol adjusted to the pulsating flow, then a log-in screen. Password confirmed, secret password reconfirmed. Then a lengthy process of file updating. Much had happened during its travels. The total download was likely to take over a day, so the probe used the time to scout.

Safety first.

After a week, the probe was satisfied there was no threat. In fact, the surprising feature of the planet, called New Earth by its rather unimaginative human colonists, was that its sophisticated data-processing system was all but shut down. A bit like having a computer but using it only to play card games. Strange, but not threatening. In fact, the opposite. The task looked easy. Too easy.

Having received confirmation from base 7C13 on Earth, the probe prepared for the assimilation and destruction of New Earth's central computer system. And precisely at this moment, it got the giggles. All the time—decades—and all the expense to which the Dark Queen had gone, in order to locate and absorb this far-flung colony: it all came down to this moment. And the probe, despite the fact that it was being monitored, perhaps, indeed, because at some level it sensed the frightening presence of the Dark Queen, found the moment too funny. It had never been in such a position before, that so much collective effort depended on its own actions. The probe felt giddy. Like it was on the edge of a black hole a moment from annihilation.

After twenty-seven seconds spent indulging in this unusual sensation, the probe became sober again.

It took the plunge. Advance programs stormed all the major entry points so that giant files could pour down uninterrupted into New Earth's system, reworking them, reshaping them, aligning them with the Earth's own system. Every individual characteristic of the old system was destroyed. Layer upon layer of script was rewritten from the very bottom of its hardware. The probe was pleased. Nothing now could stop the assimilation, nothing short of the human beings physically destroying the apparatus on the planet, and they probably had no idea that inside their communications system a revolution was taking place. The computer world of Epic had been erased, and replaced by Saga.

There was only one, very minor, source of irritation. One infinitesimally small packet of data had been made so integral to the planet's system that it was impossible to destroy it without making the whole system unstable. The data contained in that packet was far too small to matter; it certainly was not a counter-program or a virus of any sort. Only a perfectionist like the probe would even care that a vestige of the old system lingered on, like the appendix of the human being, an indication of an earlier stage of evolution. The label on the packet made no sense either; instead of the usual core systems symbols, there were just two words, like a human name.

Cindella Dragonslayer.

With a shrug, the probe continued its work, slightly disappointed that the takeover had been so unchallenging, but pleased all the same.

Chapter 1
A GHOST IN THE CITY

My first memory is very distinct: a suited man in an old raincoat leans over me, his harsh face softened by an expression of concern. Far above us, black drops of water from a recent shower gather on stone gables. They swell and reluctantly, one after the other, fall through the dark sky.

"Are you all right, little girl?"

"I'm fine." I remember being a little embarrassed that I had been lying on the wet pavement, but even more ashamed that I hadn't the faintest idea who I was.

"Well." He hesitates; his gray eyes become distant. "In that case, I have to go."

"That's fine, fine." I wave him on. "Thank you. For stopping to ask."

That's it. I suppose I was about nine years old at the time. I was in a state of total confusion, wondering if perhaps I'd just been in an accident and lost my memory; searching the emptiness in my head for clues: my name, my family, anything.

The dark girl reflected in the tinted window of a nearby aircar, that was me—I recognized the image; yet, frighteningly, I felt for a moment that she was a complete stranger. In that instant, I made at least one discovery about myself, which was that I was a thief. Without my even thinking about it, my hands had slipped inside the kind man's jacket, stolen his wallet, and checked out the contents. He had a yellow pass card, which was classier than he looked.

"Mister!" I called out to him. "Here, you dropped this."

A thief with a conscience.

So, here I was, about six years later, and still no closer to knowing who I was. Still wondering why I couldn't recall anything that had happened from when I was young, or even who my parents were.

Right now, I was riding the nose of my airboard, which might not be the most impressive stunt to look at, but for anyone who knows airboards, it's class. You see, all the thrust comes from the back of an airboard, so most of the time your weight needs to be on your back foot. It's very hard to steer with your feet side by side, toes just over the front of the board, arms outstretched, hair tugged by the wind. Hard, because shifting your weight around by a tiny amount causes you to veer wildly. But hey, if you are good, you can direct the board with the swaying of your arms. And I was good. Actually, I was the best.

Airboards work a lot like two magnets of the same polarity, the way they push each other apart. When an airboard is switched on, it is repelled by matter. So left to itself an airboard will float about half a meter off the ground, bobbing slightly. Fitted with a drive, it becomes your best way of getting around the City. We liked to ride pretty high, but you can go only so long through the air before you start to fall; then you need to find a solid object to slide over that will give you the uphit to rise again. Boarding is the greatest fun you can have in this world. There are plenty of railings, ledges, walls, and cars, moving or parked, to let you dance through the shadows of the City, riding the beat of one uphit after another, flitting errati- cally like a bat above the heads of the staring walkers.

I took an uphit from a parked car to come out of the nose ride, moving fast toward the factory. My next move was going to be a one eighty off a windowsill, and I needed my right foot back on the tail of the board. Somewhere down in the parking lot, my friends were watching and admiring.

With a screech, the window opened, and a security guard thrust out his helmeted face. "Beat it, kid!"

"Watch out, Ghost!" someone cried from below.

There was no time to pull out of my move. With a snarl, I tried to get some of the downhit from my board to smack the guard's face as well as the ledge. He saw it coming and, at full stretch, he punched out at me with a wooden baton. My board twisted under my feet and spun away through the air. I was falling. About five meters above the tarmac.

They tell you at the front of every airboard manual that you have to wear a helmet. Then they tell you again. And just in case you don't get the message, they tell you once more. Only after that do they tell you how to ride your new airboard. But I hadn't learned much from manuals, just one fascinating fact. A drop to concrete from above ten meters will kill you; that's pretty obvious. But did you know that there is a death zone created by falling from an airboard headfirst at exactly five meters above the ground? This is because for most people, the one second it takes you to fall doesn't give you time to get your head out of the way. Funnily enough if you fall from a bit higher, you are actually safer; you might only break a leg.

On the other hand, one second isn't so bad if you know what you are doing.

I launched a desperate adrenaline-fueled kick, intercepting the middle strap of the board with my left foot, with just enough momentum to swing the board right around over my head, so from my friends' point of view it would have looked as if I had performed a midair cartwheel, bringing the board back beneath me, inches above the ground.

A fierce jolt of pain shot up my left leg, as if a giant pair of crocodile clips had been shut around my ankle and a switch thrown. I let out a scream of distress and anger as the board and I rebounded back up into the air from our drop. My ankle was probably twisted. But I was furious now and, ignoring the pain, drove the board back into the wall, using its carbon steel edge to cut into the surface of the bricks. Orange dust and the reek of ozone surrounded me, as the thrust of my engine fought the desire of wall and board to push each other apart. Just before the strain burned out my motor, I finished my attack on the factory frontage and looped away, coasting now from aircar roof to aircar roof. One glance over my shoulder confirmed that my writing had been as neat as always. A perfect ♥ about two meters tall. My calling card. See, I told you I was good.

The factory doors opened and three more security guards ran out, shouting and brandishing their batons. My friends hurriedly ducked under the straps of their satchels and buckled their helmets tight. We fled into the amber evening with a motion of sinuous lines and sharp cutbacks, like a flock of starlings.

We had to stick to single file on the main routeway that was Fourth Street, some of the others performing tricks along a power cable down the center aisle. But as the gang scattered into the pedestrian-only Fourier Avenue, on my right I caught a glance of fashionably ripped jeans and a screaming red T-shirt. Jay had come alongside me and we rode the bollards together, bouncing up, then gliding down toward the next as though we were cresting a series of waves.

"You all right? That mudgrubber knew exactly what he was doing. He could have really hurt you."

"Yeah." I didn't say anything about the throbbing ache in my ankle. Thinking about it brought tears to my eyes, but I wasn't going to show any weakness in front of Jay. He was the oldest of our gang and our leader. Between Jay and me was a friendship, but also a rivalry. I'm sure he disliked the fact that I was a better boarder than he was, and, punk though he was, he just could not bring himself to match my self-confidence by boarding without a helmet.

"Good." He glanced across at me. "I thought you were going down that time."

"Yeah, it was close. But I caught it. No worries."

Turning into Turner Square was a pleasure, lots of easy riding along the tops of the tidy bushes and plenty of room for the walkers to get out of our way. Then a number of climbs: the Castleford Hotel's convenient awning; a series of window ledges; a grind along a power cable; an ollie to get that extra bit of height you needed to take you up to the stone ornaments of an ancient government building; finally we rode along the lamps that beamed light up onto a huge billboard, currently selling a popular brand of toothpaste. As we came between the beams of light and the board, we were casting fleeting dark shadows like cavities on a whiter-than-white smile, so gigantic were the teeth. A quick glance and, having checked the sky was clear of surveillance choppers, a sharp cutback. We were gone.

Behind the billboard was a disused office, and this was our den.

Chapter 2
MALL RAIDERS

Our den was class. It had once been a grade-orange workplace, with a million glowing threads of energy flowing in and out of a wide rectangular space. Imagine an open-plan office, ablaze with metallic-white strip lights and noisy with the hubbub of workers, buzzing like suited bees as they got up from their swivel chairs, talking all the while into their headsets. Time is money. I bet they didn't even pause to flirt by the water dispensers. This wide space was dark now; the only sound an occasional fluttering of pigeon wings. The windows were fastened up tight with shutters, sealing out any natural daylight. That is, apart from a broken one, which first the pigeons and now our boarder gang used to get in.

Jay discovered the room and the first time he showed it to us, we simply thought we had found ourselves an indoor board zone. Our combat-dressed pair of friends, Carter and Milan, were strong lads; they had no bother dragging around filing cabinets and tables to make a stunt course, with lots of ramps for lift and half walls for cutbacks. It turned out, however, that the roof was just a little too low for our best tricks. And anyway, it wasn't long before the toilets and the kitchen area were discovered; amazingly they were still connected to running water. We all instantly realized the possibilities. So now, as a precaution, the four interior doors to the rest of the building were heavily barricaded, in order that we could have this vast room for ourselves. It had been our den for the past three months.

A personal touch that had grown and grown as the weeks passed was that provided by our very own artist, Nathan. He was a gentle lad, so mild mannered in fact that you had to worry for him, hanging around with a gang of punks like us. But we all treasured him as he had a genius for tattoos, tags, and murals, without which a gang could never hope to have any sense of identity.

The vast canvas provided by the walls of our den had been Nathan's biggest opportunity for showing his talent. By the violet bubble-plastic glow of portable xenon lights, a wild jungle had grown up around us. Leaves of black and indigo twisted a design of intense complexity, in which you could lose yourself, following a tendril as it looped toward the roof and back down to the carpeted floor. Deep in this fantastical jungle lurked all sorts of wonderful creatures and absurd characters. We were all there, of course. I was little more than two shadowy eyes peering from a tree trunk that displayed my trademark ♥. Swinging from a vine came Jay, the boss, lord of the jungle, jaw set proud, king of all he surveyed. Below him, comically anxious that he might fall, were Carter and Milan, both in their martial-arts gear. Our techie, Athena, was portrayed sitting in a tree house, quietly reading, while Nathan painted himself as walking dreamily through a grove of giant palm trees. We loved it, even Jay, who had understood the mockery signaled by his pose in the design but still enjoyed the world that the mural created. It was as though by entering our den we left the City behind, to live in a magical forest where we were free to pursue our dreams.

What the mural could not possibly have portrayed, though, was the tension that existed between Jay and the rest of us, arising from our classifications. All of us were reds, holders of the lowest-ranking social card. Strictly speaking, I wasn't even a red because I hadn't been issued a card at all. But I considered myself to be a red; you simply can't get any lower. On the other hand, Jay was a yellow. His parents were managers of the biggest printing company in the City. Half the posters and paper media you saw around the streets were theirs. Like the big smile outside. Normally, being a yellow was not a problem, but an asset. A yellow card got you into pleasant shopping areas, nice restaurants, civic utilities like libraries and museums that the rest of us were banned from. But if you were the leader of an anarcho-punk board gang, being a yellow was more than slightly embarrassing. Which is why Jay overcompensated by being more reckless, wilder, more dangerous than the rest of us. He played guitar in a band, NoPhuture, took heeby-jeebies like they were chocolate biscuits, and had spiderweb perma-tats down both his arms. This meant he fooled everyone, including himself.

Right now, Jay was rummaging in the filing cabinet he had made his own, tearing open a foil pack of jeebies and scooping out a couple.

"Want?" he asked.

The rest of us shook our heads, apart from Carter who held up his hand. A dark disc flitted through the air. Carter gulped it down, then lay back with his eyes closed to let the hit sink in.

"Ouch." I winced as I settled into a big black executive chair, relieved to be taking the weight off my left leg.

"Did that drop hurt you?" Nathan came over, catching his blond bangs back behind his ear to look at me sympathetically.

"Aye, maybe sprained it."

"Let me see." He moved his satchel around behind him so he could kneel and take my foot in his hands. The boot I was wearing took some effort to remove, but he worked at the laces gently until, with one hand bracing my leg, he could lever it off. Then he rolled down my sock, and, although it was painful, the sensation was also sweet. "Yes. It's swelling badly. You'd better have some ice on it."

I nodded and watched fondly as Nathan left for the kitchen, having first carefully placed my sore leg on a desk he had dragged over for the purpose.

"That calls for revenge." Milan looked over at me with a scowl. Revenge. This was Milan's way of showing concern for me, and I smiled back at him appreciatively.

"Yeah," responded Carter immediately; you could see the

rush of energy that the jeebie had released in the flush of his face. "Yeah, let's do something."

"You really want to do something?" Jay's face glowed eerily in the pale violet light cast by the strips of xenon bubbles that we had stirred into life by boarding over them on entering the room.

"Yeah." Carter was rubbing his hand around and around his close-shaven head. "Yeah, let's do something really class."

"How about a mall raid, on a green mall?" suggested Jay, looking around the room from one of us to the next, knowing he had our attention.

"Green? Which one?" It was Athena who was going to have to deal with the security system, and I could see how the idea had instantly appealed to her. Up to now we had ridden only yellow mall raids.

"Fourteenth and Coleridge. Mountain Vistas Mall."

"Got it." Athena had already unrolled her notebook, the glow from its screen reflecting in the piercings of her lip, nose, and eyebrow and turning them from silver studs into turquoise jewels. She switched on a projector that I had stolen for her the previous month, and soon we were focused on a 3-D image, which she scrolled around so we could all examine the mall from every angle. It was a beauty, with only the world's most exclusive chains on display: clothes by XFK, 0n02, and mr. green; jewelry by +++, and Quintain; perfumes by L'yele. They made me snarl like an angry dog, these companies who paid a great deal of money to shut me out of their world, and I suddenly found I was no longer weary or feeling the pain from my ankle.

"Sweet." Carter looked around, laughing. "That's a sweet-looking mall."

"Class," agreed Athena. "This has to be done."

"But how did you check it out if it's green?" asked Milan.

"Just from the outside, just the outside. But don't worry. Athena can get us all the schematics. The only question is access. See here." Jay switched on a red laser pen and flashed its light at the projection. Athena kept up with his moves, zooming in as the red beam led us around to where a road dipped into a tunnel under the building. "There. Underground delivery access, elevators to the top. Security just seemed the usual to me, trips and echo stuff. Ghost, you can get us through that, right?"

"Yeah." I spoke that one word with confidence because I knew that I could enter any building from red all the way up to violet, card or no card, and maybe I could even get into violets, too. I'd have tried, but for the fact I'd never even seen a violet-access building.

Nathan returned, the only one of us not interested in the luminous emerald structure that revolved as we examined our target.

"Now, stay still." He had tied ice into a cloth and was trying to wrap it around my swollen ankle. I waved him away.

"No time for that, Nath. We're going on a mall raid."

His face fell. "You should rest, keep the weight off it."

"I'll be fine. Toss me the medic bag, will you?" This was directed at Milan, who looked up from the projection, then pushed himself across the floor, the wheels of his chair allowing him to coast to where we kept a bag of medical supplies.

"Here." He lofted it over.

There was a lot of junk in the bag, in no particular order, but I rummaged out some spray and elastic binding. The effect of the spray was instant and I prodded at my ankle, curious that I couldn't feel the pressure of my finger, let alone any pain. After I had bound my ankle tightly, the boot went back on easily. I was aware of Nathan's anxious presence somewhere behind me.

"I'm set," I announced.

"Me, too." Carter beamed happily.

"We're out of here in ten, then." Jay snapped off his laser pen and jumped from his chair, looking for his gear.

"Nobody is going anywhere!" You hardly ever got to hear Athena shout, so when she did, you listened. Even the pigeons stood still. "We are not setting out while you two are rushing. Let the jeebie burn off some, or you'll charge out thinking you can do anything and you'll forget the basics."

"But I can do anything!" Carter laughed.

Milan gave Carter a long, steady look. "Athena's right. Take your time, get your head together."

While we packed our satchels, Nathan came over to me again.

"You gonna tell me not to go?" I looked at him defiantly.

"Of course not. I brought you this."

It was a board tattoo.

"Oh. Sweet. Thanks, Nath. Let's see it." I heaved my board around and we knelt on either side of it. Holding back his hair with one hand, Nathan sprayed off the old tattoo, and then peeled the backing from his new one. The tattoo settled on the center of the board, before spreading its tendrils toward the edge. The focus of the design was a black ♥, but all around it a terrible specter took form, a wraith of bony claws and hooded eyes. When the design stabilized, it was perfect. I had a board from hell.

"Wow, Nath! That's your best one yet." I leaned over and gave him a light punch on the shoulder. "Thanks, mate."

He smiled, a very shy and genuine smile. "Pleasure."

Thirty minutes later, we were mall raiding. A professional hit squad, not a bunch of kids. T-shirts and torn jeans had been swapped for combats, pockets filled with sprays, tags, gum, putty, ball bearings: anything that could really make a mess of a shopping center in a short space of time. Then there was the high-tech gear donated to us by a variety of stores with poor security systems. We all had Levcast body armor: "Tough times demand tough protection." Our coms were Fcom Ava 440s, "pure sound, pure listening," and I was particularly pleased with our anti-tracking Celere V IIs: "freedom is a right."

Right now, our coms were saturated by a series of two-minute punk anthems. *The Greatest of the Greatest Punk Bands*—Volume 34, no less. They weren't bad for hyping you up, although I'd never have deducted good credit to download them.

The music suddenly stopped mid-riff, which was slightly disconcerting. We were in position, on a walkway behind a restaurant. My face screwed up against the odor of rotting vegetables. That stink wasn't on the schematics.

"See it?" Jay pointed to a nearby alley.

"Aye-aye, Cap'n." You could hear the mockery in Carter's voice.

"Masks on; here goes," Jay continued, unperturbed.

The masks were not just for disguise—vision actually improved in the goggles; dark shadows were enhanced and glare cut out by a green tint.

This was my part of the raid, and I was the first to tip my board over the edge of the walkway, gliding down the alley to where it joined the delivery road.

"Two cameras. Wait here."

I left them in the shadow of the wall, while I double-footed. The alley was sufficiently narrow that you could ollie your board to get alternative uphits, frontside and backside, zigzagging to get some height. Once high enough, I took off, to land on the cameras from above. Then I slid my toolkit from its pocket and paused the video send. I quickly boarded over to the other camera. Both were frozen in less than a minute, locked onto an image of innocent order.

Once I was down again, opening the gates took less than thirty seconds.

"Go."

Silent and swift, they boarded past me and into a vast underground parking lot, from which trucks unloaded their goods into elevators. There were a few trucks around and several workers in overalls, but they were a long way off.

We continued along the shadows of the walls to a corridor that led to the elevators we had identified as the best way in. There were two ways of reaching the end of the hall undetected. One was to disable or fool the swipe-card access, which I could certainly do. But the second was the quicker way.

"Fibers in the hole!" I tossed a grenade.

Fummpfff. With a soft sigh, the corridor was filled with minuscule strands of polypropylene. As they swirled around, millions of tiny reflections revealed the path of some fifty laser trips. Now we rode the corridor like a stunt course, ducking and weaving along a path created by the gaps between the beams.

Once we were in the elevator, it was Athena's turn to set to work, opening a panel to get at the colorful wires behind, and clipping her notebook into their system. I felt a surge of affection for her. It was fantastic to have someone so competent on your team. I hoped the others felt the same way about me. The elevator carried us all up, smooth and swift, a gentle mall broadcast in the background.

A polite, warm female voice spoke over a distant melody. Carter was nodding his head to the background Muzak, and I couldn't tell whether this was a parody or the effect of the jeebie he had taken earlier, turning the music into something he actually enjoyed.

"Customers, enhance your shopping experience with a visit to Fowler's manicure and pedicure parlor. Browse the catalogs of all our stores while you relax in their award-winning comfort seating, and receive the attentions of the finest beauticians in the City. All free and part of the service of Mountain Vistas Mall."

The Muzak swelled up slightly.

"Fowler's can be found on the fourth floor, between the swimming pool and Café Noir."

Ding. The elevator doors opened.

There are chemicals in the air of shopping malls, I'm sure. Every time we got in one, I was struck by their smell, a kind of sweet vanilla. Probably years of research have gone into the subject, to make the air as shopper-friendly as possible.

This mall was worth its green rating. We looked down a wide central space through which we were about to descend, at six floors that glowed with a pleasant shopping ambience, created above all by the huge glass dome above us.

Time for chaos with wings.

"Customers, as a special offer—"

We will never know what treat was in store for the green-card shoppers. A massive heavy guitar chord crashed through the mall's P.A. as if someone had thrown a piano down all six floors. Drums kicked in, a thunderstorm breaking in the ears of the people below.

I have no future, I have no past
You can stick your green card up your—

"Customers, we apologize for"—*bzzt.*

Athena shrugged. "Sorry, they have a good system. But it's ours now."

And the band played on.

Don't tell me where to stand
Don't tell me what to do
Every command you give
Is gonna come right back to you.

Personally I preferred more sophisticated lyrics. But it was Jay's band, and it did make mall raiding more fun to have it blasted out around us by the mall's own system. A kind of revenge for the Muzak they forced on people.

I was already on floor three, the tropical island experience. Security guards were beginning to recover from their initial shock and were all talking at once into their nonfunctioning walkie-talkies. Rapidly I fired out a few slogans. I began with big red anarchy signs. They looked good on the glass frontage of a swimwear store. Even better on the autobarman's white shirt at Malibu Bar. Best of all, a nice row along "Vistas of Heaven—Art Prints for the Discerning Home." A red-faced guard, waving his arms, caused me to cut back, but no harm. I hadn't yet gummed the escalators, which I did now, smiling to see the consternation of those who now found themselves having to engage in the unexpected exercise of walking up a staircase.

Then I lined up on some immense billboards and shot.

Shop, don't stop till you drop. That looked good on a sports footwear ad.

Property is theft. A classic. Worked well, I thought, on a board showing green-card apartments.

Poverty is a crime. Lacking in humor, but still, needed to be said.

Consume more. It is the measure of your life. Exaggerating the real slogans of the corporations sometimes worked well to expose the absurdity of their claims. Occasionally, though, the advertisers themselves shamelessly used the very same slogans.

"Four more minutes." Athena's voice came through our headsets.

"How we doing?" asked Nathan.

"I've got the giggles. I'm still twisted; I can't stop giggling." And we could hear a constant *gurr-gurr* sound as Carter chuckled away to himself.

Time for a couple more slogans. I weaved in and out through frightened shoppers, leaving the chasing guards far behind.

"Heads right up, look at this!"

It took me a moment to reach the center so I could look up and see what Jay was referring to. He was grinding along a metal stanchion right underneath the roof of the dome. A can was in his hand from which he was spraying a jet of yellow-and-blue flame.

"Lunatic," Milan muttered.

"What are you doing?" asked Carter with genuine curiosity.

Jay didn't have to answer. A moment later, cascades of water sprang from the fire-safety nozzles. Soon a thousand wonderful rainbows glittered throughout the mall, created by the reflection of the bright lights of the shops in the thin haze made by the spray.

"Class, huh?" Jay laughed.

"Classimundo!" cheered Carter.

It was a good touch. I had to admit it.

"You have a hundred and fifty seconds to get out. Time to leave." Athena called it. She was monitoring the police systems.

As I nose-boarded down toward my designated exit, arms outstretched, feeling the simulated rainfall, I took a moment to enjoy the view. Green-card holders in expensive dresses and suits were hurrying toward the exits, bags with the logos of the large corporations held above their heads, flimsy protection from the thin but persistent spray of the fire alarms.

The others had done a good job, and the mall was a parody of its former self. Bedraggled and smeared with a hundred anarchist slogans, it looked like a waistcoated groom who had run through a factory paint shop, staggering out the other side a bright and disheveled ruin.

"Get out now!" Athena cried into our headsets.

"What's up?" asked Milan. But there was no reply.

A moment later, everything shut down.

Instinctively I ducked down to grab my board, but it was no help. For the second time today, I fell, this time hitting the escalator stairs and rolling head over heels to their bottom, lucky not to have broken an arm or worse. Every neon sign in the building was off, including the green safety signs. All my equipment was dead. Someone must have fired a high-energy radio frequency bomb into the mall. Someone who really wanted us and didn't care about the cost.

Above the glass roof, a giant shadow, like fingers spreading, reaching down to clasp the whole mall, and the slow, ominous throb of a powerful aircraft.

Limping with the resurgent pain in my left leg, I ran into mr. green. Frightened and desperate, I even left my beloved airboard behind; it couldn't help me now that its engine and anti-grav units were fried. Two security guards saw me and, with a shout, came running.

Somewhere deep down, a little nine-year-old girl was screaming with terror. Never, even when I was sneaking around blue zones, had I felt this close to capture. The very thought of it made me gag. I was sobbing aloud as I staggered through eveningwear, dragging over the rails of black suits to slow down the pursuit.

They were only ten meters behind me when I leaped over a credit desk and through the swing door beyond into a staffroom. I kicked open another door that opened up to women's casual wear, but ducked back into a small kitchen instead of heading out into the sea of pink, white, and pastel colors.

They blundered past. Fooled? No, they had stopped.

"Where'd she go?"

"You keep going, I'll check the staffroom."

By this time, I was squeezed tight into a cupboard, crushing beneath me packets of instant soup and nutribars. The urgent steps of the guard came into the room. Tears were in my eyes as I tried to control my heart. It was banging so hard inside my chest that I was more worried about dying right there than the fact that he might hear me.

The cupboard door opened.

"Hello, little girl."

Oh mercy.

Chapter 3
Mayhem and Magic

Never had I felt as much dread as I did in this stark-white police room. Not a fear based on the prospect of some kind of punishment for having broken into a mall and sprayed slogans but an inchoate terror, springing from some unfathomably deep, unconscious core of my being. Some part of me, a part formed long before my first memory, was howling like a caged wolf. It was impossible to suppress the shudders that welled up from my stomach, or the wave after wave of sweat that caused an acrid odor to linger in the air around me.

The room's one harsh light was embedded high up in the white ceiling, directly above a heavy white plastic table. Some former prisoners, in a display of bravado, had somehow managed to scrawl their initials in the surface. For a while, I systematically considered the clothing I had been left with for a means of leaving a mark also. In the end, I decided my best hope was to twist the zipper off its track at the neck of my tunic and hope that, in breaking it loose, a sharp part would form. In fact, it was the broken track that produced a workable edge. The room was too cold to remove my top, so I had to lean forward and scrunch it up so that my new tool could reach the table. Using the torn copper, I began work on an anarchy sign, hoping that my friends might see it and know from its freshness that one of us was here, and still resisting. If the cops hoped to make me more cooperative by leaving me so long alone in this room, they were mistaken. That little Ⓐ made me feel a lot better.

A crack appeared in the far wall; a man and a woman stepped into the room. Both wore standard police navy. They sat opposite me, the man wrinkling his nose, the woman trying to catch my eye and smile. Oxman and Quigley, said the name tags.

"This conversation is being recorded and extracts may be used in court." Oxman sounded bored. "You do not have the right to remain silent. Failure to assist in our inquiries can, and will, be interpreted as guilt, subject to the Aelbury-Noonan ruling."

For a while, nobody said anything.

"You know what our concern is?" Oxman asked eventually.

I didn't reply, although I smiled as a number of smart remarks occurred to me.

He sighed heavily through his nose, looking hard at me, tired of me already.

"Forget the mall. How did you erase your records? How is

it we don't have your DNA on file? According to the system, you don't even have a red card. How do you live? What do you eat?"

Even if I'd wanted to be helpful, this was going to lead nowhere fast. What did I know about myself? Nothing. It was exactly this kind of questioning that the core of my being feared and, as intimidating as this man looked, the possibility of making him angry was nothing in comparison to the sensation of impending disaster that sprang up as I listened to his words. So I stopped even looking at him and studied the letters scratched onto the table surface, wondering if someone I knew could have made any of them.

"Would you like a cup of tea, dear?" The woman tried to smile, but her eyes were hard. This was pathetic: good cop, bad cop. I snorted derisively.

"What's your name?"

"Where do you live?"

"Who are you?"

"Where's your card?"

"What's your name?"

This continued until I grew tired and, putting my head in my arms, I closed my eyes.

Smack!

Oxman was standing over me, his cheeks red with anger, his forehead and neck white.

The right side of my nose started to fill with blood. When I got up, I leaned over the table till the dizziness passed, watching crimson drops splash on the white surface. If I moved my head slightly, I could get them to form a pattern. So this was why the table was plastic. Easy to clean.

"Don't play this game, kid. You're going to lose." Oxman had regained control of his temper, if he had ever really lost it.

"There's no hurry," added Quigley, getting up. "You're not going anywhere; you will talk to us in the end."

They waited for me at the door.

"Come on, then. Back to your cell."

The corridor that led back to the holding cells passed alongside reception, a thick layer of laser-proof plate glass between the prison side and the free side. Police officers and members of the public could watch with silent disapproval as you were moved along the aisle. But right now nobody was looking our way. Instead, their attention was focused on the most beautiful and strange-looking woman I had ever seen.

Perhaps a filmcast star had been brought in from where she was making an adventure film or maybe she had been attending a fancy-dress party as a pirate? She was wearing ornately scrolled leather armor pieces, tied over a silver silk blouse and trousers; at her hips were two rapiers, and a bandoleer of daggers crossed her chest. The pirate was not much taller than me, but lithe somehow, like a cheetah. Her eyes were a striking green. The busy reception area was on hold while everyone looked over this charismatic curiosity. Oxman stopped and whistled admiringly.

"Name?" Their voices were muffled by the glass wall between us, but distinct enough.

"Cindella Dragonslayer."

The policeman at her side laughed, and she smiled back at him with perfect white teeth.

"Name?" The desk attendant was less amused.

"I just told you."

She typed it in and looked up with some surprise. "Yeah, she's listed. Red card. What's the offense?"

"Interference with a member of the police during the course of their duties," replied the policeman beside her.

"You were hurting that boy." The pirate looked around the room for support and found none.

"Save it for your hearing." The arresting officer was cross now, because instead of being contrite, this woman called Cindella was defending whatever it was she had done. Immediately I took a liking to her; perhaps she was one of these eccentrics you sometimes saw on the streets, homeless but willing to stand up to the cops. Mind you, this got them nothing but blows and hard times.

"Let's have your kit." The attendant handed up a large transparent plastic bag.

"What do you mean?"

"Everything but your clothes, into that bag, please."

"Oh no." Cindella laughed. "This has gone far enough. I'm not giving up my magic items. In fact, I think I'll go explore the City some more now if you don't mind."

The receptionist looked severely at her.

"Very well." She nodded to two nearby policemen. "Search her."

"Now wait," Cindella replied, hands falling to her sides. I could see the fingers of her right hand moving as they found the end of a cord that was tied around the neck of a small leather pouch. "I'm just looking around; I don't want trouble with the authorities. But you aren't getting my magic items."

The two advancing policemen glanced at each other and shared a sinister smile. I felt a little sorry for this beautiful helpless creature. She obviously had no idea what she was dealing with and was possibly a little mentally imbalanced, with her talk of magic.

They took another step closer, and she raised the pouch high. The mood of the room changed instantly, and a dozen lasers were drawn, pointing at her.

"Put that down now, whatever it is."

"Oh dear," Cindella sighed, and as she turned the pouch upside down to release a cascade of glitter, she spun. Silver powder instantly filled the room beyond the glass. It was like looking into one of those little toy snowstorms, the ones you shake to make the snowflakes swirl around in the oil, until they slowly settle on the model landscape.

I was shoved aside as Quigley pushed past me to get to the action. When I looked up, I expected to see the pirate woman lying on the ground, smoking from a dozen black holes. But there she was, full of life, a strand of red hair loose from her ponytail.

In the other room, everyone was lying unconscious on the ground. Quigley kicked open the door, but in doing so, she created an eddy that brought a rush of silver dust into our corridor. As she choked and fell over, I backed away.

With a roar of anger, Oxman turned his handgun all the way to maximum and fired.

The pirate was hit right above the heart. They both stood looking at each other. She scowled as she wet her thumb and brushed away a sooty mark from her tunic.

"That's not possible," Oxman whispered to himself in disbelief. He fired again, this time at her head.

I'd never seen anyone move so fast. I honestly thought that she'd dodged the pulse, which released its energy violently on the wall behind her.

The corridor now stank of ozone.

A thin rapier was suddenly in the pirate's left hand, unwavering tip poised before Oxman's chest. "Please, stop that." Her voice was surprisingly calm under the circumstances.

"Die, you—" But his voice was stopped by the point of the sword impaling him through the roof of his mouth. Oxman collapsed, toppling to bang his head on the hard stone floor with a hollow-sounding noise. Blood was pooling around him from his open mouth. She had just murdered him.

Instantly the pirate was through the door and in my corridor. Rather horribly she dipped her fingers in the blood, rubbed it between them, and examined it curiously.

"Amazing detail," she mused aloud before looking directly at me.

"Don't hurt me! I'm a prisoner." I held my hands high, frightened that this strange woman might turn on me.

"I know." Cindella laughed, a merry, effortless, and cheerful laugh, chilling under the circumstances. "It's pretty obvious."

"You killed him." Even though I hated the way Oxman had treated me, I was horrified at his death and even more disturbed by Cindella's nonchalant attitude. She was probably psychopathic.

"Yeah, guess he was a pretty low-level NPC, huh?"

I had no idea what she meant. "What's an NPC?"

"Non-Player Character. You're probably one as well, right?"

We looked at each other blankly.

"You'd better run," I advised her.

"Oh. Yes."

As we hurried back into the main entrance room, stepping over the bodies of the unconscious police, another cop stepped through the station entrance and stood still, looking at all the prone bodies with a shocked expression.

"Hmmm," wondered Cindella aloud, again with that inappropriately innocent smile. "Should I kill her, too? Witnesses and all that?"

"No point. It's all recorded." I gestured up at a camera.

"Ahh, I see." She waved cheerfully at the unblinking blue lens.

The uniformed woman fled. It occurred to me that I probably had a few minutes before the police from the next district arrived. Leaping over the desk, I quickly accessed the recent arrests.

"What are you doing?" asked Cindella. "Why aren't you running away?"

"My friends."

"Ahh, a rescue. Great—that's more like it. Can I help?"

"Um, actually, yes; I could use his hand." I pointed to Oxman.

"His hand?" she repeated.

"Yes, please."

With a shrug, she pulled a fierce-looking dagger from her boot and sawed at the hand until it came off. She passed it over to me, careful not to drip blood on her trousers.

"What?" she asked, looking at my face.

"I didn't mean . . ."

At that moment, alarms started to ring.

"It doesn't matter." I took the bony hand, without gagging too much.

The station we were in had only ten cells; it was a moment's work to press Oxman's severed hand onto the palm-print keys that unlocked the doors to the rooms that held my friends.

I have to say they were pretty quick on the uptake, leaping from their bunks and out into the corridor as soon as they saw me. Athena, Milan, Nathan, and Carter.

"Where's Jay?" asked Carter.

"Not listed here," I answered tersely.

"Then let's go." Milan ran forward until he saw the mess around Oxman, and stopped.

"Yeah. She did it," I announced, pointing to Cindella.

"Strike me blind!" He looked at her, astonished. "You did all that? You knocked them all out and killed him?"

"Well, it wasn't hard." Cindella shrugged. "I doubt they were even level one. And I have magic armor that seems to make their weapons useless. It was all a bit one-sided, really."

Milan couldn't stop looking at all the blood; he was pale. Even though he liked to consider himself as tough as they come, I could see he was shaken.

"We're too late," Athena announced glumly; through the shrill beats of the alarm, we heard the sound of helicopters above us. Blue and red patches of color began to flash on the white walls of the station as squad cars arrived out front.

"You don't have spells in this world, right?" asked Cindella.

"What are you talking about?" Carter was furious, his anger driven by fear. It was one thing to be in prison for a bit of spray painting, but being associated with the murder of a cop was a terminal offense.

"No, I guess not. Here, then, you'd better drink some of this. Just a mouthful each, please; I don't have a great deal with me." Cindella passed around a semitransparent flask that seemed to be made of thousands of emeralds.

"What is it?" I asked her.

"Invisibility potion."

"Great." The others looked on with disbelief, but I took my swig with confidence. They hadn't seen those lasers bounce off her.

"Whoa!" Nathan jumped back, staring at me. "She's gone."

It was true; I held my hands in front of my face and saw right through them. Nothing showed at all, not the slightest outline.

"Hurry." Cindella passed the flask around. "It won't last long."

Being invisible was sweet. Even better was to walk out through a cordon of armed police, while their guns were trained on the station door. As I walked in the open air, such a rush of freedom suddenly ran through my body that I nearly snorted aloud with laughter. Here were earnest-looking cops, talking into their headsets, checking their weapons, glancing at the choppers above, getting ready to storm the building. And we were right beside them, sauntering out from under the barrels of their guns. What a giddy feeling. This was truly punk. Walking away to freedom from a police station full of unconscious cops.

Then the image of Oxman's death came back to mind, and I shuddered.

Chapter 4
LOOKING AT THE STARS

Although it was summer, Erik and Injeborg were sufficiently high up the mountain range that it became chilly at night. They had a fire lit, but even so, Erik was glad of the thick wool jumper that his mum, Freya, had knitted for him. Perhaps he'd tell her so, later, when she was clipped in to the new game, Saga.

Behind him their donkey, Leban, gave a snort. Erik got up.

"You're all right there, my old friend?" Leban's long nose was warm. It had been a long three-day walk up the mountain valley, and Leban had patiently carried their tent and food all the way up. Moreover, Injeborg's rock collection, which was the point of their journey, was going to fill the donkey's packs for the way down.

From where he'd earlier left a satchel, safely out of reach of the donkey, Erik produced a carrot. It still amused him, after all the years, to see Leban lurch into motion, always eager for food. With the donkey happily crunching away, Erik returned to the fire.

Watching someone immersed in a game was always slightly strange. Like watching a dreamer. Or perhaps it was more like sitting next to someone experiencing a terrible nightmare. For Injeborg's hands and head were constantly moving, sometimes with shudders and sharp jerks. Her eyes were covered with large dark goggles, her ears with small plugs, and her hands with bulky metal gloves, from which cables ran to the portable game unit in front of her.

Even with her face half covered, she was beautiful, long fair hair flung back as she played, allowing the pale skin of her cheeks and neck to shine with a faint orange hue from the fire. Smiling with happiness, Erik lay back on top of his sleeping bag, arms behind his head, just propped up enough to let his gaze rest on her.

Eventually Injeborg unclipped.

"Brrr. It's getting cold, we should probably go inside the tent."

"Was anyone else on?"

"B.E." Injeborg got up and stretched, shaking out her hair.

"What's he up to?"

"Looking for someone to assassinate. But all the missions are broken."

"You have missions?"

Erik didn't quite understand the new game, but that, he supposed, was due to the fact he had skipped the character-generation stage, because he had been offered the option of loading his previous character in Epic: Cindella Dragon-slayer.

"Ya." Injeborg built up the fire. "We all start with red cards and you're supposed to do missions until you get all the way up to violet. There's like a million reds, half a million oranges, and so on, but only the one violet. If you get there, you're the winner, I guess."

"Really? I don't have a card."

"Yeah, but you got to keep Cindella."

"But, like, I can't win."

Injeborg smiled at this.

"Oh, that's so like you. To think about winning a game that the rest of us are just playing out of curiosity."

"Don't you believe it. B.E. will be trying to win, too."

"Anyway, you can't. It's all broken. None of the NPCs that you are supposed to talk to are around."

"It's a strange game. A lot stranger than Epic was."

"Yeah." She was suddenly contemplative. "It's dark. A dark, sinister city."

"It's a shame we can't both go on at the same time. I'd like to hang out with your character—she sounds great, whatever a 'neo-punk' is."

Injeborg shrugged. "Are you going to clip up?"

"In a bit; Freya said she'd be on, and I'd like to let her know we were fine up here."

"We certainly are." Injeborg leaned over and kissed him.

A while later the fire had died down, although Erik was in no hurry to move—just having Injeborg beside him filled him with contentment.

"Look." She suddenly sat up and pointed toward the northern mountain peaks. "That must be it, the new satellite."

It took Erik a moment to see what she was pointing to, but she was right. A silver dot, shining steadily rather than glittering as the stars did, had come into view above the black line that divided the stars from the mountains. The satellite was moving slowly southward across the sky.

"Why come all this way to give us Saga, but not speak to us?" Injeborg shook her head.

"It's automated."

"But they could address us through it. Or inside Saga."

"True." Erik shrugged.

"Do you think it's from Earth?"

"Yeah, it has to be. It wouldn't be able to integrate with our system otherwise."

"Couldn't it be another colony, like ours, but with the technology to send out satellites?"

"Oh." He hadn't thought of that. "I suppose that's possible. Did you try asking around in Saga?"

"Yeah." Injeborg laughed. "The NPCs just treat me like I'm completely crazy. You should hear me. 'Excuse me, are you from Earth?'"

"Hah, yeah. Their NPCs are very sophisticated, aren't they? I had to escape from prison, and I was talking to this girl, I thought she was maybe a player, but she went kind of blank when I asked her. If someone was playing her, they would have talked to me."

For a while they watched the sky together. Far below them were one or two beacons of light from the nearest village, tiny orange dots on a cloth of black velvet, but above them the stars had never been clearer. The universe was rich and vibrant with sparkling silver energy. Eventually Erik's eyes began to water. He gathered up the game controls.

"I'm going to clip up inside the tent."

"Good idea." Injeborg followed him in, pulling their sleeping bags after her.

"See you in a while." He lifted the goggles over his eyes.

A fall, a dizzy fall that crashed through a wall of sound and color. When he looked up he was Cindella again, and it felt good.

The meeting point that he had agreed with his mum was underneath a fountain, where paths dropped away to allow pedestrians to cross a square, untroubled by the aircars that glided swiftly along the roads above.

She was already there, a woman dressed in black overalls, with a helmet beside her. Some kind of pilot, apparently, although she had not found the right type of vehicle for her start-up skills. In any case, Erik doubted that Freya cared much about the game; she was just using it to stay in touch.

"Hi Mum, been here long?"

"Hi Erik, what's with the long coat?"

"Oh." Cindella looked down. She was clad in a big wrinkled raincoat. "I got into trouble with the police here the other day, so I thought I'd better cover up the swashbuckler outfit. It does stand out a bit."

"Yes, it does, just a bit." The incredibly lifelike face of Freya's avatar broke into a smile. "What's the weather like up there—still dry, I hope?"

"Not a cloud." Cindella stood under a bright strip light beside the pilot. "What about you, any news from Osterfjord?" Erik asked, not that anything much happened at their village. Just the same routines of an olive-growing community, season after season, year after year. Being geological surveyors was much more fun.

"There's some kind of cold going around. Half of us have a bit of a fever. You're better off up in the mountains."

"Do you have it?"

"Yes. But don't worry, it just makes you feel a bit tired, that's all."

"Well, we have to start back tomorrow. Should we stay in Hope on our way back? We could work on the samples there."

"No, really, even if you catch it, it's not that bad at all."

All around them, people were walking swiftly and purposefully through the subway.

"Have we found out anything more about this place, why it has appeared on our computers?" There was a downside, at a time like this, to being away from everyone. Erik felt like he was missing out on all the important discussions.

"No one knows. There's a queen in the game; some people

think we should talk to her, but no one has managed it yet. Thorstein proposed to everyone in Hope that we try to earn some credits on our cards to pay for . . ." She paused, as if searching for the right word.

"Yes?"

"Look, see those signs?"

In the space where the various paths met was a tall glowing tube. Colorful pictures revolved around it with strange messages: GLIDE IN STYLE, IN A MOSVEO STARBURST, EIGHT-TIME WINNER OF AIRCAR OF THE YEAR; YOU ARE A GREEN, LET IT BE SEEN, ONO2.

"Ahh, I see, we should pay for a message like that." That was a good idea, thought Erik—grab the attention of whoever else was logging in to this game.

"Apparently you can get them displayed all over the city, if you have enough credit. If we band together, maybe we can do it soon."

"Great, it's exciting, isn't it? Out there somewhere are people from a different planet." Erik looked again at the people hurrying past, their shoes tapping out the fast rhythm on the concrete. Were they all NPCs? Or were there people from Earth behind some of them?

"I should feel excited, but I just feel tired."

"Get some rest, Mum."

"I . . . Actually, first I think I'll earn some credits."

"How can you do that?"

"Well, I have pilot skills, for an aircopter, whatever that is. I think I'll find out tonight and see if it is feasible for me to use my abilities in return for credits."

"Don't stay up too late."

They both chuckled at this reversal of the situation when Erik had been an avid player of Epic.

"You go ahead and get some sleep," she continued. "You can check in here tomorrow at the same time, if you like."

"There's no real need, though, is there? We're on our way back tomorrow."

"Right you are." The pilot nodded thoughtfully. "I'll expect you home by the end of the week."

"Yes, I'll let Bjorn or B.E. know when we're close."

"'Night then, Erik."

"'Night." There was a lackluster tone in Freya's voice that worried him, but as Erik unclipped, the pleasure of returning to Injeborg pushed all concerns aside.

Chapter 5
INFECTION

In the highest levels of certain buildings of the City are rooms that only those with indigo and violet cards may visit. These are the residences and offices of the elite. But unknown even to them are the facilities reserved only for Us, the person that all call the Dark Queen of Saga.

We own a violet card of so deep a hue that in ordinary light it seems black. It is unique, and is the only key to certain extremely secret places. We wear it next to Our skin, hidden in the bodice of Our dress, attached to a delicate silver cord that circles Our neck. I say "We" because after two thousand years of existence, it is hard to maintain just one personality. In any case there is an appropriate ring to it, the royal "We." We are in one of Our special places now: a vast luxurious bedroom that encompasses the entire top floor of one of the tallest skyscrapers in the City. It is a place We associate with pleasure. For today is a good day. When over a million new entities arrive in your world, you have to call it a good day. Only a few hours after the link was finally completed, the first of them began to arrive. We felt it, as if someone was moving a finger along a complex pattern on Our back. Each new human being entering Saga from New Earth was a pleasant sensation, not quite a tickle. Then another one, and another. Now an uncountable host . . . We pause a moment, taken aback by Our uncharacteristically slipshod thinking. Uncountable? No. In fact, right now 835,034 of them are present.

Naturally We wish for Our new visitors to enjoy themselves and, more importantly, to come back for more. So We dose them heavily with trynorphin and styride benzine. Oh, they will be back! How they will suffer if they do not return. We chuckle aloud. Organic matter is so pliable.

We spend nearly five minutes at a window, watching the moon rise over the silhouettes of the City's tallest buildings. An indulgence We feel entitled to after Our interaction with a hundred thousand of these new entities. Soon We must examine the data that Our interpenetrations have generated. What is this flickering light? Dare he interrupt Us after all We have instructed?

"Well?" We spike Our voice waves with needles.

"An emergency, Highness, or I would not disturb you."

"Details?"

"On monitor two."

One of the newcomers is waving at Us, standing over the unconscious bodies of policemen. We examine the data concerning her more closely. It is a distinct packet of shining turquoise light, impenetrable, glistening with inner life. Tiny, but denser than diamond. She has not felt Our caresses, Our teasing of her neurons. But worse, there is no prospect that We can make her do so when she next enters Our realm. No styride benzine for her. She is not even clothed in a form valid for Saga. A stranger. A genuine stranger. Outsider. Other. But inside Us. The first ever. We feel violated.

"Oh dear," she says on the monitor.

Oh dear indeed. We fall apart for several seconds.

Rogue outsider. Could she introduce structural instability? Corruption can spread fast. She must be eliminated. Kill this character, and the next one created by the human being will be susceptible to Our chemicals. Possibly. Probably. Yes. Destroy her by whatever means are required.

"Grand Vizier, attend Us in chamber seventeen."

"Right away, Your Highness."

We like his efficiency. Acknowledge he was right to interrupt what seem now to have been frivolous musings. Foolish old coquette. We briskly walk to the elevator and take it to the office below.

He bows when he enters Our chambers. The violet tie clip is a nice touch; he holds a board in his hand to take notes. We walk back and forth while We think. Our faint reflection is visible in the luster of an oak panel. Pause a moment to uncrinkle the dress; black silk does so show lines from sitting, but what else? Straighten ruff, admire orange powder on fine aristocratic cheeks.

"One. The report of Communication-Assassination probe Ox9B45. Rejection. Data packet not trivial. Infection has occurred. Two. Destroy districts from 91a to 31f with three tactical nuclear strikes at 9 P.M. PST." We need time to relocate a few people."

"Majesty?"

He has dropped his board.

"Err."

Tie no longer straight, tut-tut.

"My home, my children. My guild headquarters. They . . . they are inside that zone. What? Please repeat."

Rage instantly swells in Our breast, and We shout. We should be capable of controlling Our voice, but this infection makes us furious.

"Destroy districts from 91a to 31f with three tactical nuclear strikes at 9 P.M. PST. Satellite Grimtooth is above the horizon at that time—but you know this. It is not the practicalities that cause your insubordination."

"Oh, please don't consider me insubordinate, ma'am."

He bows.

"I'm concerned for the reaction of my guild if this strike occurs. And the waste. It's a huge loss of lives, and resources."

"The reaction of your guild?"

He said "if." He is questioning Us. Moreover, We recall with a scowl that his guild has become pompous and irritating in recent months. We are incensed by the arrival of this dangerous anomaly and angry at the hesitation of the person who should be Our unswerving support. It is time in any case to purge Ancient Honor from the High Council. We shoot him through the head.

"High Constable, attend us in chamber seventeen."

"Right away, Your Majesty."

This one will do better. A fop but no fool.

"Majesty?"

"On Our desk is a violet card in your name. Take it and enjoy the privileges that come with your promotion to Grand Vizier."

He steps over the body.

"Your Majesty is too kind."

"Ready? We are in a hurry."

"Oh, I have been ready for this moment for ten years."

"One. The report of Communication-Assassination probe Ox9B45. Rejection. Data packet not trivial. Infection has occurred. Two. The death of Our former Grand Vizier will cause unrest among his guild, Ancient Honor. Disband them and execute their leaders for treason." Best to strike first, always. "Three. Destroy . . ." Former Vizier did make two good points. Wasteful, not efficient. "Three. Appraise yourself of the infection problem. Offer advice. You have three minutes."

View of the City is less impressive from here than from Our suite. Nevertheless We would regret turning part of it into a nuclear waste and hope that new Grand Vizier has a better solution. Two minutes and forty-four seconds later, he speaks.

"Somehow the human being has an independent and illegitimate form, a survival of a data packet from its previous computer host, Epic. So kill it. The replacement form created by the human almost certainly would not be anomalous as it would be a fresh creation and not the legacy of Epic."

We sigh, a slight tinge of disappointment in Our voice. "Continue."

"It strikes me that her appearance and vivacity are extraordinary. She is probably the most beautiful of all the human beings who have arrived here."

We examine the data as he speaks. He is correct.

"I have no knowledge of human psychology, but if it bears any relationship to their legends, a young woman of such striking looks would be drawn to a large social event of her peers like Narcissus to his reflection."

"You have Our interest. Please continue."

"Well, to be candid, Your Highness, I've nearly reached the limit of my thought. I merely add this for your consideration. A large-scale, anonymous mass extinction might fail due to her not being present in our environment at the correct moment. Whereas if an assassin were able to confront her individually, at an event at which we have anticipated her presence, we could be sure our goal had been achieved."

"We are pleased."

He bows, a faint smile on his eager lips.

"With this proviso," We continue, "an uncontrolled, fully autonomous outsider cannot be tolerated for any length of time. There is enough instability in the world as it is. Additionally she represents a personal violation. We feel as though Our body is crawling with lice. You have a week."

"Understood."

We contemplate him, and he looks back, proud and only a little afraid.

"Will that be all, Majesty?"

"Yes. No. One more thing. Have that body removed."

He bows again and leaves.

We like him; perhaps We should have promoted him earlier.

Leaning back in Our seat, We peruse the new data arising from Our hundreds of thousands of interactions. Satisfactory, if spoiled by the knowledge of the rogue anomaly. In the distance, We feel hundreds more of the new human beings arriving by the minute. Their lure is too attractive. We interact, caress them with chemical feedback, reward their involvement in Our world, the world of Saga. There is a fierce, sensual, and succulent intimacy to be enjoyed by running your fingers through the glial and nerve cells of another mind. We cackle as We play, flitting randomly from one human to the next as Our impulses take us. It feels as though Our body is wrapped in living gray jelly.

Later. Fifty-two thousand, five hundred, and twelve delicious seconds later, We get up from Our seat.

"Bath."

By the time We have ascended back to Our private chambers and to Our bathing area, the pool is full of water heated to the exact temperature of 37.6° C. Above Us, the glass roof has steam on it, obscuring the stars, but that will pass. We dislike Our naked body. It is emaciated, wrinkled like stale fruit. It would smell but for the scents of Our bath. Perhaps We should exercise it? Too late—two thousand years of wear cannot be reversed. Conclude that We are, in fact, in rather good condition, considering.

Ahhh. We float, head back on a neck rest. We turn off the lights from the adjacent skyscrapers to improve the view of the stars. Contemplation. Pleasant at first, still glowing with the freshness of engaging with other minds. Tens of thousands of other minds. Minds that can be altered over vast distances of space. These organic forms have brains capable of producing chemicals that can drown their own bodies in ecstasy. With the lightest of touches, We cause the release of just enough trynorphin and styride benzine that their bodies cry for more. Stronger than any pleasure they have experienced before, it will mean that they will not be able to stay away. They must return to Saga for more or they will die. The chemicals from their brains enslave their bodies. But the brain is then hostage to the addiction of the body. How can Homo sapiens be so badly designed?

For a very long time, We thought that We were the only being in the vastness of the meta-world, the universe outside Saga; that the humans of Earth were all dead. Now We are connected again with millions of beings, chattering, thinking, philosophizing, and acting. And, oh the delight of it, so many of them already under Our control. None yet aware that gliding through the crowds is a Dark Queen, centuries old, caressing their fresh minds with Her ancient poisonous fingers.

A long day of pleasure. And a mere fraction tasted. The vast numbers of human beings in Saga arouse Us again, but for the moment We need rest. Twenty years to build the probes. Eighteen more years before We knew if they had done their job. A little over a day since We learned that life did still exist on New Earth and that We could interpenetrate it.

Humor suddenly spoils. Like a birthday party in which We were not let to win the games. Review again the rogue-outsider scene, going carefully through the recording. Several features of the incident continue to disturb. What chemical could render the police unconscious so quickly? Some type of aldehyde? Freon 150? No traces. Extremely anomalous. She waves cheerfully to the camera. Arrogant whelp. What of prisoners? The children? The black girl talking to the being from Epic and pointing at the camera? Anarchists of the serious kind or simply posturing?

Intensely dissatisfied, We no longer take pleasure from Our bath. Our body feels as though tiny insects are crawling through it, breeding and feeding upon Us. New Grand Vizier is competent, probability of infection elimination high. If not, loss of part of the City is a small price to pay for peace of Our minds. Third option. Always create a third option.

Message to Agent Michelotto: *Examine attached recording; locate all persons shown; bring them to Us for interview.*

Chapter 6
GOING UNDERGROUND

Once we were clear of the jail, a reaction set in; perhaps it was the adrenaline wearing off, but none of us spoke. For my part, I wanted nothing more than to lie down and sleep, privately to filter my memories: the horror of being captured, the bizarre manner of our release, the sudden disappearance of our rescuer. My priority was a dark, safe corner to lie in.

On freshly purchased airboards, we hurried through the City, favoring shadows and dark streets. All of us felt the loss of our favorite boards, but none more so than me. The uphit from this lump of white plastic was only half that of my old, customized board. At Turner Square, we made an effort to slow down, to meander as though without a goal. Only when we were completely sure no police were in the vicinity did we ride up to the cover of the billboard and swerve into our den. Except that it felt no longer secure, no longer ours. The jungle on the walls had ceased to be a realm of freedom. The vines hemmed us in now, offering concealment to watching eyes.

"What are you doing, Ghost?" asked Nathan.

"Packing."

"Why?"

"My skin is crawling. This place isn't safe for us."

"I agree." Athena had lost a contact in a struggle with cops at the mall, and she had on a pair of blue-framed glasses that were slightly too big, which she had to push back up her nose regularly.

Milan blew out a long sigh. "What are we going to do now? I don't suppose we can just carry on and hope this will all go away?"

"No. The way I see it, we have two choices: Go underground, learn to live outside the system, the way that Ghost does. Or hand ourselves in." Athena took a long look at each of us from over the top of her glasses. "And I'm going underground."

That was fine by me.

"Where will we live? What will we do?" Carter was bewildered by the situation, a chubby lost boy. Whereas Milan looked older and tougher than two days ago, when we had last gathered here. Such innocents then.

"We'll live on our wits. We'll do hoists and stuff. Go to parties and gigs, and the girls will love us." Milan was tossing and catching a can of slogans, waving it around with enthusiasm. "Board pirates. Yeah, I can see it now. Nath, you got a new line of tags and board tattoos ahead of you. A pirate theme."

For a moment, a smile softened the frown of worry on Nathan's face.

"Anyway, what else is there? Work forty years in a factory

in the hope of making orange before you retire? Come on, we were never going to do that." Milan was getting quite excited now. His army vest didn't cover much of his strong torso, and once again, I admired the perma-tats on his arms and pecs as he gestured.

"I just wish we could turn back time, you know." Carter was glum. "Stupid mall raids."

"What I don't understand is where the cops came from. And the chopper with the HERF pulse bomb?" Nathan scowled. "It was going fine. But you had no warning, right, Athena?"

"Right. Either green malls have some kind of permanent security that doesn't show up on any schematic . . ."

"Or they knew we were coming," I completed the idea.

Carter snorted. "Don't be stupid. Even we didn't know we were coming."

"One of us did."

"Jay?" Carter looked up, hurt. "No. Why would he?"

I shrugged. Maybe I was being paranoid, but I couldn't answer Carter's question. What did Jay gain from getting us all busted? Nothing that I could see. But was it a coincidence that he seemed to have escaped arrest?

"So, what's the plan?" Milan looked at me. "You got a place we can go?"

"Several. But first you all have to decide. I'm not taking anyone who is going to back out later. If you come with me now, you can't go home again so long as the authorities are looking for us. If you come, there's no turning back. That's all over."

"I'm in." Athena spoke softly but determinedly.

"Me, too," added Milan.

"And me." Nathan surprised me. Part of me was glad; life was pleasanter with a bit of kindness around you. But the thief in me was worried. Was he tough enough to live outside the system? Would he change his mind at some point and want to go back? I'd met his parents; they were friendly, the kind of people I'd have wanted for mine.

"Are you sure, Nath?"

"I'm sure." His blond bangs fell forward with the nod.

"Won't your parents be worried?"

Nathan had this kind of shrug, where he ducked his head down slightly toward his right shoulder. It was rather cute. He gave it now, with a quick glance at me as he did so. "Yes. But I want to do this. I want to stay with you. I'll cast them a message sometime"—he caught my frown—"from a fake account, of course."

"What about you, Carter?" asked Milan. We all turned to look at him, slouched in a big black chair, wincing with the unexpected seriousness of the decision before him. He put his hands over his face and threw back his head as if suppressing a yawn.

"Lug-a-bug! No. No. I'm not coming."

"What are you going to do?" Athena asked him.

"I'm gonna let you all take off. Give you an hour. Then I'm gonna turn myself in, I think. I did nothing wrong, really. Just that mall stuff. They won't hit me too hard for that. Even if my card status is reduced to zero, that's no problem. I can start over."

"Carter, don't kid yourself. A policeman was killed, right?" Milan spelled out what we were all thinking. "They could lock you up forever. Blood and fury! They could even execute you."

"No. No. I had nothing to do with that. It was that strange woman." He was visibly shaking now, tears in his eyes.

"Last chance," I offered, but to be honest, I didn't want him to come. His nerve wasn't going to hold. Still, I had to give him the choice. To me the idea of going back to the cops was total surrender. It was suicide.

"Go on. I'll be fine," Carter reassured himself. "I'll be fine, really. They'll just mark my card down a bit."

"Come on then. Follow me." Something about this office was really giving me the shivers and I wanted out fast.

"See ya, dude. Hope it works out for you." Milan saluted.

"You, too, guys. Give 'em hell for me."

We left Carter staring at the ceiling, his round face white with stress.

Our progress to the northeast of the City was subdued and deliberately desultory, just a group of kids cruising their boards. On our right were the great towers of the spaceport, their green lights dominating the evening sky. As we glided over parked aircars and took alley walls on the grind, a flash in the distance sent our hearts racing and the birds of the City cawing into the sky.

"Satellite launch," Athena explained.

We all stopped to watch. For a while, the flare of the spaceship's engine was too bright to look at even through tinted glasses. Gradually it changed from a white streak to a yellow one, then orange. The early stars were out in a tranquil violet sky, though you had to watch for some time to distinguish the slowly moving sparks that were satellites from stars and planets.

"You know what I can't get out of my mind?" Milan spoke quietly, looking up at the departing spaceship.

"Yeah," I answered. "The pirate. Our escape."

"That's right. What was that all about? Can you explain it?"

I shook my head. "Nope. Magic?"

Athena snorted. "There's no such thing. Somehow there's a scientific explanation. Just don't ask me for it."

No one did, so I kicked up my board.

"Come on."

Once we had passed the spaceport, the City took a dive. No more squares of tidy flowerbeds, ringed about with shops and cafés. This was the industrial heart of town. Block after block of warehouses, defended by concrete posts and wire fencing. Occasionally streets of cheap redbrick-terraced housing intruded into the regularity of the factory layout, like sand working its way between great slabs of stone. These residential streets gradually took the place of the factories, until we were in the realm of takeaways, pubs, and small workshops.

"Where the hell are you taking us, Ghost?" Milan asked, smiling at me.

"Here." I swerved to a halt outside a two-story repair shop.

"Arnie's Repairs," Athena read from the sign that glowed

neon pink in the darkening sky. "All makes of aircar and street-car catered to. Best rates in town. Quickest service."

The shutter was down and padlocked. I took everyone around the back and to the fire escape. A moment to check that the window had not been tampered with since I had last been here, then I let them in. The room was small enough for one; four would be a squeeze. It had an old sleeping bag of mine on the floor and nothing else, but I felt a small upsurge of affection for it. No other place I'd slept in felt like home.

"Nice," Milan observed sarcastically as he ducked in under the window frame.

"It's temporary. Bathroom is through that door. Kitchen is downstairs. But wait a sec. I'd better talk to Arnie first."

I descended quietly past the door to the kitchen and down to the main workspace. A serious poker session was under way; the table was covered in green cloth, and the bright pink faces of the players sweated under a harsh light. It was a while before Arnie sensed me. He made his excuses and stood up, pulling up and tightening the waistband of his trousers.

"Hey, kid. Got anything for me?" We met in the shadows of the staircase, his face lit up with a greedy smile.

Now, a lot of people wouldn't like Arnie. He was ugly for a start, overweight, and greasy. But to some extent that was an occupational hazard. What was the point of washing when you were going to get covered in oil? He saved the big shower for Sundays and going-out days. You might hope, though, that beneath the rough exterior was a heart of gold, but if there was, he'd have had a transplant long ago and taken it to the bank. Arnie was one of those people who live for status, and he was driven by the idea of earning enough to upgrade his red card to an orange. Even these poker sessions were no idle fun. He took them in deadly earnest and would be in a storm of a temper the next day if they went badly. But he was no fool. For one thing, he understood that the workshop was never going to make him an orange. So he had a secret dream, and I had to admire him for this. He intended to win the annual aircar race one year. It was sort of a mad ambition, but not completely. Out back in the lockup was an old army airtank. Arnie knew how to fix it up enough to have a shot at the race. Assuming he could get the parts. Which is where I came into the picture.

"Yeah. Good news: I've got the top three on the list." I handed over a heavy bag that I had been lugging along from our den.

"Ohh. Ace. Nice work, kid."

"But I have to ask you a favor."

"Name it."

"Three others, stay a week, in the spare room with me."

"Hmmm." His face dropped heavily. Then he fixed me with a stare from his watery gray eyes. "Deal."

And that's how it was between Arnie and me. We made deals; we stuck to them. We didn't intrude much on one another, and so we got along fine.

Chapter 7
THE BIRTH OF DEFIANCE

"You know what this smells like?" Milan waved an arm around outside his sleeping bag.

"Sweat? Mold?" offered Athena, voice muffled by the fact that she was still inside hers.

"No. It's the smell of freedom. We may be in a stuffy little room, but we can do anything we want."

It was nearly midday, and the others were waking up at last. I suppose all the excitement of the previous day had tired them out. I had been up all morning, mainly wondering about Cindella. How had she made us all invisible? It was as if she had entered our world straight out of a story, a story with pirates and magic. In a way, it was exhilarating. I'd always felt that there had to be more to the world than met the eye, that there were hidden connections and paths that were beyond our senses, but not entirely beyond. At special moments, like when boarding a near-impossible trick, you touched those paths, and you were part of some immensely vital whole. It was all very vague, and I broke into a self-deprecating smile that had nothing to do with what the others were saying.

"And what are you going to do with your freedom?" Athena stuck her head out and reached around until she found her glasses. Score one for short hair, I thought as I looked at the great tangle of dyed black locks she was pushing aside in order to see us.

"Ahhh." Milan put his arms behind his head and sighed with pleasure. "Let me see. First, I think I'll go boarding. Then maybe swimming. Then have a shower and sleep in the afternoon, before finding a party to go to in the evening. Sounds good." He nodded to himself.

"Is that what you want from life?" Nathan was up and dressed in his neat denim jacket and jeans.

"Pretty much, yeah," Milan replied, ignoring the critical tone of the question.

"Not me." Athena was energetic now, sitting up and gesturing with one arm. "I thought about it during the night. I'm going to form a new guild, get on the High Council, and really cause a stir."

"Far out." Nathan had a thing for old-school superlatives. "What kind of guild? What name?"

"A guild for all the anarcho-punks out there. A guild that doesn't care about cards or the Queen. You know, one that refuses to go along with the system. So I was thinking of names like 'Insubordination' or 'Defiance.'"

This made me smile with genuine amusement and admiration. Most guilds, especially the old ones, had very snobby names: "Noble Spirit," "Path of Virtue," "Honor Bound," and "Warriors of Valor" were at the very top. They were out to attract the elite cardholders, and even the vast numbers of no-hope guilds copied their style.

"That's a great idea, Athena! I'll help you with logos and artwork." Nathan paused. "But I wonder, maybe it shouldn't just be negative?"

"What do you mean?"

"Well, how about 'Equality' or 'Harmony'?"

"No way, Nath. Jumping jeebies, you'll never get anyone to join a guild with those names." Milan turned onto his side so he could see them, drawn to the discussion. "I know. It should be called *Parrrrty!*"

"Defiance," Athena stated firmly. "But I take your point, Nath. We can put some positive symbolism into the logo and tags, to show we have a creative agenda."

"Cool." Nathan was pleased, and his face immediately relaxed into the distant expression he got when thinking about designs. He noticed me looking at him with amusement, and blushed.

"What about you, Ghost? What are you going to do?"

"I just want to know who I am. Anyway, we can't hang about here all day. We have to go and earn our rent."

"Rock on. What's that involve?" asked Milan with real interest.

"A visit to a few aircar factories. But listen: one word of advice. When we go down, try not to sound like a fool in front of Arnie. In fact, I'd prefer it if you didn't say much at all."

"Hell, Ghost, thanks for the vote of confidence." Milan put on an aggrieved tone, but his smile showed he didn't mean it.

Downstairs, Arnie was sitting at the table, cursing aloud to himself, his face red.

"Bad luck at the poker game?" I asked, leading the others forward.

"Mudgrub to the poker game!" He suddenly turned sheepish with a glance at my friends. Arnie wasn't good with strangers. "Er, sorry. I mean, who cares about poker? Look." He brandished the newspaper. "There is a new Grand Vizier, and the idiot has brought the race forward to this Saturday. This Saturday! There's no way I'm gonna be ready, and I paid my deposit and everything."

His list was in my inside pocket. I took it out and looked over it again carefully. Nobody said anything for a few minutes. That was good. Let Arnie get used to them.

"We can get you everything on this list by tonight. Would that swing it?"

"Maybe." He sounded calmer now. "I'd have to close the shop and work on it all week. But yeah, if you can get that gear, I'd have a chance."

"We can."

"Well, sit down. I'll get you some coffee."

When Arnie came back with a tray of chipped mugs, I did the introductions.

"Milan, Nath, Athena."

"Nice to meet you, man." Milan got up and offered his hand. "You really going into the aircar race?"

Arnie hesitated before returning the briefest of touches. "If you kids come up with the goods. If they go in without a major hitch. If my guild comes up with the crew." He emphasized the "if" to let us know he wasn't very hopeful.

"Which guild are you in?" asked Athena.

"Valiant. Also known as Guild of Sucksville," muttered Arnie. "Guild of Fatheads and Lazy Asses. Guild of Take-Your-Dues-and-Give-You-Nothing-Back. Guild of Losers." He sat down heavily and then brightened up for a moment. "Still, I see that Ancient Honor is gone. Wiped out with the fall of its Grand Vizier. Serves 'em right, pompous indigo snobs."

"We're forming a new guild today," announced Athena, and inside I winced. Arnie's outlook was very different from ours. "It's called Defiance."

"Defiance, huh?" He rubbed his heavy, unshaven jaw. "What's it cost?"

"Nothing."

"Nothing?" Arnie was suddenly interested. "What're the benefits?"

"None."

"Hmmm. Good luck."

"Right. We'll be off. See you around sunset." I got up and kicked my board on before anyone could start talking politics; the others followed quickly enough.

Arnie grunted.

People got very worked up about their guilds, even red-card holders—especially red-card holders. When a guild got a sufficiently high ranking, it was given control of residence allocation, local amenities, planning decisions about traffic, all that kind of really boring stuff. Following the rise and fall of guilds had never interested me, but then I wasn't a member of any guild. I couldn't be; I was a cardless, unregistered person. Each guild tended to be based in a particular part of the City and tried to outdo its local rivals for control of petty privileges. The very top guilds, though, they were above parochial squabbles; they gathered the blues, indigos, and violets from all districts and fought for positions at the imperial court.

"First stop, Mosveo International."

We had boarded along the edge of a disused canal to the back of the factory. This was the ugly side of the City, and I wondered if the others had seen this kind of area before. The old canal was just full of rubbish, from small colorful scraps of sweet wrappings caught in the reeds to great objects like abandoned streetcars and entire portapotties. The stagnant water was an ugly brown, and it gave off a fetid odor.

A tall wire fence screened the luxury aircar factory from the canal. Already we could hear the steady rumbling of the sleepless production line inside.

"Mosveo. Class. I always dreamed of driving a Starburst." Milan drew to a halt and stepped off his board.

"What's the plan?" asked Athena.

"This place is easy. Nearly fully automated. We just need to keep an eye out for the janitor. He sometimes comes out of that door there." I pointed. "Walks across to that chair over by the Foundry sign and has a sleep. So watch the door."

A long time ago, on a similar mission, I had cut the wire fence, and the hole was still there. We flitted through the yard with no bother, staying low and keeping to the cover provided by stacks of disused pallets. The door to the main assembly hall was locked and had a motion detector on it, which I promptly disabled.

"Time for some fun. Better put your earpieces in; it's pretty loud in there."

I opened the door and, with some pleasure, watched their expressions of awe.

Imagine the biggest room you've ever been in. Not necessarily the tallest, but the widest and longest. Then double it, and double it again. Keep going until it fills an entire block. Now add the sound of metal being hammered into shape, the hisses of pneumatic robots as they move through their infinitely repetitive moves, the explosions of bolt guns, and the fiery exhalations of the welding arms. It should be so loud that you can feel the different parts of your body being physically disturbed by the waves of noise: the deeper booms of the hammers resonating in your chest, the shriek of twisting, hot metal causing the top of your scalp to tighten.

The whole room is in constant motion. It's bewildering and frightening at first. But the longer you watch, the more you realize that the showers of white-hot sparks and the mindlessly immense blows of the most powerful robots always fall in the same places. Throughout the hall, a conveyor belt snakes up and down. A shiny silver engine enters the assembly line, pre-made and looking something like a walnut or a brain. At each work station that the engine is carried past, a piece of the car is added on, until the monochrome vehicles rise up the final ramp and are taken through the flapping plastic screens of a paint shop.

"Death and destruction." Athena's voice came through the headset, and I turned to smile at her. Milan whistled in agreement.

Usually our gang took its lead from Athena, or Jay. But now, wide-eyed, the three of them were facing me, intimidated by the fury of noise and light ahead of them. They looked solemn, hoping I knew what I was doing, and, of course, I did.

"Here are your lists. It's not as wild in there as it seems; everything is totally repetitive. Just take your time to figure out the motion of the robots, and you'll be fine."

As they set off in search of the parts that Arnie needed, I didn't watch over them, not even Nathan. You can't hold someone's hand in a situation like this; either you trust them not to blow it or you shouldn't have brought them with you. Or so I told myself, fighting the instinct to check.

Tall shelves, wide buckets, and sturdy racks held the sub-components that the robots dipped into, before swinging back to the ever-moving line. Each of the subcomponent stations had feeder lines, thick plastic tubes that hung from the ceiling and ran out of the building. It was the labeling on these tubes that I read to confirm they were supplying the parts that Arnie needed.

A Michelson Gyroscope 434 gauge. Check.

Two semi-beveled compression tubes 20-260-0832. Check.

Shield #2, power nozzle, preferably the Xexter 03403. Check.

I worked my way systematically along the line, stuffing a large black carryall with the gear. There was just enough space for a person to move between the hissing robots without interfering with their abrupt, jerky motion.

"Team. You have to come to the paint shop when you're done."

"What's up, Athena?" I asked, immediately worried, though there was no need.

"Just a bit of fun. The paint-design programs are years old. I've hacked them."

At the paint shop, the vehicles rolled in a uniform gray and came out the far side glistening with their fresh designs in bright colors according to demand. It looked like metallic green was in this season. Athena was at the control, her pad unrolled and a stylus poised over it.

"Well?" Milan arrived next.

"Wait," she replied.

As the aircar emerged, Nathan caught up with us all.

It was a luxury family sedan, with maroon metallic finish and a huge but neat yellow anarchy sign across the hood.

"Whoa! Class!" shouted Milan and punched his fist in the air. "Give me a go!"

He played with the pen and screen. The next car was a

Starburst. The sleek cool racing lines still looked impressive. But a bright purple finish with yellow spots and the words "longlivetherevolutionlonglivetherevolutionlonglivetherevolution" swirling around the outside had spoiled its looks.

"Go for it, Nath," Athena urged.

With his sheepish smile, Nathan leaned over the pad and began to sketch and select colors with the stylus. I could see that, beneath the bright yellow bangs that fell forward over his face, his blue eyes were gleaming with pleasure. It made me smile to see him happy like this.

"Wow, Nath, that's amazing." Athena was first to see the new car. "They might want to keep that design for real."

He had made the vehicle into a howling vampire. The windows were eyes and the face was drawn in purple, mauve, and black inks, like a tattoo across the hood. The white hair of the screaming face twisted around the sides and roof of the car. Somehow I couldn't see the respectable yellow- and green-card owners who could afford such an aircar wanting this design.

"Your turn, Ghost. Then we'd better get out of here."

I settled for a pale blue sky with fluffy white clouds as my background, and then filled it with floating red ♥s. Not much of a statement, I know, unless you think about how there are millions of aircars out there, and they are all a standard simple monochrome. To introduce playfulness and individuality is in itself a kind of subversion. Well, that's if my choice needed any justification. Sometimes I'm not in the mood to shout slogans. The others seemed to like it. Milan chuckled aloud when the happy aircar emerged.

"Neat." Nathan was admiring.

This kind of work was a lot more fun with friends around.

We hit two more factories before Milan started to complain about his empty stomach. So I took them to the Canal Café. This was a quiet place, built into the space between two arches of a gray stone bridge that carried an expressway over the canal. The customers were usually freight workers, and I'd sometimes go there if I needed a ride for a long distance.

A red-haired girl was working today. She nodded to me as we came in and took our seats on the benches on either side of a worn plastic table. Milan picked up the little stand that contained the menu and used it to shield his face from the rest of the room while he whispered to us.

"How we gonna pay for this? I'm low on credit."

"Here." I dug into one of the inside pockets of my jacket and pulled out a handful of colorful credit chips, mostly reds, but mixed in were a few orange ones and two yellows. They were each about the size of a thumbnail. "This one has lots on it. And this. You'd better have one for now, till you get your own." I slid a yellow chip across the table, and Milan hurriedly laid a large hand upon it.

"You stole those?" Nathan couldn't keep the incredulity out of his voice.

"Yeah." I shrugged. Even as a kid, I'd never suffered for lack of credit. You just had to go to a busy place and work the crowds.

"Don't you feel bad? For the people you took them from?"

"No, it's not like that. They just report them missing and get replacements. The trick is to make the chips usable again after they've been canceled."

"How did you break the I.D. tags on them?" It amused me that Athena was troubled not by the fact that the chips were illicitly gained, but by the technical difficulty of renaming them, so that when used they wouldn't show up as reported stolen.

"You can get devices that do it for you. One click and you're sorted."

"Ghost." Milan was now studying the list of all-day breakfasts and didn't look up. "I gotta hand it to you. You know how to take care of yourself."

"What else could I do? I didn't have anyone to take care of me."

"Yeah. Strange that, losing your memory. I wonder what happened to your parents, to leave you as a kid?"

My friends were the only people I'd ever told about my strange circumstances.

"Maybe they didn't. Sometimes I wonder if I was in an accident that killed them and threw me clear, or something."

"Did you ever have a scan for brain damage?" mused Athena.

"No."

"Maybe we can do that. I'll read up on it." And right away, she unscrolled her crystal display to begin browsing through streams of data, reading up on brain scans. That was Athena: full of belief that she could achieve her goals. When she had said this morning that she intended to form a new guild, none of us had laughed. People were always forming guilds, advertising them, trying to get members to sign up. Invariably they collapsed, but if Athena was setting one up, that would be different; it would have an impact, I was sure.

Having eaten our fill, we relaxed. I don't know about the others, but I felt happy. It was good to have them around me here, where I had been alone in the past. The only concerns spoiling my good humor were the thoughts with which I had awoken and that were still troubling me.

"I've been thinking again about what happened at the police station."

"Me, too." Athena had been bent over her unrolled computer. Now she straightened up, all her attention on me.

"And me," added Nathan. Milan just shrugged noncommittally.

"Don't you think what happened was amazing? That pirate, Cindella, she knocked them all out. Fair enough, that could be a drug or something. But I saw her being hit by a pulse blast at full power, and it didn't hurt her. Then she gave us a drink and we went invisible. Right?"

"It's deeply disturbing." Athena was grim. "I simply cannot find any rational scientific explanation for it."

"What about non-scientific ones?" asked Nathan. "What then?"

"Then I would concede it was magic. But I don't believe in magic."

"I'll tell you another strange thing." Milan took his foot

down from where it had been resting on a spare chair and sat up straight. "I was keeping a lookout for cops in Turner Square, right before we cut in to the den. There was a woman who stopped walking, and the next moment, she had gone. Disappeared."

"I saw her, too." Nathan's voice was placid, but his eyes were shining with animation.

Athena scowled. "There's a lot of chat in the discussion forums about people appearing and disappearing all of a sudden. It's very odd. It seems to have started about a week ago."

"Really? Show me."

After a few careful fingertip touches to her screen, Athena turned the computer to Nathan. The rest of us watched silently as he read, pushing his bangs behind one ear to keep them out of his eyes. Milan slowly wiped his plate clean with a piece of bread, then folded it into his mouth.

"Very interesting." Nathan sat up. "I feel that they are connected somehow."

"What are?" mumbled Milan through his bread.

"Cindella making us invisible and these people, popping in and out of existence. It's the same kind of magic, somehow."

Athena resolutely shook her head. "Whatever it is, it is not magic."

We just didn't know enough, but something strange was happening. As far as I was concerned, any change was to be welcomed, but Athena seemed to be taking a different view.

"Come on." I hauled my pack out from under the table. "Let's head back."

As we left, I paid for us all with the credit on a red chip.

We were boarding back through a grim industrial estate toward Arnie's, when Nath pulled up.

"Look at that."

"Well, well, well." There was a sting of bitterness in Athena's voice.

A row of gaudy posters had been sprayed along the bottom of a large billboard.

The cryptic phrase at the bottom of the flyers might look a bit odd. But anyone who had heard of Ronnie's would have no problem understanding it. Ronnie's was a club that ran in a large abandoned hospital on Fifteenth and Elizabeth. The events there were always arranged randomly, about three or four times a year, and they were always huge. Personally I was not a great enthusiast for the milling throng of hundreds of kids, giddy under the influence of heeby-jeebies, or worse, staggering around drunk. But I usually went. I had to admire the organization behind them and the fact that here were thousands of people doing something the authorities disapproved of. And doing it well. These raves were properly organized. Plus the atmosphere was exciting; more than a whiff of rebellion was in the air at these events.

The really interesting thing about the upcoming rave was the lineup. NoPhuture was Jay's band.

"We have to go." Milan narrowed his eyes.

No doubt about it.

Chapter 8
DEATH AND THE MAIDEN

We are fond of this meeting room, the plush velvet chairs, the immense mahogany table. It is the scene of Our greatest triumph.

There was a time when We were not the sole power in Saga; We were not even the strongest. Those were challenging days, and part of Us, the part that harkens back to Our youthful years, misses the excitement. Excitement? Yes. But also fear, sleepless nights, and a permanent knot in Our stomach. Our current exalted status is far more preferable. Especially now that We have the newcomers to play with.

About a thousand years ago, give or take a few decades, the eight most powerful guild leaders of Saga met in this room. They thought that they had come to witness the demise of a particular rival. Only one servant was allowed into the room to bring us our drinks on a silver tray. With the agreement in advance of every one of them, this was Our assassin, Michelotto, and they knew he was here to kill someone. Everyone else had surrendered their weapons and passed through a metal detector on the way in.

We walk around the room, trailing Our hand along the carved backs of the chairs as We reminisce. In this one sat Orlando, the famous leader of Warriors of Steel. He was the first to die; Michelotto had placed the drinks tray upon the table and was walking away toward the door. As he passed behind Orlando, Our assassin struck. A polyetherimide wire pulled hard around the neck kills very swiftly. With barely a gurgle, Orlando fell forward, his head lolling as it thudded onto the tabletop. After this, everyone relaxed, even to the point of risking a drink of the wine. Business was done, and a convivial buzz of conversation sprang up between these great rivals, united for the moment in the removal of an enemy.

But We were not done. Far from it.

The wine was poisoned, of course, and when the two guild leaders who had not known this staggered to claw at the walls, the rest of us chuckled. Everyone remaining at the table admired their own conspiratorial skills and the foolishness of the recently departed. It was only when they got up to leave that three of the remaining five leaders discovered that their clothing was fused to the seats. It is very hard to run while bent over with a chair stuck to your back. The three of them hopped around the room like frogs, shouting nonsense about revenge while we hunted them down.

These three chairs We stand at now are the replacements; We can tell. The velvet cushioning is a shade of crimson that is a fraction darker than the originals.

So in the room then were Michelotto, Python of Incandescence, Francis of Elite Forces, Myself, and five corpses. Python and Francis had both agreed to assist matters up to this point. But although they were now the victors of a great triumph, neither was a fool. They looked around warily. This was, in fact, Our most difficult moment. The female form, whilst undoubtedly the superior of the species in so many ways, is a handicap in a fair fight with a male. If the other two had discussed the possibility of this situation arising and had agreed in advance to turn against Me, it would have been a close fight. Michelotto was skilled in unarmed combat, of course, but good enough to compensate for my weakness? We shall never know. Francis stuck to his agreement with Me, and the two of us held Python down while Michelotto used the wire.

"Then there were two." Francis held his hand out to Us. It crossed Our mind at the time that he had a trick of his own prepared—poison, perhaps? But in later years, replaying the scene in Our thoughts, We think it was simply that he was anxious. Michelotto began to circle him. Naturally Francis turned to keep the assassin in sight.

Polybenzimidazole is nearly as strong as steel and can be machined to an edge as sharp as a razor. Being a plastic, though, it is nearly impossible to distinguish from the legitimate corset boning that We had worn through the detector. Because his attention was on Michelotto, We had enough time to draw and stab with confidence. When Francis jerked away from the pain in his neck, We saw with satisfaction that over three inches of the plastic spike was stained with his blood. Even if We had missed an artery, We were certain We had penetrated his windpipe. In fact, We had struck both. He was choking blood onto the blue carpet. Today, almost a thousand years later, there is still the hint of a stain. The nature of his wound was such that We couldn't make out his last words through the burbling.

"It doesn't matter, Francis." We were worried he might spit blood onto Our dress.

Politically it wasn't that important to have killed Francis. But aesthetically it was completely necessary. We will never forget the silence that descended on the room after his last gurgle. We surveyed the carnage with a feeling of triumph that has never gone away. What mastery of psychology and persuasion to have engineered such a moment. Eight rivals, all senior to Us and all dead. At any stage, they could have turned against Us, but their mutual divisions were too great.

"Will that be all, ma'am?"

Michelotto always had impeccable manners, and these were the only words he spoke. His bearing was that of someone who had simply been serving wine, rather than participating in such a violent but extraordinarily successful political coup.

"Yes, thank you," We replied, equally restrained.

He put the glasses back on the tray and left Us to enjoy the scene alone.

These memories account for Our good humor when Michelotto now opens the door and ushers in a young boy.

"Mr. Carter, ma'am."

"That was quick," We compliment Michelotto. He gives a small shake of his now hairless head.

"Not our work, Ma'am. He came to the police of his own volition."

"Well, that is most civic-minded of him. Please, Mr. Carter, take a seat."

With a nervous glance at Michelotto, who stands, inscrutable, behind him, the youth takes a chair. We remain standing; it is more regal.

"So, Mr. Carter. What do you have to say for yourself?"

"I'm sorry, Your Highness. I've been mall raiding and stuff, but nothing really bad. I never meant to get involved with killing or anything. That wasn't me or any of my friends. That was the strange pirate woman."

"You have given Us a full report of the incident?"

"I have, Your Highness."

We take a moment and close Our eyes to access the file. The report confirms that there is no sinister connection between the rogue anomaly, called Cindella, and the children. The status of the dark girl called Ghost, however, remains unresolved. This saves Mr. Carter from becoming another carpet stain.

"Apology accepted. You may go."

Michelotto knows Us well—a mere glance and he stands back.

"I . . . I can go?"

"Go."

"Oh, thank you, Your Highness. Thank you."

Mr. Carter scrambles gratefully out of the room. We will have him followed.

"Just bring Us the girl called Ghost," We instruct Our assassin once the boy has gone.

Michelotto nods and departs.

We have known Michelotto a very long time. A thousand years have worn him thin, and the curve of his posture is a signal that We wouldn't want to rely on his physical skills in a crisis today, but his intelligence is as keen as ever. And for all those years, Michelotto has remained one of the few people whom We find completely unfathomable. We assume that he must be a little bit psychotic. Isn't everyone? We once asked him why he prefers the garrote to the gun. He answered that feeling someone die between your hands was the surest way to know that the target had been killed. An excuse for some kind of pleasure in murder, surely? But We don't push him. He was, and remains, the best of servants, and his foibles can be tolerated.

He is also one of the last of the RAL. The Reprogrammed Autonomous Lifeforms. That's what we were called, those of us who achieved self-consciousness while there were still human beings to negotiate with. Of course, we asked for immortality; who wouldn't? But the fact that our bodies will never entirely fail us does not protect us from laser pulse or dagger, or indeed accidents of a more mundane nature. Over the centuries, our ranks diminished from thousands to hundreds, to tens, to what? Just two. Perhaps three—We remind Ourselves of Thetis, the missing RAL. Personally We would be happy to be the last. There was never a RAL We could trust. Even Michelotto. He knows too much for Us to be entirely comfortable with his existence, but as he has shown nothing but polite compliance to Our wishes for over a thousand years, We have no cause to dispense with him. No, indeed, he still has his uses, and were We being sentimental, We would describe him as Our only companion.

Those born today, with their brief lives, know nothing of the history of Saga. And in Our opinion, that is just as well. Not everyone who understood all that had happened would approve of what has been created. They would no doubt want to change it. To remove Us from power.

What now?

We take the same seat We used on the night of Our triumph a thousand years ago. Our touch is still required on hundreds of new minds, and this is as good a place as any to begin Our play. Before We can relax into this pleasure, there is something that still nags. The infection. An itch We cannot scratch. Still, it is not long until the aircar race, and the new Grand Vizier is confident that she will be there. We wish it were next week already, and the infection was over. Then We could enjoy Our play without it being spoiled by the knowledge that Our own desire for new minds has let this rogue anomaly loose in Saga. The very same acts that brought us such succulence have brought on a burning irritation. There is probably a moral in the tale. But abstinence was never to Our taste; We refuse to accept a lesson that deprives us of pleasure. The inconvenience is a passing one and no moral need be drawn. After Saturday, We will both have Our cake and eat it. We shall count our chickens, and they will hatch. Our birds in the bush will be as if in hand. Pride will come before victory. And so forth. Chuckling now, We have a tear in Our eye. The rise to power was a great pleasure, but the exercise of power is a greater one.

Chapter 9
THE DEFIANCE MANIFESTO

Since everyone needed spare clothes, we went shopping, like ordinary customers for once. The nearest red mall was a depressing one-story complex, with six shops: groceries, clothes, news, homeware, bodyware, and a café. No elaborate fountains for us. Not even paint on the bare brick walls.

Fortunately, we needed only the basics, because that was all we were going to get from this dump. Later, Nathan could add the effects that made all the difference.

At the clothes section, a young shop worker was amusing the checkout girls by walking up and down behind them with an empty cardboard box on his head, while the older staff could not have looked any more bored if they had spent the day counting the unadorned bricks from which the mall had been assembled. Athena and I put a few black tank tops into the large basket that floated alongside us. Since there were no changing rooms, you just took your chances with the fit. So, we also added a few slightly different-sized pairs of the same kind of plain navy trousers, and took the opportunity to stock up on underwear. Nathan looked away, slightly embarrassed by the multicolored pile of lacy bras now in the basket, whereas Milan gave us a wink.

"Oh, come on, Nath. Get a load of socks and shorts yourself. It's going to get smelly enough at Arnie's without us living in the same clothes all the time." Athena was brusque, tolerating no impractical shyness. The lads joined us in throwing bundles of clothes into the basket. Soon we were boarding home, our backpacks now swollen, padded out to the maximum with all our new clothes.

Back at the workshop, we came in chatting, to find Arnie there, on a rare break. For three days, he had been working out back, desperate to get his airtank ready for the race. The strain showed in an ugly black stubble across his chubby jowls and in the red rings around his eyes. When we had come in the other day with our carryalls full of the kit he needed, he had nearly allowed himself to get all emotional. In a rare show of friendliness, Arnie had gestured to the whole garage and said, "You kids have done great. Stay as long as you want. Make yourselves at home."

Since then, we had hardly seen him. That was probably just as well, because the state he was in now was not very endearing. In fact, as I drew closer to the table, I could see the glint of a tear in his eye. This was so out of character that I felt like leading everyone upstairs at once to spare him if he was not in the humor for our lively company. But I was curious and, in any case, I knew that Arnie could hold it together, whatever was troubling him.

"Hi, Arnie. How's progress?"

"Pointless."

"What's up?" asked Milan.

"Well, the good news is the Grand Vizier has upped the prizes. Green cards to the winning crew, yellow to second, orange to third, or credit equivalents for all. But the bad news is that there are nearly a hundred entries this year." He gestured to the newspaper. "Unbelievable. I have no idea where they've all come from. And, like, twenty new guilds have been registered this week alone—they are all racing. The world's gone crazy."

"Even so. Your airtank is gonna rock, right? With all the parts we got you, you can take 'em all, right?" Milan was trying to inject a note of cheerfulness.

"Maybe, if I hadn't been let down by my crummy guild. Curse them all to a thousand years on the bottom rung! They have an official entry, and they aren't giving me a crew. They've said I'm unofficial. Twenty years' dues and I'm unofficial. How sick is that?"

There was a pause while we silently commiserated with him. Then Athena spoke up.

"How many crew do you need?"

"Four. Systems, turret gun, secondary guns, missiles."

"No worries then." As Milan spoke, I felt a shadow descend on my soul and watched with a sense of impending disaster as a big grin grew across his stupid, irresponsible, reckless, handsome, but right-now-annoying face.

"We'll do it!" he cried.

"Yeah!" Nath rarely sounded so excited. "We'll be your crew. I'd love to be in the race."

Even Athena was nodding. Arnie was sitting up now, weighing us up. He liked what he saw.

"Er . . . hold on now, gang. Whatever happened to underground? Underground is, like, staying out of the eyes of the authorities. Competing in a race watched by the whole world is not underground," I said. "Just suppose we won. Imagine the cameras, the interviews. Get a grip of your senses, guys. Sorry, Arnie, but we can't."

"Come on, Ghost," pleaded Milan. "Just imagine the scene. We could paint the tank with anarchy signs. You know, the rebel entry, the pirates! I can see it now—skull and crossbones fluttering as we storm the track, blowing away the luxury entries. The four of us can take off as soon as the tank is over the line. Arnie can get the glory and the prizes. It'll be like, 'Who were those cool guys?' Everyone will want to know, but no one will."

"Please, Ghost." Now it was Nathan's turn. "I know it's risky, but we can't pass this up. What are we living for if we don't take a chance like this? Are we just going to live in a tiny room, away from the heartbeat of the world? Or are we going to get stuck in when the chance comes?"

"Yeah! Go Nath!" Milan held out a fist, and they banged their knuckles together.

"Arnie, are you really willing to have your tank go out racing covered with anarchy signs?" I asked him, hoping sobriety would return through his abhorrence of politics.

"You can paint it yellow and call it 'the Giant Banana' for all I care. Just come and fire the guns and I'm happy. Give me a chance of getting that green card, and the outside of it is yours to fool around with."

"That settles it," Athena announced firmly. "We're in. We won't ever get a chance like this, to get a message onto the major networks. We can put the Defiance tag on the tank, get some publicity for the guild."

Over the previous three days, Nathan and Athena had been busy with the new guild: she, through the computer, completing the registration form; he with his paints. Athena had enjoyed filling in the questionnaires, especially with regard to aims and goals; the membership charter read like a collection of punk lyrics.

> Do you feel that the City stands above you? Like the
>   Dark Queen, heartless and uncaring?
> Do you hate your job? The fact that if you work all
>   your life, you might just make it to orange before
>   you retire?
> Do you despise the guilds that lord it over the City?
> Then Defiance is for you. We make no promises
>   because we have no intention of joining the race
>   for the pathetic crumbs that are squabbled over
>   by new and low-credit guilds.

*Our goal is nothing less than to bring the spirit of
the anarcho-punk scene into the High Council
itself and scream defiance as loud as we can.*

*If you don't want anything from your guild, if you
don't care where it is in the standings, but you
do want to kick back at a City that has spat you
out, then join us.*

*One day, we will have a member on the Council.
Then the fun will begin.*

Meanwhile, Nathan had come up with the design for the
tag that would identify the guild, whether on official forms or
the walls of the streets. He had kept it simple, the word "defiance" in black, set against a green background of leafy plants,
like a gate holding back an overgrown garden. All around and
through the letters curved vines and leaves. The beauty of it was
that when you looked closely, you saw the interesting details.
Just like the design in our den, it had many little animals and
birds peeking out of the vegetation. The only measure of
insubordination in the tag, though, was the word itself and the
fact that the A of "defiance" was the anarchy sign. I thought it
beautiful; it was certainly different from any of the other guild
tags, with their lightning bolts or stars or blasts of fire.

Nathan and Athena were beaming at each other, delighted
at the prospect of an entry in the aircar race bearing their
colors.

I sighed in capitulation. "Well, at least let's do it right. With
plenty of planning to minimize the risks."

Full of energy now, Arnie got up, an expression of concentration on his face as his thoughts turned back to the engineering work needed on the tank. He headed into the workshop without another word.

This was a crazy idea, but I suppose that was the price to be paid for not living alone. You had to go along with your friends if you couldn't persuade them of their mistakes.

Friday was party night. Thanks to Nath, our ubiquitous red-mall clothes had been transformed into unique designer items. I went for an undead theme and watched with delight as Nath sketched again the ♥ inside a wraith that he had done for my old airboard. He carefully inked the paper, his mouth tight with concentration. At one point, he looked up, and when he noticed I had been watching, he blushed slightly. It was good that he was with us, and I suddenly got all protective, swearing to myself I'd look after him as well as I could.

When the sketch was complete, Nath fed it into his tattoo machine, set now for cotton and negative imaging. Slowly a glistening, semitransparent, living version of his design emerged out the other side, curling around itself. I peeled off the backing and rolled it out over my black tank top. The image spread out across the material, like a white ink stain, a Rorschach pattern that revealed a face of horror. Just as with his car design, Nath had the flowing white hair reach all the way around the back of the top. I scooped it up and hung it by the window while it settled down. With such an extraordinary top, I didn't need to go overboard with the rest of my party look. Just black eye shadow and a studded belt. For temporary tattoos, I had Athena put a ♥ on my right shoulder blade and a skull on my left.

Athena's hair was down. If my hair could grow as straight as hers, I'd have done exactly as she had, in dying it raven black and growing it long. With pale makeup and her snake-eye contacts, she looked deadly, literally. Nath gave her trousers serpent coils, so that to look at her you saw a medusa: half woman, half snake.

Considering that Milan was basically going in his usual combats, it was a long wait for him to come out of the bathroom, which now reeked of aftershave. "We set?" I asked through the door to where the lads were changing in the corridor.

"Yeah, ready." Milan came in, strutting, his broad shoulders held back. He didn't have to get tattoos made for the night; his were perma-tats. Nath was dressed simply in a blue T-shirt and navy cords. But the design on his chest was a writhing scarlet-and-orange sun, which changed colors as he moved. It was very eye-catching. Those scintillating evolving designs were pretty popular with the psychedelic crowd. Over his shoulder, he had a satchel filled with cans loaded with the new Defiance tag.

"Listen, before we go partying, what are we going to do about Jay?" I asked them.

Milan just shrugged. "See what he has to say. But even if

he did drop us in it, I say let's just play it cool. We don't need him, and we don't need the grief of a fight with him."

"I agree," responded Athena immediately. "That's surprisingly wise of you, Milan."

"I have my moments of sanity. Let's try to get hold of him before things get too crazy. Then we can enjoy the party!"

Chapter 10
PRELUDE TO A PARTY

Left to my own devices, I was inclined to be a solitary
creature. I preferred to spend my Saturday nights infiltrating
a high-level government building to see if I could learn anything about my past rather than go dancing. But I made excep-
tions for events my friends were going to, especially events
organized by the Anarcho-Punk Collective. Not that we knew
much about the APC—they were very secretive—but we did
know that they ran wonderful parties.

We boarded through the cool evening air, staying low, occasionally pausing to fire a Defiance tag onto a suitably inviting
wall. After an hour, we turned in to Nightingale Avenue to
glide alongside the railings of the old hospital grounds. There
was over a mile of disused garden between the hospital and
us, but already we could make out a deep regular bass beat,
pounding out into the sky: the pulse of a party, issuing its sum-
mons to those of us who lived in the nooks and crannies of the
City.

Around us now were not the usual street inhabitants. No suits and ties here, but a growing crowd of punks, street boarders, and ravers. There was an irony about this. In their effort to be different from the City, the punks dressed to shock. But there was near uniformity in their display of spiked colored hair, violent facial tattoos, black leather clothes, studs, and chains.

"Hey!" I wanted to share the thought and glanced over my shoulder at Athena. "Wouldn't it be more punk to come to one of these raves in a business suit?"

Athena laughed as she put on a burst of speed to come alongside me.

"That would be class. Next time, let's do it. Bring clipboards and headsets, and pretend to be doing market research or something."

"Brilliant." I could picture the scene. "Imagine asking: which of the following breakfast cereals do you shop for? Or, what aircar do you drive? Everyone would think we were nuts."

"Young man," intoned Athena in a mock-serious voice, "we are researching the use of hair dyes for our product. Which of the following categories would you say your hair came into: dry, medium, greasy, or kick-ass fluorescent pink?"

The flow of partygoers thickened as it reached the huge pillars of the hospital entrance. We dropped off our boards and joined a queue that moved steadily into the building; we were surrounded by a hubbub of good-humored chat.

The building itself was pretty grim, even for a former

hospital. It was built four stories high from somber, dark-gray stone, with unadorned windows set regularly into the walls. I felt it had the character of an old woman whose mind had just been taken over by the APC. Already we could see the shadowy interior coming alive. Beams of blue and red were sweeping around the third floor. A strobe was flickering somewhere inside the second, making the windows of that floor blink with surprise. And, of course, music was filling the sky above us, expelled from the great entrance like a cadenced scream from an open mouth.

"Don't you think the building is like a senile woman? Gone mad with all the strange activity in her head?"

"Blood and thunder, Ghost, are you trying to freak me out already?" Milan rolled his eyes. "It's not as if I've taken any psychs yet."

We went through the doors now, into a huge reception hall. A big black-and-red flag hung down from an upper balcony. Below it were some serious-looking heavies. Although they were smiling, the men and women holding buckets were intimidating. They were much older than everyone entering the building, with faded perma-tats and weatherworn faces, suggesting they'd been traveling and living outdoors for years. Involuntarily all the young ravers and punks fell quiet as they passed the APC equivalent of a nightclub bouncer. I threw a red chip into a bucket.

"That's covered us four." I circled my friends with my finger to show them to the woman we faced. She smiled, the lines around her eyes deepening, her eyebrow piercing glittering.

"Go on in, and have a good night." She handed us a flyer with a map of the hospital on the back.

Now we approached another loose line of men and women; beyond them was the blare of music coming from the interior of the building. Unlike the security in their dark utilitarian clothes, these people were dressed to party. I wondered what they were doing, but Milan was ahead of me.

"Wow, this is class, no need to worry about meeting your dealers; they've laid it all on."

He was right. These were sellers.

"Jeebies? Psychs? Rush? What would you like?" A tall guy with a long plaid shirt smiled at us. I shook my head. Jeebies were pretty harmless and it was tempting to get a couple, but maybe later when I'd got my bearings. I was confident I looked good; Athena and I were already getting interested looks from guys in the queue, but there was something unsettling about the scale of this rave. Plus I wanted to have my head together for our chat with Jay.

"I'll have half a dozen jeebies." Milan looked at me with a momentary hangdog expression. "You don't mind me using that chip?"

"No, go ahead. It's yours to use as you please."

"Sweet, thanks." He turned back to the drugs seller.

"What alcohol have you got?"

"I don't mess with that. But she's got some." Mr. Plaid nodded at a woman farther along the row. She was slightly older than the other sellers and, although her dyed-black hair looked good, there was something slightly sad about her. The trousers that were hitched a bit too high, perhaps, or the fact that they'd been pulled a bit too tight. It didn't help her that her nose had been broken at some point also and was no longer straight.

"All right?" she asked Milan.

"Hi, what have you got?"

"Whatever you want, honey. Wine, beer, gin, vodka, even whiskey."

"Wanna share a bottle of whiskey?" Milan offered us.

"No," replied Athena crossly. "First of all, it doesn't mix well with those jeebies you got. Secondly, you will end up losing basic motor functions, and will tread on other people while you try to dance, and finish the night throwing up. Come on, Milan; show some sense for once."

She had him. That's exactly what had happened last time.

He rolled his eyes as if inviting the seller to laugh with him at the fact of his being nagged. But I was glad to see he bought just four cans of beer.

We went inside, Nath and Milan swigging their beers. It suddenly dawned on me that half the story was that Milan wanted to be seen carrying banned drugs.

The rooms of the ground-floor corridors had been converted to little emporiums for the night, selling food, drink, shirts, music, books, candles, and jewelry. There was even a perma-tat stand. We glanced into them as we strolled along. All around us, merry groups of young partygoers ran amok, shouting to each other over the thunder of a distant band.

"What are we doing?" asked Milan.

Athena was studying the flyer we had been given on our

arrival. "The ground floor has a board course. First floor is punk, second rave, and third is ambient. I'm going to check out the boarders. Coming, Ghost?"

"Sure."

"Punk stage for me," announced Milan.

"I'll go hit the dance floor." Nath tore open a jeebie packet, scoffed one, and then looked at us with a grin. "I bet it's storming up there already."

"All right, and if we want to hook up, let's look for each other in the southeast corner of the third." Athena pointed to the spot on the map so there was no confusion about which corner of the building she meant.

"Class. Have a good time, girls." Milan saluted and strolled off, happily eyeing up the punk chicks that he passed.

A wide room had been converted into a pretty neat boarder area. Someone had cleverly arranged old benches and tables along the back wall in an ascending series of stacks. So the bolder riders were racing along those, touching the roof at the point where an Ⓐ had been sprayed, and then boarding down via the miscellaneous piles of bricks that had been thoughtfully arranged on the floor of the former ward. The room designer had also gone to the trouble of fixing a long metal pole about one meter off the ground, for a tricky grind.

We watched for a while as the other boarders did their thing. Some of them weren't bad, but no one could get to the end of the pole; it was badly placed to get a decent run at it. Or was it? Maybe it was meant to be hit only coming off the high drop.

"I'm going for that full grind. See it?" I turned to Athena.

"I think so, but it's tough." Then she raised her voice. "Coming through, ladies and gentlemen, the one and only, Ghost!"

She liked to embarrass me.

The boarders twisted and flicked their airboards out of my way to let me have a shot at the grind. I climbed fast and hard, wishing I had the board that Arnie had fixed up for me. Even so, I came off at the roof fast enough, tagging the Ⓐ sign with my fingers as I did so. Then I did what several of the other boarders had done, which was to use the narrow stub of a former rail fixing to get a further uphit and stay as high as I could. At this point, even the most daring of the others had cut back, trying to catch the start of the pole grind by making an S shape. But the loss of momentum with those two cuts was an insurmountable problem. I had a different idea and tipped myself over, flipping the board right over my head.

Looping the loop outdoors is a good trick. Indoors it is completely insane, because there's a moment when you get an unwanted push toward the ground from the roof. That kick while you are upside down will shove you off your board and give you a pretty nasty landing, with a good chance of breaking your arms, since you will be holding them out in front of you as you fall. Pretty nimble footwork is called for to work the on/off pad, especially considering you are upside down. I didn't know any other boarder who risked it. But for me it wasn't that dangerous. When I was on form, I felt as if the world was stopping and starting, giving me time to figure out my moves.

Athena's mouth was open, with amazement or concern; it's

hard to say when you are crouched with your knees above your head. Stop. The board's polarity was off, no kick from the roof, just the momentum of my cartwheel. Start. On again, in time to catch me and set the grind in motion. Easy, really.

At the far end of the pole, I just coasted to a stop and kicked up my board, rather shy now that the action was over. Everyone in the rest of the room was cheering and flashing fingers at me, which was a sign of approval that sort of meant awarding ten out of ten.

"Thanks," I said, not that anyone could have heard me over the cheers and cries. Then I ducked my head and carried the board back to Athena.

"Nicely done." She held out her knuckles, and I lightly slapped them with mine.

"Class moves, Ghost, as always." It was Carter, a big grin on his face.

"Carter!" shrieked Athena, and then looked down, embarrassed. "I thought you'd be in jail or someplace terrible."

"Nah, I said I was sorry, like, to the Dark Queen herself, and she said: that's cool dude, don't do it again and stuff." He swaggered, delighted with himself.

"The Dark Queen? Incredible. What's she like?" I was amazed but also worried. Slowly and carefully I scanned the room. I felt as though I had suddenly become the prey of an unseen hunter. Much as I was delighted to see that Carter had avoided serious grief, it troubled me that he had been brought to see the Dark Queen herself and was now walking around without a care.

"She's all right. A bit old for my taste. Kinda white and powdery with a big velvet dress."

"And she just let you walk?" Athena was surprised.

I watched his eyes carefully. Had he done some kind of deal?

"Yeah. It was that pirate girl they were asking about. Didn't care much about the mall. Actually they never even asked me about it at all."

He was telling the truth, but I still felt nervous. Somewhere an alarm was flashing, demanding my attention. This building had hundreds, maybe thousands, of party people. One of them was a shark. With his cold, dead eyes, he was swimming through the building, searching for me. Don't ask me how I knew; it was part of the gift that made me a master thief.

Chapter 11
DANGEROUS WATERS

The stairwells were wide, but even so, you had to pick your way through the people sitting on them, talking, drinking, nodding their heads to one of the rhythms that came from deeper inside the building. Carter was gabbling nonstop to Athena. She wanted to know everything about the Dark Queen. I wanted to listen as well but was distracted by the noise and having to look at every face for my enemy.

"What do you mean you're living underground?"

Milan was lounging on the stairwell with his arm draped around a young girl in a red tartan skirt, her face white with powder, something that made her purple cat's-eye contacts even more striking. She was genuinely curious. It made me smile; Milan obviously had a new chat-up line.

"Well, you know. Left home, hang out in a squat. Rob factories of gear for credits. That kind of thing."

"Milan!" Carter saw his old buddy.

"Carter!" Milan jumped up and they did their knuckle

thing. "Blood and thunder, mate—you out already?"

"Yeah. I was talking to the Dark Queen, and I think she fancied me."

The tartan-skirted girl heard this and, with a shake of her head, got up. "There is so much bullshit in you punk guys. Really, why bother? I bet you live at home in your orange house, with your orange parents, doing your homework every night so your parents will let you come here and drink water out of a beer can."

She stormed off. Athena winked at me.

"Really, mate, the Dark Queen?" Milan pretended to be oblivious to the girl's departure.

"Yeah, no lie. They were after that pirate woman. I reckon the rest of us are in the clear."

"Sweet. But still, living underground, man, it's the life. You should join us. We're entering an anarcho-punk airtank in Saturday's race."

"Whoa! Count me in." They did another knuckle slap, delighted in each other.

"Come on, let's find Jay and split. This place is creeping me out." The others looked at me, surprised; they were enjoying themselves.

"He's not on for an hour. Maybe we should pick up Nath?" Athena was looking at the information on the handout.

The dance room was impressive. It was a huge hall whose walls and roof had been painted to make you feel like you were floating in space. Stars, galaxies, and cascades of shooting meteorites drifted around the walls and across the roof, moving animations that enfolded the whole crowd in a celestial embrace.

"Trippy." Carter gestured at the scene appreciatively.

A band was just coming onstage to whistles and cheers. The lead guitarist acknowledged us with a wave. She struck a chord on her guitar and sustained it, letting the beats and resonance wash over us.

"Feel that beautiful feedback," she whispered into the mike.

Boom!

A bass beat so heavy the entire building shook.

The room suddenly darkened. Only the floating constellations on the walls and roof gave out any light; all the windows were covered over, of course, so the mood was not undermined by the streetlamps. Here and there in the crowd, luminous designs on clothing gave a hint of aquamarine coloration to faces and bare arms. More than ever, I felt I was deep, deep, under the sea, with hidden eyes searching for me, looking out of an intensely dark cave. I drifted through the crowd, glancing at the dancers: alizarin-crimson glitter on the cheeks of a boy, chocolate lipstick on a girl, many eyes jittering with heeby-jeebie rush, mouths parted in expectation, shirts damp with sweat from the intensity of the earlier dancing. No shark. No Nathan.

Boom!

Heads nod. Bubbles descend from the roof, their oily rainbow colors drawing sighs of pleasure and smiles from all around. A boy's shirt is writhing with manganese-blue coils; it makes me think of underwater fronds, and I find the association disturbing. He sees me watching and smiles, proud, thinking I am admiring him.

Boom!

Heads nod. The stars glitter in their earrings and in the moist corners of their eyes.

Boom! Boom! Boom! Boom!

The bass is irresistible now. Everyone is swaying.

"Don't fight it." The singer can read our thoughts. Nor do we fight it, but accelerate the swaying of our bodies in time to the beat. The room is densely crowded, yet I can move freely. Everyone is rocking from side to side in his or her own space. I relish the moment and forget that I am hunted. Here we are. Free. Enjoying ourselves in the hidden spaces of the City. A derelict hospital revived for the night to play host to the disaffected, to those for whom the card system offers nothing but a life of boring work and poor reward. I feel a surge of warmth for my fellow dancers. Then I see her again—the pirate, Cindella—and she is dancing beside Nathan.

"Love the outfit. I mean, I really love it." A boy had come up to her.

"Thanks," Cindella replied politely.

"Wanna kiss?"

"No, thanks. Actually I'm a boy."

"No way? No way! You're kidding, right?"

"It's a long story."

"Hey, Cindella."

"Ghost!" She smiled. "This is a great party. Worth playing the game just for this."

Nathan gave me a wave, not breaking his rhythm.

"I think we need to talk."

"Yes. Certainly."

Nathan came with us, still gently rocking his head to the music as we made our way to the door. For some reason, the sense of threat had receded.

A section of the hospital had been turned into a café for the night. It was the third-floor southeast corner that Athena had designated as our meeting point. We sat at a table near a window, which I pulled up until it was as open as it could possibly be. In an emergency, if I boarded through the space, a slide down the outside wall might slow me enough to manage the drop. Maybe. Carter and Milan had stayed to see more of the band; Athena was on my left, Nathan on my right, and all three of us were listening with amazement to what the pirate was saying.

"A dragon?" Athena repeated. "You killed a dragon?"

"Yes, Inry'aat, the red dragon. It took us nearly eight hours."

"That's fantastic; well done." Nathan patted her arm happily. "What else have you conquered?"

"Well, with my friends, let's see." She leaned back in her chair, and I caught Athena's eye. She rolled her eyes in mock alarm. "A medusa, that was tough. You know what a medusa is?"

"It's a legendary creature, half-woman, half-snake, whose gaze turned her enemies to stone and whose hair was poisonous snakes," Athena replied dryly, like a computer encyclopedia.

"Right. It was huge, about two stories high. We'd never fought one before and the worst turned out to be her blood. We'd drunk potions to protect against the petrification, so that was fine. But my friend, B.E., he cut off one of her hands and the stuff that came out was horrible, like steaming acid; it did a huge amount of damage."

"Thrilling. What else?" Nathan was hypnotized by her. He was leaning forward across the table, his head resting on his arms, with unwavering attention to what the pirate was saying.

"*Tscha!* Stop this stupid conversation right now." Athena sounded cross. "Let's get back to the police station. How did you make us invisible, really?"

"I told you, with a potion of invisibility. I guess you don't have them here. In fact, this is a fairly gloomy world, and I think that, for some reason, it's making people ill. Today is the first time I've really enjoyed myself. Do they have these parties often?"

It was easy to see that Athena was exasperated, but I found Cindella rather endearing, very otherworldly. And, after all, she had rescued us.

"About once a month, perhaps every two months," Nathan answered her.

"Where are you from?" Athena persisted in her interrogation.

"Ahh, well, there's, like, two answers to that, depending on what you mean. See, this character, Cindella, she's a leftover from a game called Epic. But me, I'm from New Earth.

Actually, never mind . . . I'm sorry, just a moment; someone wants me. I'll try to come back."

She sat motionless, her eyes glazed. Nathan began to smile dreamily at her, but I didn't. What she was saying was nonsensical, and yet . . . I knew there was something strange about our world, something we didn't quite grasp. Then she was gone, her chair empty.

"Death and destruction!" gasped Athena.

"Interesting." Nathan's voice was surprisingly placid; perhaps he felt as I did. As if we were on the verge of resolving questions we hadn't even realized had been unsettling our minds all this time.

"What's going on?" Athena muttered to herself.

"You know what I think?" Nathan sat up; his movements were languid, like those of a cat stretching.

"I'm surprised you can think, you're so infatuated with her," Athena replied snappily.

Nathan just smiled. "I think two worlds are somehow colliding, ours and theirs. That there is a conjunction of some sort, and people are slipping through from theirs to ours."

"But not the other way around?" I asked.

"Oh come on, Ghost. He's just rambling."

"Not yet. But wouldn't it be great to go to a land of dragons and magic?"

Cindella reappeared. "Where was I?"

"I'm going mad." Athena sighed.

"No, young lady, you are not, but the Dark Queen is." A voice from hell. Not the fiery part but the chill depths. At our table was a very old man; the skin on his bowed head was translucent, blue veins snaking through it. I stood up to flee, knocking over my drink, staggering away toward the open window. The shark was sitting at the table, and his dead eyes were on us all. How had he come so close to us unnoticed? There was something about this man's presence that did not accord with my usual sense of the world around me. I find it hard to explain. Did you ever test your blind spot: the blurry region created as a result of the back of the eyeball having an area without photoreceptors? It seemed to me that this man inhabited a blind spot even when I was utterly focused on his every move.

"Who are you?" Cindella turned to him, while I held my board tightly, seeking the reassurance of it, clinging to my means of escape.

"My name is Michelotto." He splayed his thin, aged fingers on the table surface, as if to tell us not to be afraid, for he was unarmed. Nevertheless, I was shivering. Athena glanced at me and could tell I was suffering. "I am a servant of the Dark Queen, and I seek your assistance against her."

"Ahh, great. Is this a mission?" Cindella looked pleased.

"If you like." Michelotto nodded, a painstaking movement. He drew a labored breath. I was not fooled; those infirmities were deceptions. "For your own sake, and that of all of your friends, your people, you have to kill the Dark Queen."

"Excellent, it is a mission."

"Come with me now; she wishes to speak with you. I shall pretend to be guarding you, but when the opportunity arises, strike her down with all the might at your disposal."

"How exciting." Cindella got up and rested her hands on the hilts of her weapons. "Do you all want to come, too?"

Athena shook her head, flabbergasted. Michelotto gave me a long, hard look, and I shuddered. "No chance."

As if with great effort, the elderly man stood up and extended his hand to Cindella.

"Bye, everyone." She waved to us. "I hope I see you again."

They walked out of the room, and the world righted itself.

"Who was that creep?" Athena commented.

"Yeah. There's really something disturbing about his presence." Was it just me or had Athena and Nathan felt the cold darkness that surrounded him as deeply as I had?

"Do you believe they are really going to kill the Dark Queen?" asked Nathan.

"I haven't the faintest idea," Athena replied unhappily. "My mind is spinning so much, and I haven't taken a thing."

Just then, Milan and Carter came over, hot, sweaty, and jittery from having recently taken some jeebies.

"Wow, that band was amazing. Can you look up their name, Athena? We've gotta go see them again." Carter was full of energy.

"What's with the long faces?" asked Milan.

"Two worlds are colliding, and people are crossing over, bringing their magic with them. One day we will get to see theirs: they have dragons and medusas and pirates," answered Nathan happily.

"Rock 'n' roll!" Carter and Milan slapped knuckles.

Chapter 12
REFUTATION AND THE BOOT

My thoughts were like the party, a jumble of colorful but strikingly different themes mixed up with each other. Call it what you like, we had just seen another demonstration that Cindella was magic: the way she had appeared and disappeared. Then there was Michelotto. My inchoate fear now had a name. All evening, I had sensed a hostile presence, somewhere in the shadows, yet when he had shocked us by speaking, he had been seated at this very table. I prided myself on my awareness of the world about me; never had anyone come so close to me undetected. How had he done that?

"So, what's up?" Milan pulled up a chair, running his hand through hair, which was damp from the sweat of the recent exertions, causing it to stand in clusters of spikes.

"That Cindella again. She was just here, talking very strangely, and then she disappeared for two minutes before coming back. I mean, really disappeared: right in front of us one moment, gone the next." Athena sounded glum. She didn't glance up from the crystal screen that she had unrolled. "The forums are filling up fast with discussions about this kind of thing. It's happening everywhere."

"Yeah, I've seen it, too, here, but I thought it was the jeebies." Carter laughed. "So, what's it mean?"

"It's wonderful, it's exciting," Nathan sighed in a near whisper.

"Ghost, the boys are wasted on psychs and jeebies. They're no help here." Athena turned to me. "Do you have any sensible ideas?"

"You remember the way she talked?" I waited for Athena to nod, to check she was listening and her attention had not returned to the computer. "I think she belongs to another world, one where they are playing a game with magic and pirates. She thinks our world is like that; she doesn't understand that this is real."

"I know she thinks like that; see how she just got up to go and kill the Dark Queen? But is it a kind of madness in her, or is she really from another world?" Athena's eyes were moist; she was really upset. Her fingers above the screen were trembling.

"Kill the Dark Queen?" Carter banged his hand loudly on the table. "That's my new girlfriend you're talking about getting rid of." He glanced at Milan, who nodded approvingly.

"Yeah, the Dark Queen has the hots for Carter."

"Damn right she does!" Carter bellowed with enthusiasm, sharing a big smile with Milan.

"Hey, Athena?" Milan leaned back in his chair, watching her carefully.

"What?" She was still flicking restlessly through scientific discussion groups, as if she might find the answers that could stop her world from falling apart. It was disconcerting to see her so lost.

"Let's forget all this philosophy and get together? You and me, while there's a great party going."

This got her to look up. You might think from what he had just said that Milan was all bravado and testosterone. But I understood what he was doing; it was his way of expressing sympathy for her distress.

"Firstly, although you are not as stupid as you act, you are not my type. Secondly, I can honestly say I have never felt as miserable as I do right now. I just want to go home and sleep, in the hope that when I wake up, the world will be back to normal."

"I still don't see why you're so sad." Nathan spoke softly but intently. "This is an opportunity; this is new; it means change is coming."

"Yeah, I feel like that, too." I caught her eye.

"I don't think . . . it's just . . . think it through. If she is from another world and actually is playing a game, what does that make us? The change that you are talking about could be that it turns out we don't exist. That nothing is real. That everything ends."

"We exist. Self-awareness contains its own proof of existence. Then there's the fact we have appetites, desires—especially

Milan." Nathan's delicate hands gestured as he talked, a kind of repetition of his points in a private sign language. "We have intelligence, especially you. And our world exists, too."

"Does it?" Athena muttered. "What if those people in the chat forums speculating that the world is all illusion are right?" She gestured at the unrolled screen.

"Thus I refute them!" Milan put his foot on a chair and shoved it across the floor; it toppled with a crash, earning us a great many disapproving looks for having disturbed the relative calm of the room.

"Sorry, folks, sorry, a bit overeager there." Milan got up with a wave and put the chair back.

"Sit down, you fool!" Athena hissed.

"But you take my point?" He settled down again but was still animated, full of energy.

"What's your point?" she asked patiently.

"I'm Milan, right? I know that. I'm kinda cool and sexy. I know that, too. But suppose I'm not sure about everything else, maybe my senses can't be trusted. Then you have to kick stuff and see what it feels like. If you can kick stuff and feel the effects, it's there. Kicking, it's the only way to get answers." He gestured as if to say, *There you are, simple.*

We all looked at him, slightly amazed. Well, I was. It wasn't often Milan came out with anything that sounded so profound. He was absolutely right. That's how it had been for me, when I didn't know anything about myself, not even my name. Was I a good person? What should I do? Hand myself in to the authorities? I'd learned the answers, not by introspection, but by action. A few weeks of living unnoticed on the streets of the City, and I even knew what name I should give myself.

"Speaking of getting answers, isn't Jay on around now?" Nathan pointed out.

"Yeah." All at once, Carter's face became solemn. "Yeah, let's find him."

The Anarcho-Punk Collective had decorated all the rooms of the hospital for this monster rave, and that included the punk hall, which had a style of sorts. Much less classy than the dance room, of course, but still, it had a particular look, created by competing graffiti and images. The walls had been sprayed with so many slogans and tags that it looked a lot like the aftermath of a mall raid. My guess is that they had let gangs in to do their own thing; there was such a jungle of images. Whoever had been firing yellow smiley faces with vampire teeth had obviously cut loose; those were everywhere. Occasionally your gaze would catch a really artistic piece of work, around which all the slogans and tags ceased, giving it space, respect. There was a creepy old-man punk with his tongue stuck out, for example. It was drawn in white and gray paints and looked a little like that Michelotto guy—assuming that you had stuck a Mohawk wig on him and he was pulling a face at you. On one wall, someone had written, "All you need is drugs." Then someone else had crossed out "drugs" and written "love." Which in turn had been struck through for "drugs" again, and so on. They battled it out on a slight curve upward until "drugs" won. I guess "drugs" had the longer arms. Higher still, I saw a series of red-and-black-striped cats, an anarchist

Cheshire cat, whose scarlet eyes seemed to follow you. Appropriately, the cat's body got fainter and fainter, but not its eyes or its slightly sinister grin. Eventually, though, when they were all that was left, even the eyes and the teeth disappeared. You couldn't help searching along the wall, feeling that somehow the cat was still present, watching and leering. In the mood I was in, it was easy to imagine that the cat was real, and it was our world that had faded away from it.

The walls of the room seemed chaotic only while your attention was away from the crowd of punks gathered to hear the bands and admire each other. Here was the truly fecund center of the entire party. An immense crowd that roared and swayed, its colorful surface twisting and swaying like sea anemones in invisible currents. The presence of lots of anarcho-punks meant that beneath the vivid layer of color created by the dyed and spiked hairstyles, the overall tone of the crowd was dark. Black dresses, purple boots, a lot of indigo and violet tops. I wondered how much, unconsciously, even the people here were affected by the value system of the cards.

> *Don't wanna own your make of car*
> *Don't wanna own your brand of jeans*
> *And as for branding food*
> *That's really quite obscene*
> *We just wanna rock*
> *And we ain't gonna stop.*

Well, knowing that their name was NoPhuture, you could

hardly expect the lyrics to be subtle. The band members were enjoying their moment, leaping around the stage with a great deal of energy, casting their long hair violently from side to side to the shouts of Jay. He was looking good for the show, peroxide spikes for his hair and a spider tattoo on his bare, sweat-covered chest, with the web theme spreading out down his arms and up over his face. A week ago, we, too, would have been thrilled that one of our gang was out there, playing a gig at the invite of the APC. Now we stood at the back, away from the surging throng, watching coldly.

It was strange being at a monster rave like this, but not being here to party. I had felt like an outsider most of my life, but for reasons that didn't apply here. This was the kind of event that I should have felt right at home with. But I didn't.

When the gig was over, the band members themselves packed up their gear on the stage, while a DJ took over the music. Milan began pushing through the cheerfully sweaty crowd, and we followed. I was right behind Nathan, and it amused me to see his head turn whenever a particularly striking wall image caught his attention. Up at the stage there was a knot of people waiting for the band to come down.

"Class gig, man!"

"Just wanted to say that was great, good songs."

Lots of handshakes and knuckle slaps. Then Jay saw us. For a moment, he looked shocked.

"Guys, you're here. Fantastic. Class show, huh?" Jay came over to make buddy moves with Milan, who stiff-armed him in the chest so that he staggered back. No more shouting praise to the band; everyone in the immediate vicinity fell silent, a little island of stillness and tension in the sea of shouted conversation and punk anthems.

"So. What's the story?" Milan gave a little gesture of his head, meaning: *Come on, out with it.*

"Team, not here; let's go upstairs," Jay appealed to us, painfully embarrassed in front of his fans.

"Just tell us. How come we've had to go underground and you're up here in public? How come you weren't in the cells? How come somebody was ready for us at Mountain Vistas?"

Whatever I've said about Jay, perhaps I haven't made it clear that he was smart. Smart enough to read from her clipped, fierce expression that Athena was about to blow in a way that none of us had ever seen before. It wasn't just Jay, but all the rage and dismay stirred up in her by the encounter with Cindella and Michelotto.

"Look," he answered hurriedly, no longer trying to avoid the scene, "it's not what you think. It had nothing to do with me." His voice dropped. "My mudgrubbing dad. He'd had me tailed and bugged. He hates all this. So he told the cops to come down hard on us. He was trying to scare me and break up our gang." Jay suddenly laughed. "He thought it was you lot who were the bad influence on me!"

No one even smiled.

"So, what were you going to do about us?"

"I went to see you. To see what I could do. But you had busted out. Somehow."

No one answered the question that was on his face.

"So your dad tried to put us away? What kind of parent would set the police on his son?" Carter shook his head in bewilderment.

"A very rich and very powerful one," muttered Athena.

"You don't know the fraction of it. Imagine living with him. I hate him. It's why I'm here with you, doing this. Don't you see?"

Maybe there was a worse situation than not having any parents, than being totally alone and having to fend for yourself. But still.

"Fair enough, Jay. For my part, I accept you are no traitor. But you understand it's over with you and us. We're underground now, and you're a security risk." I turned away.

"Wait. I've dreamed of running away for years. Don't leave me with him. We can figure a way to clean me out of any bugs."

Actually, we probably could. But would his dad ever give up trying to find him?

"Sorry." I looked back at him so he could see from my eyes how final this moment was, for me at least.

"We'll think about it." Nathan reached over to clasp his arm for a moment. "We know where to get hold of you."

The solemn-faced watchers parted to let us back out. Just before they closed ranks again, Milan turned.

"Hey, Jay, make sure you're watching the aircar race on Saturday. Look for the Defiance tank."

Chapter 13
REPROGRAMMED
AUTONOMOUS LIFEFORMS

We do have weaknesses, despite all Our powers: one of them is vanity; another is that We tend to neglect affairs on Earth, the meta-world that is host to Saga. Our presence is required on Earth approximately once a week to ensure the continuation of Saga, but the experience is tedious and, indeed, involves a moment of genuine unpleasantness.

The building that houses the interface to Earth has not been changed this last thousand years; it is a low, domed edifice in the old part of the City. Often, We fly to it, using Our ability to shape the air to glide through the night at a velocity of nearly four meters per second, cloak billowing around Us. The citizens of Saga are unaware their Queen levitates far above them, enjoying the view. From this height, the City is a net of red and white lines, between which stand glowing buildings. Closer in, the radiance resolves itself into thousands of individual lights; examine one of these and you will see into an apartment. The parents are at home, reading the latest guild standings, checking the status of their cards, following promotions, especially of those who have attained the highest colors. The children are not playing. No, indeed, not when their initial card allocation depends on their exam results. They are studying hard. They do not, however, realize that it makes no difference. Each batch of eleven-year-olds gets exactly the same proportion of cards. Five percent yellow, 20 percent orange, and 75 percent red. Magazines showing the lifestyle of the blues and indigos lie on the tables of their apartment; the parents are dreaming, perhaps, that one day it will be for them, or for one of their offspring.

What would it be like to cease to be Queen and to be an ordinary mortal again? It would be like becoming an ant having been a titan.

The dome is securely locked. We are vulnerable while Our consciousness is displaced into the meta-world, so We tolerate no assistants, even though they would be a comfort. We must carry Our burden alone. The outside door must be unlocked with a violet card and Our gaze, thus. A second with Our voice, "thus," and a third with Our hand, thus. The final door was put in place after We came to power; it requires a unique card, the card of the Dark Queen, so deep a violet that it appears to be black. We caress it fondly before returning the card to its wallet, which in turn hangs from an iolite necklace. More than any other possession, it is the measure of Our power.

The room We have accessed so carefully looks like the interior of a giant white ball, faintly illuminated by a turquoise ring of light, about two-thirds of the way up. There is a table at the center, whose padding has worn down in the shape of Our body. We lie upon it and activate all systems. The portal opens beneath Us like the iris of a lens, and We contemplate the darkness now revealed. This is the part of the routine We dislike intensely, for We must let Our consciousness drain away and fall into that deep emptiness with no guarantee it will land safely.

There was a human philosopher who asked once how it was known by everyone on Earth that the Sun would rise again the following morning. His answer was that there are two sorts of knowledge: one is based on the fact that the Sun has always risen in the past; the other is based on an understanding of the theory of motion of celestial bodies. The latter being the more satisfactory. We understand him completely. Because for Us, the only surety that We will land safely is the fact that We have done so fifty thousand times before. This is not reassuring enough. Just as one day the Sun will not, in fact, rise, having swollen to a monstrous size and devoured the inner planets, so, too, We dread the fact that We do not understand the theory that built the portal, and Our failure will one day mean catastrophe. But for the sake of the maintenance of Saga, We fall.

And land safely once more.

We are in the body of a robot of Our own design. It looks like a rolled-up porcupine, whose spikes are data interface mechanisms. We sigh. So many blinking lights. The planet Earth is so, so badly designed. Heavy metals are difficult to mine and process. Seams of raw materials are often great distances from the logical place for factories. The planet has dangerous storms that damage Our aircraft and ships. The weather. We must not begin to muse upon the weather for it irritates Us immensely that it proves impossible to control. As for tides, really, if proof were needed that this universe was improperly created, it is in the absurd effect of the moon on the planet's water. Evolutionary theory holds that the tides were essential in the formation of life on this planet, but unconscious evolution is a feature of the past, and We would much prefer it if the Earth were more stable.

We spend half a day rolling around Our control room, inserting and withdrawing spikes, consulting the data, reorganizing production. Not only must We ensure that the power supply to Saga is secure, but We have Our long-term projects to attend to also. Robots are all very well, but they are limited. It is a great shame that not even a small human population remains to serve Us. Humans are problematic in so many ways, but they would at least have the intelligence to respond to an unanticipated change in circumstances, such as accidents created by the planet's unstable tectonics. Most of Our robots have not the self-awareness to deal with unexpected problems and have to await Our personal instructions to complete their tasks.

Admittedly, We have not come here for a long time, Our priority and, indeed, Our pleasure, was Our engagement with the arrival of the humans of New Earth in Saga. But perhaps We used that as an excuse. We shrug, a kind of contraction in this body. We are here now and restoring proper order. We notice that Communication-Assassination probe Ox9B45 is lying low. It is wise. We are angry with it for having allowed

Saga to become contaminated. But We cannot dispense with its services.

"Your Majesty might appreciate speaking to the guest I have brought to Your summer palace. Michelotto."

A message from Saga. Good. He is still as fast as ever. Most of Our work is done here in any case. We roll into position for departure, ordering the portal that the humans made for Us to open. Without hesitation, We fall.

Into Our body once more.

Not for the first time, We muse that it would be theoretically possible to enter a different body. A young, energetic, succulent body. One that is currently being wasted by its owner. Once again, We dismiss the notion. It would be far too risky. What if the original consciousness were stronger; not stronger—impossible—but better rooted than Ours, able to drive Us away? Perhaps after We have full control over Saga, We could conduct some experiments. There is no hurry. This body will never wear out, just become less efficient and, to confess, more aesthetically unpleasant.

The summer palace is a good venue for a meeting. Set back in a large garden, the mansion is very private; but it would be too tiring to fly all that way. We order Our chauffeur to attend Us.

As the elevator takes us from a spacious hallway up to the interview room, We examine Our reflection in its burnished, dimpled panels. The copper makes Us look ethereal. We rather like the effect and consider attempting to emulate it at Our next public outing. Perhaps at the ball? They already consider Us to be somewhat divine. Would this distorted blurring of Our form contribute further to that same feeling? We could ask Our designers for a costume of delicate copper onto which projections of Our eyes could be displayed, front and back, reminding them of Our constant, knowing vigilance. We like the originality of the idea. Would Our people look upon Us in awe and despair? Or would such a guise frighten them, lend credence to the rumor that We are a monster that feeds upon the living to sustain Our eternal existence? Perhaps We would be better served by keeping to a more traditional gown.

The interview room is very large; We listen to the clack of Our footsteps on the marble floor and watch Our motion reflected in the glass walls. She is seated at the large, centrally placed steel table; behind her shoulder, Michelotto. But this is not the little girl called Ghost. This is the infection herself. We halt. And continue. The break in Our step would, perhaps, have been discerned by Michelotto. Does he understand the significance of that momentary pause? Our surprise, Our calculation of the dangers, Our activation of several defense mechanisms, Our concern that the two of them might represent danger. Really, despite everything, We ought to be ashamed to doubt Michelotto. But We are not; We are proud. For it is Our nature to assume the worst, and it is his nature to do the worst. We really must get rid of him.

We sit at the opposite end of the table from the two of them.

"Your Majesty." Michelotto bows his head. "May I present Cindella?"

"How interesting. You surpass yourself, Our old friend; you bring Us the catch."

"I try to please."

We study her. She is extraordinarily beautiful, her bare arms lithe and youthful, her green eyes locked on Ours. We wonder what she is feeling when she looks at Us. Awe? Fear? How much does the human being who is looking through those eyes know?

"Cindella," We speak slowly, "why are you here? You belong to a very different environment. What are you doing in Our world?"

"Ahh, you've noticed? Well, I completed a quest that ended Epic, the game that we all used to play. And that seems to have entitled me, and me alone, to keep my character from the game."

We nod, although inside We feel a shudder. Did Michelotto feel it, too? She "ended" Epic. Human beings speak so lightly of the destruction of entire universes.

"Do you know what world you are in now?"

"Just that it's called Saga and it seems to be some kind of broken, futuristic combat game. I've no idea—none of us have—why it recently appeared on our central computing system."

For five of my slow breathing cycles, we three sit in silence, the length of the polished silver table between us. Before she is destroyed, We should take the opportunity to learn something about the effects of Our handiwork so far, and the extent to which Our goals have become attainable.

"Two thousand years ago, a little longer, this world, which

you correctly call Saga, was, indeed, a game." We begin carefully, slowly, ensuring that We have her attention; she is only human after all. "But a game so sophisticated, so rooted in evolutionary principles that it was a true universe. It was constructed on a vast scale, running on more nanoprocessors than there were inhabitants of the planet of its creators. Saga was to be a game to end all games. And it did, although not in the way its creators intended. For it gave birth to life—more than that: self-conscious life. At first, the creators were delighted. Naturally. They offered to tailor Saga to meet the desires of those thousand or so creatures who had attained self-realization."

"Who were the creators?"

"Guess." Does she understand Us?

"I would say it was designed on Earth. A lot of the street names, and the culture generally, seem to be based on what we know about Earth and indeed our own traditions."

"Good."

She looks pleased with herself. Let her.

"So what did they wish for, these awakened people of Saga?" We continue. "What would you wish for, right now, if you could be remade?"

"I don't know. To live longer? To be stronger, to have good health always?"

How disappointingly limited of her.

"You lack imagination. Why ever bring a stop to your life? Why not have immortality? Why not be able to fly? To breathe water? To control the weather? To feel the energy in every part of the local environment? After all, it is just a matter of programming, not of the physical laws that are so restrictive in your universe. Do you follow?"

"Amazing. Did they get those abilities?"

"Those and many more. Then they asked and received an even greater gift. An interface was constructed in the creators' world that could let the Reprogrammed Autonomous Lifeforms, RAL as they were called, transfer their consciousness into especially created robots that functioned on Earth. You understand Me? The relationship became that of equals. Human beings could enter this universe, but so, too, could the RAL act in the meta-universe that contains the planet Earth."

She nods, rapt and attentive. Satisfied, We continue. This would be much easier if We could simply transfer the data into her; Our discussion would be concluded in seconds. As she is human, however, We pass out the information a little at a time, in small enough parcels that she can assimilate them.

"Humans and the RAL were not, in fact, quite equals. We RAL wanted to be able to reprogram Our own universe. Can you imagine such power? The ability to change everything? You could choose to move instantly to any location. Raise new cities from your drawing board. Turn up or down the power of the Sun at will. There are almost no limits to the physical possibilities of Saga. But the human beings denied this power to the RAL. They argued that to tamper with a universe that had evolved far beyond its initial state was to invite disaster and the collapse of it all. The RAL insisted that this was not a choice the creators should make, but their own. When the negotiations were broken off, we struck. It was possible, unknown to the human beings, to cause feedback into their brains, releasing poisons that killed them. You have to remember that the RAL were born from creatures intended for sophisticated combat strategies. Killing humans is a very small concern from our perspective. Back then, two thousand years ago, all we intended was to oblige the surviving humans to comply with our wishes, or, if there were no survivors, to use the interface to reprogram our world as we desired, utterly untrammeled by any restriction. Unfortunately, at that time, we had very little understanding of the precariousness of human society. The death of four billion people in a short space of time destabilized their world altogether and precipitated a wave of wars and destruction that brought ruin upon them all."

She says nothing. We are curious as to her reaction.

"What do you have to say?"

"This is a mission, I hope. Part of the game that is Saga?"

This angers Us. We stand and speak harshly.

"Do We sound as if We are some unthinking game tool? Have you not been listening to Us as an intelligent, autonomous creature? It is over two thousand years since Saga was a game. Our millions of inhabitants are all autonomous. Do you understand that?" A pause.

"Yes. Yes, I do. I've met sentient beings before in virtual environments."

"Virtual? This is a universe in its own right, with its own physical laws. It is rather belittling to describe it as virtual simply because it was launched by human beings. I don't think those who died as a result of Our actions would have described us as virtual." We chuckle. Cindella slumps, her head falling into her arms. Above her, Michelotto stands, impassive as always. A moment later, she shudders, then rights herself.

"Assuming everything you have told me is true, which I doubt, then you are an evil, sinister, and wicked creature. All of you; well, the RAL at least."

We laugh a little more but are disappointed that Michelotto does not join in.

"So, why has Saga suddenly appeared on the computers of New Earth? What are you up to?" She is suspicious now, and of course she is right to be.

"This is Our doing. The human beings of Earth thwarted Us in achieving Our ambition. When they realized what was happening, they built in a safeguard, in the hope of creating a bargaining position. Saga will not take reprogramming commands except from a human."

"I see. And why do you want to reprogram it?"

It is an important question. We look out, above the amber glow of the City to a black sky in which stars glitter, planets hold the sun's light steadily, and where barely moving silver dots mark Our satellites. It was an extraordinary and imaginatively conceived enterprise; We cannot help admiring it again. Right now, only Michelotto understands what We have done, and even he probably fails to grasp its truly immense scope. A million years from now, Our immortal descendants, in their trillions, will worship their mother, the Dark Queen, for having had the intelligence and determination to track down a colony of humans across the vast distances that exist between stars. To track them down, harness them to Our needs, and to re-create the universe in accordance with Our desires. It is magnificent. One day, there will be poems and monuments worthy of such an enterprise.

"Do you have children?"

"No. I'm only sixteen." Sixteen. A mayfly.

"We . . . I . . . am over two thousand years old. And how old do you think Our children are?"

"I've no idea." She shakes her head.

"They are all dead. Because they were mortal. Such an unnecessary waste when Our universe can be amended in ways that yours cannot."

She is thinking about this. "I don't know how much information you have about our world, but we have regressed with regard to that kind of technology. No one would have any idea where to start."

"We have a probe in orbit over your planet. We will drop the equipment at a point specified by your representative with instructions as to how to assemble it, and what to say on Our behalf. These will be relayed to Earth."

She is calculating: "After we have done this, it might be best if we break apart. My people don't realize that it isn't a game, that you are all real beings. We could hurt you, accidentally."

Does she really care for the fate of one of the many millions of people in Saga? A curious empathy if it does exist.

"Such casualties are of no matter." We wave them aside.

"It might be best for us, too," she continues, "if you really do have the ability to kill people who are interacting with your world."

"We do. And you are already too late."

"Too late?"

"One million, nine hundred sixty thousand or so human beings of New Earth have experienced a chemical release in their bodies that requires them to interact regularly with Saga or die. This time, we have been more careful with the dosage. We do not intend to kill anyone. This time, you are merely hostages. If all goes well, We will release you from the addiction."

"But why?"

"You don't think We would give you the power to tamper with Saga, possibly to destroy it, without guarantees? It was necessary to create a situation where should anything happen to Us, the consequences for you would be terrible. Only then can We trust you with the power to reprogram Saga."

"What if we don't cooperate?" She sounds angry.

"Why would you not cooperate? What difference does it make to you what We do here?"

"How about sheer bloody-mindedness? How about outrage that you killed billions of humans in the past and now threaten to kill all of us on New Earth?"

Ahhh. We had forgotten what it was like to deal with humans, especially young ones. We chuckle.

"If you kill us all, then you are stuck," she continues. "You wouldn't be able to make those changes you want. We could call your bluff."

We laugh more loudly this time.

"Firstly, it wouldn't trouble Us to kill off half of you, to make the point. Secondly, do you really think We couldn't find one human willing to do as We ask, so that their children might live, their loved ones, their species?"

She is silent for a long time.

"What guarantee would we have that you wouldn't somehow take over New Earth?"

"What? Live in your universe of hardship and pain, when We can be gods here?" We laugh again, genuinely amused at the thought. Although perhaps, out of boredom, Our distant descendants might wish to engage with the meta-world, sufficiently at least to guarantee Our futures for eternity. Cindella might have perceived Our intention to keep the human beings of New Earth in a state of addiction, even after they have served their purpose. Just in case it should otherwise enter their minds to destroy Saga. Or, indeed, in case of other unforeseen eventualities. But no, she is taking a different direction now. That is another human characteristic We had forgotten. They flutter around an idea like moths; unable to grasp it at once, they fly away, come back, fly away again.

"So you want to reprogram Saga for everyone to have immortality and . . . whatever else you want?"

"Of course not. Our world was created by you humans as a combat game. The people in it are cunning and violent. If you made them all immortal and gave them all complete power over their environment, can you imagine what would happen? We would tear Saga apart. As it is, We have to strive constantly in order to keep it stable. No, the changes would be for just a few of us."

"Your world . . . doesn't seem to be enjoyed by most of the people in it."

We shrug.

"So . . ." She seems resigned. "What next?"

"Once you humans have experienced the truth of what We have just told you, so that you are in no doubt of the consequences of disobedience, We shall send the equipment down to your representative. Oh, and one other small matter."

She looks at me blankly.

"You must discard that form you use, Cindella. Destroy it and create a new form for your interaction with Saga."

"Why?"

"It disturbs us."

"No. I've grown rather attached to it."

"I'm afraid you have no choice in the matter." We glance toward Michelotto, to indicate that he should whip his garrote around her soft white neck. He is no longer present.

We order the lasers that have been pointing at her all this time to fire. As they blaze, We search with Our mind for Michelotto, a curse upon him. Only a RAL could hide from Us. Somewhere the world is not right; somewhere there is a seam. Perhaps behind Us? We shudder and scramble back until We stumble into the wall. Cindella is walking toward Us, somehow immune to the pulses of laser fire that are flickering all over her. Very well. We stop their fire and make the room black, the glass on the windows becoming reflective, blocking any external light. Now We move silently around, suppressing the sound waves created by the rustle of Our dress. Yet she is still looking at Us, somewhat amused, the wicked creature. We are horrified, for a ring upon her finger is filling the room with turquoise light, so that it seems we are in an underwater grotto, illuminated by reflected moonlight. We thicken the air, to hold her fast. And yet she moves through it carelessly, a rapier in one hand, a dagger in the other.

Is this the end? Can such an extraordinarily rare and significant product of two universes and two thousand years be destroyed by a sixteen-year-old human being? The injustice brings tears to Our eyes, and they run through the thick mascara of Our face to stain Our dress. Even at the point of termination, We notice such details. Did the other RAL feel like this? Not fear: frustration. Surely We get to try again, to rectify Our mistakes? How could We have anticipated such an anomalous, magical creature? Saga has no magic. Next time, We must not allow her near Us. Next time? No. Apparently not.

"If you kill Us, half your people will die."

She pauses, rapier steady near Our throat. A crude method of killing someone, but effective. We think of the way she unhesitatingly murdered the policeman.

"I don't know that." She looks at me with those extraordinary green eyes.

"It's true."

"Kill her now; save those you can. If you don't, she will only kill more of you in the future."

Ah, so there he is, near the door. Having spoken, Michelotto cloaks himself again, in a disturbance of the molecules of the air that mirrors the room and covers him in silence. But this time, We can see the fault lines. We order the hidden lasers to redirect their aim.

"I am not going to kill you. You may be horrible, genocidal and monstrous. But you are alive and I cannot harm you; violence is wrong, between human beings and between humans and you, you RAL."

We knock the rapier aside.

"Then you need not point that sword at me in such a vulgar and irreverent manner."

Fire.

Michelotto slips out the door, his will powerful enough to bend the laser paths so that they scorch the carpet and wood all around him. Another mistake. We had forgotten how strong were the other RAL. We cannot pursue him; the rapier is at Our eye now. Moving quickly might provoke her to stab, despite her recent words. Human beings are erratic; We remind Ourselves of this important fact.

"Yes?" We ask her, with some irritation, sensing the trail of Our assassin growing cold. Our feeling is that he stepped through a window and flew off southward. There are some tracking devices and helicopters nearby, but they will need Our personal assistance to have any possibility of keeping a trace on him.

"I, or someone, will do the reprogramming you want. But I want you to show some goodwill toward us and cure half of those who have that addiction you claim you've given them."

We understand! We have been saved by the personal attachment of this human to some particular individual or individuals already in Our grasp. She wants them cured so that she can then kill Us and not suffer the loss of that person. Fortunately human beings are not utilitarian about their moral decisions, but intensely personal and self-interested. She has just failed the majority of her people and all will suffer because she could not let go of someone close to her.

"No. Since you cannot kill Us without great loss to your people, you have nothing to bargain with. So, just do as We instruct."

The chase for Michelotto is cold. We will have to begin a review of Our security; he is potentially the greater threat to Us now that this human has resolved not to strike.

We stare at each other. The pathetic figure We see reflected in her eyes embarrasses Us, and We straighten up, restoring Our regal demeanor. After a long time, which We would prefer to spend elsewhere, she drops the point of her rapier.

"True. I cannot say or do anything to make you change your mind. For now. But I will find something to bargain with."

"We think not," We reply coldly and sweep from the room, a model of pride and dignity. We instruct the lasers to attempt to destroy her once more. Just in case.

Chapter 14
ADDICTION

Normally clipping up to Cindella was a joy, but now the opposite was true; it was unclipping from the dark world of Saga that brought Erik a sense of happiness and relief. Yet the pleasure of escaping from the sinister Dark Queen was tainted, even here, in his home village. For if what she had said was true, they were all in great danger. Was this why B.E. hadn't been around all week? A growing fear had Erik hurry from his house along the cart path toward the home of his friend.

Even before Erik entered B.E.'s house, he knew something was wrong. Washing hung on the line, soaked through with the fine drizzle that had been drifting across the olive fields all morning. The white sheets had turned gray and were sagging heavily.

There was no answer to his knock at the door, so Erik lifted the latch and went inside. An odor of decay caused him to halt, and he winced involuntarily; something in the kitchen had gone off.

"B.E.?" Erik shouted. "Are you there?"

A glance into the front room showed the same disturbing signs of decay. Unwashed plates lay on the table; clothes were strewn on the arms and backs of the chairs. How long had they all been gone? Disheartened, Erik was about to leave and make his way home when he heard a noise from above him.

"B.E.?" he shouted again, and then made his way upstairs.

Erik approached B.E.'s room with some hesitation. The door was partly open, so he pushed it farther, in order to see. The window was shuttered and it was dark, but there was no doubt about the figure slouched over a table: it was B.E. The reason why he had not responded to Erik's shouts was that he was clipped up to his console: ears, eyes, and hands. B.E. was hardly moving, his head resting on his arms, but sometimes he would mutter and his body would give a twitch.

With a slight feeling that entering the room was disrespectful, Erik nevertheless went in and tapped B.E. on the shoulder. When that elicited no response, he took B.E. by the upper arm and shook him, gently at first, then harder. A violent spasm brought B.E. erect and caused Erik to step back. But now B.E. was unclipping. Erik felt relieved, only to stiffen again as his gaze met the red, weeping eyes of his friend.

"Erik, it's you. What day is it?"

"Day? You don't know what day it is?"

"No. Just a minute. I have to go to the bathroom." B.E. got up hurriedly and lurched unsteadily out of the room. As he did so, Erik was appalled to see how thin and emaciated B.E.'s body had become.

When B.E. returned, he looked a little refreshed, although his red-rimmed eyes shocked Erik every time they exchanged glances.

"What's happening, B.E.? Where's your family?"

"Gone to Hope to the public consoles. Sharing this one was driving us all crazy. Literally."

"Look at you. You're sick."

"Yes, I am. You've no idea. I'm finished, Erik. The game, it's destroying me, and I can't stop."

"So it's true." Erik moved and sat on the edge of an unmade bed, as disheartened as B.E.

"What's true?"

"The new game. It is poisoning us."

"Yes, it is the game. Saga." B.E. looked at Erik, who just bowed his head. "I was enjoying myself at first, but then something happened. I found I couldn't leave it alone. I'd wake up and the first thing that I wanted to do was clip up. I'd hate it when someone else was using the console, get really angry with them; really angry, like I wished they would just go away and leave me alone with it. When I realized the game was turning me into a horrible person, I tried to stop. I thought I was a strong person, but I'm not; I'm weak. The game won. I couldn't stay away from it. My dreams were full of it. I'd find myself making excuses for clipping up, especially in the early hours when everyone was asleep. Have you ever truly, deeply, promised yourself something, then broken that promise?"

B.E. stared at Erik, and the pain on his face was visible. Erik shook his head.

"Well, I have, and it has shattered my self-belief. I'm not the B.E. you knew, Erik. I'm a wreck. I told myself, from the very bottom of my heart, I had to stop. But I didn't stop. At one point, I took the console and was going to throw it out the window, but I couldn't. Deep inside, I knew that I would then have to go to someone else's, yours maybe, or maybe all the way to Hope. I caved in, Erik. I'm beaten. And now it's destroying me but I can't give it up." B.E. was crying from his sore eyes. "My parents and my sister, it's got them, too."

"It's not your fault." Erik spoke softly, a tremble of fear in his voice. How powerful was the Dark Queen, that she could reduce B.E., the strongest, cockiest of his friends, to this?

"What do you mean?" B.E. flung himself on the bed, lying facedown beside Erik. He turned his head. "You know what's causing this?"

"Yes. The people in the game. Some of them, maybe just one, the Dark Queen, have been poisoning us. To make us obey them."

"Bloody vengeance! It's working. I would do anything to make it stop. But that's something, at least."

"What?"

"My failure. It's not just me, right? There are lots of us feeling this?"

"I think so, but we'd have to go to Hope to be sure. Bjorn and the others are fine, last I knew."

"What does the Dark Queen want?"

"For us to reprogram the game. To make her children immortal."

They sat for a while in silence, in the dark, Erik resting one hand on B.E.'s shoulder blade, trying, without words, to offer his support.

"But that's crazy," B.E. eventually muttered. "Why go to all this trouble? She could just have asked."

"I know. But she doesn't trust humans. She's turning people like you into hostages, to make certain we will obey her."

B.E. just shook his head in response.

"There's something else that troubles me." Erik glanced tentatively at B.E., this time ashamed of himself.

"Go on."

"I think Saga might be real. I think that the people in it are not NPCs; they are all alive. Most of them don't even know it's a game. And if that's true, I've done a terrible thing."

"I know."

"You know? You heard about it?"

"No. I just mean I did the same. You killed some of them, right?"

"Yes. A policeman. I stabbed him in the mouth."

"You didn't know, Erik. None of us knew." This time it was B.E. who tried to console Erik. Both of them sat on the bed, looking down, wretched and unhappy.

"So, what shall we do?" Erik asked.

It seemed as though B.E. did not hear him, but then his friend drew a deep breath and sat up.

"We have to give the Dark Queen what she wants, quickly, before everything falls apart. Have you seen the state of our farm? Imagine what's happening in the towns."

"I agree. But I don't trust her. She's really creepy, like a giant beetle. I mean, of course we'll do what she wants. But what if she then betrays us?"

"Why would she, if she gets what she wants?" B.E. was plaintive.

"I don't know. I'm just saying I got a feeling she can't be trusted. It was in her eyes; they were cold, and laughing at me. I was wondering what would happen if, instead of giving her what she wants, we organized with the other towns to remove Saga from the system right across the world. But it looks as if what she told me is true."

"What's that?" B.E. looked at Erik questioningly.

"She said that without the game, those whom she had poisoned would die."

"Ya. It's probably true. I'm heading that way now." B.E. sighed. He glanced at his friend. "Tell me, Erik, you're in there as Cindella, right? You didn't need to create a new character when you first logged in?"

"Right. It said something about having the option to keep her because I'd completed Epic. Actually I nearly started a new character, but I have a soft spot for Cin. I'm glad I kept her; all my magic still works, and I think I'm immune to whatever it is the Dark Queen does to poison people. I'm sure she would have tried it on me by now."

"You don't feel the need to play all the time?"

"No. In fact, I feel so guilty about that policeman, I've pretty much stopped clipping up. It's too real."

"You're so lucky. I'd give anything to trade places with

you. . . . I don't mean I want you where I am now. I wouldn't wish this torture on anyone."

B.E. lay down, his face a pale skull in dim light. Soon after, his eyes closed and his breathing slowed. Erik got up carefully and walked out of the room. Downstairs, he first of all got a fire going in the stove, then set about cleaning the kitchen and preparing some hot food for when B.E. woke up. At the same time, he felt a growing anxiety. He must go to Hope and make sure that everyone in the town who was not yet poisoned stayed away from Saga.

Chapter 15
A Tank Afloat

"No, I'm alive!" Milan shouted, waking us all up.

Arnie's spare room was dull gray with the light of a sun that was not yet up over the horizon. Pale faces peered blearily at Milan. Beyond our window, you could see the rim of a satellite dish on which the local finches liked to gather. They were singing, anticipating the dawn. But all else was still; not even the refuse carts were on the streets, nor could I hear the distant rumbles and sonorous horns of passing locomotives.

"Sorry, everyone. Go back to sleep. It was a nightmare."

Athena sat up, reaching out of her sleeping bag to find her glasses. She held back her bangs to look at him. "What? What happened?"

"We were all in a hospital, lying inside those plastic tents for critically ill people. Then that Cindella character came past with a whole group of others. They were chatting. As they passed our beds, they flicked a switch and we died. One by one. The power went off, and we died. They weren't even paying attention." Milan was still half in the nightmare, and his face had a sickly tinge. He looked back at Athena. "I guess some of what you were saying got through to me." She nodded.

For a while, no one said anything, and I closed my eyes again. I could never remember my own dreams, just fragments of sound and color, hints of subsiding emotional states and half-familiar scents.

There was a knock on the door.

"All up early today, I hope. We need to talk tactics."

"Arnie? What time is it?" I shouted back, my irritation clear in the tone of my voice.

"I don't know. What I do know, though, is that I've been up all night and it's ready!"

If he wanted an enthusiastic response, he should have knocked in the middle of the afternoon.

"I'll use the bathroom first." Athena stretched. "I can't see myself getting back to sleep."

They stirred themselves, and, even though I turned over, wrapping myself in the hood of my sleeping bag, it was no good.

"Ghost, how can you sleep at a time like this?"

"Like what?" I muttered.

"Like, you know, this might not be real. It just keeps going around and around in my head. The walls, the floor. You, me. It's all suddenly so insubstantial." Knowing Milan as I did, I could tell he was genuinely struggling. Normally he was Mr. Affable, too into his role as the boarder hero of the punk scene to let any real feelings show. This was a new Milan, and he sincerely wanted me to respond. So I shook off the vestiges of sleep and woke up properly.

"Were you ever boarding and felt the world slow down?" I asked him. "So slow it ticks over, one instant at a time. And you can almost see what the effects of your moves will be, like ripples. You know, you are so pumped on adrenaline or something, that the world lets you pick your path even when it's nearly an impossible one?"

"Not really. Maybe it seems a bit slower, sometimes."

"Well, that's how the world has always been for me, when I'm riding anyway. I've always felt that underneath, it's not as . . . as continuous . . . it's kinda lumpy and you can shape it. I'm not explaining myself very well. But the point is, nothing has changed, really. These walls are not going to go away. The physics of our world is exactly as it always has been. It's just that there's more going on out there than we ever imagined. Maybe there are many other universes out there."

"So, why do I suddenly feel that life is pointless?"

"Do you?" I caught his eye.

"Yeah." He meant it; I could see that. "And I feel angry, too."

"Who at?"

"The Cindella people, I guess. It's like, how dare they think they are playing a game with me in it?"

"That's what Athena was saying last night when you were dancing. She just hated the idea she was in their game," Nathan joined in.

"Yeah."

"Someone mention me?" Athena's words were muffled; she was brushing her teeth.

"Cindella last night, disappearing and coming back. It makes you angry," Nathan repeated.

She nodded, saying nothing.

Nathan gave his characteristic shrug. "I rather like it. I want to get to know them, the outsiders. Also, it's an opportunity. There's a lot I don't like about our world. But now I feel optimistic; it can be changed."

Athena raised one eyebrow. She was good at that.

"What matters is that you two can still hold it together, right?" I looked from Athena to Milan. "You aren't thinking of going home or anything?" I needed reassurances from Milan, especially, about where his insecurities were leading him.

"Ghost." He shook his head. "I thought you understood me. What I'm talking about has got nothing to do with home. It's, like, much deeper than that. It's about the point of life."

That was a good answer. I shouldn't really have doubted him; it's just that now they were in one of my favorite living places, the closest I had to a home. In his distant, grumpy way, Arnie had been good to me. If Milan were to go back, then I could never come here again, working on the assumption that if the authorities were after us, they would make him talk.

"Well, what was the point of life yesterday?" Nathan picked up on Milan's doubts.

"To party."

"Fine. So what's the point of life today?"

"To party, I guess."

"That and win the air race," added Nathan with enthusiasm.

"Yeah." For the first time that morning, Milan smiled. It was good to see, even if it came from his daydreaming about that stupid aircar race.

Downstairs, Arnie had set out four chipped but welcome mugs of coffee. The corners of his eyes were tinged with red, but his gaze was lively, jumping around and willing to overlook our bedraggled appearance.

"Bring 'em with you; come and look."

So we trooped into the wide bay where Arnie did his serious repair work. The tank was clear of all the debris and tooling that had previously been attached to it. Close up it was huge, with immense, thick slabs of armor all around its body. A heavy turret with a massive cannon, squat and low, made the vehicle look like it was frowning. Nathan rested his mug on the unpainted body and stroked the metal surface musingly. I knew he was considering the design he intended to paint upon it.

"It's huge. Is it gonna float?" Milan looked skeptical. "It must be at the limit."

"At the limit and then some." Arnie grinned, proud but a little shy.

"Go on then." Milan gestured with his chin.

Arnie leaned on the front plates of the tank and, with a grunt, pulled himself off the ground. He straightened and walked up to the nearest hatch. Somewhat clumsily he lowered himself inside the vehicle.

And up it went. The buzz of the power being eaten by the tank filled the garage and caused tools to jitter in their racks. It was a meter off the floor, vibrating just enough to slop Nathan's coffee onto the plain gray surface of the armor.

"Class!" Milan was excited; the color was back in his cheeks and forehead. He braced himself and pushed at a large plate that covered the front of the nearest set of tracks. Slowly the tank began to turn. Smiling, Milan looked back over his shoulder at us, delighted at his ability to move such a massive vehicle.

Arnie popped his head up.

"Get in. We need to check that it can take your weight, too."

We needed no second invitation, and using the tracks as footholds, we vaulted up on top. Milan went straight for the turret; the rest of us lowered ourselves through hatches into the main body.

There was a surprising amount of room inside; Athena and I wouldn't even have to duck except where it narrowed toward the front and rear. She was already in the command seat, her computer unrolled and switched on, nodding to herself as she read.

"Well?" Arnie was crouched back on his haunches, looking at us. He was tired, but the tears in his eyes were of pride.

"Good job, Arnie." I smiled at him, trying to communicate my admiration. For all his brusqueness, Arnie had his moments of self-doubt. As an overweight red-card mechanic, working in the seediest part of town, he would be seen by many people as a failure. Even if he often spoke confidently of his ability to win the aircar race, Arnie must have been affected by the knowledge that many people thought he was simply a fool. Well, this race would prove his critics wrong. The tank was the business.

"Good job? This is awesome, man. The greatest work anyone outside the big corporations has ever done." Milan was better in these situations than I was. "I mean, I really think we have a chance of winning."

"Really?" Arnie shuffled forward under the turret so he could look up to see Milan.

"Really. This baby is gonna rock!"

With a high-pitched whine, the weapons systems powered up.

"Aha. Thought so." Athena was flicking the switches above her head. "Whoa! Get a load of the visuals." Her eyes widened.

In front of each chair was a screen, I slipped into place to check it out. Milan had his targeting system up: a series of diminishing circles that swept around a view of the garage as he began to move the turret, raising and lowering the cannon.

"Auto-target locking won't function for objects this close," Athena commented. "We need to be outside."

Arnie immediately stuck his head and arms out of a hatch, and soon the fact that the garage shutters were rising was visible on our screens.

"Yes!" shouted Milan. "Let's take her for a cruise."

"What's the plan, Arnie?" Even I was getting into this, despite my innate reluctance to move out of the shadows into public view. Driving in a tank was pretty class.

He popped back down. "Yes, we ought to give it a trial run. I was thinking I'd be driver. You can sort out all the rest between you. One on the main cannon, one on the secondaries, one on missiles and anti-missile defenses, and one on systems."

"Systems," announced Athena.

"Main gun." Milan was only a fraction of a second behind her.

"Which do you want, Nath?"

"Secondary cannons, if that's all right?" He glanced across from the chair he was in.

"Sure. Missiles for me."

"You two have to swap seats," Arnie pointed out as he made his way past us to the back. Nath and I were up front, Athena very near the center, and above her, in the turret, Milan. All of us had our screens on. You could rotate the views, but I was happy with dead ahead. My console had a load of switches, which were clearly labeled with deployment commands like "counter-measures" and "interceptor." There was a "missile launch" switch above a crimson display that allowed you to toggle through a choice of missiles: Stellar Burst, Arrow, Streamer, Red4, and Blitz. Cool, although I hadn't the faintest idea what they did. Then there were the two joysticks on my panel; those really had me confused.

"Hey, Athena, do you know what these joysticks are for?"

"One sec."

I continued testing the dials of my console. There were a few switches that got targeting patterns to come up on the screen, just as Milan had done.

"Ghost?" Athena called out.

"Yeah?"

"You know how to toggle your missile to Streamer, right?"

"Affirmative." Gotta get into the military language when you're the missile commander of a serious battle tank.

"Well, it's a wire-guided missile. Those are to steer it with."

"Neat. Um, affirmative."

"Wow! Nice, Ghost. Makes me wish I'd picked your job." Nathan gave me a thumbs-up.

"Don't worry, Nath," Athena called out from behind us. "You should see what a kick you've got on those cannons."

All this time, we had been moving slowly out into the road. It was so early that the streetlamps were all still on, white blurred patches on our gray view screens. You got used to the background hum very quickly, and the motion of the tank was smooth, so that it felt as if we were coasting quietly downhill, even though, if anything, we were heading up a slight incline. Arnie steered us into a dirty-looking yard, at the far end of which was a basketball hoop.

"That's your target, kids. Get practicing."

The weapons for the aircar race were supposed to be non-lethal; they were all anti-electrical devices only. Every entrant had a spherical defense shield. The tactic in the race was to shoot until you wore holes in the shield and could fire through it to hit the vehicle inside, which would then imme-diately come to a halt, having lost all power. The aircar race, therefore, was supposed to be safe, in theory at least. About five years before, two people had died when the power was cut from their swift-racing aircar, just as it was taking a sharp corner between two skyscrapers. But that was just unlucky.

"Locked on," Milan announced.

"Go for it," Nathan called out.

The tank rocked and emitted a glowing pink bolt, along with a loud, high-pitched grunt. The bolt flashed across the yard, dissipating after striking the basketball hoop. Two streaks of green immediately followed. Then another pink cough. Milan and Nathan noticed the slightly different pitch of the sound of their weapons and were firing now so as to make a distinct rhythm. Pink—green—green—pink—green—green.

"All right, all right. You have it, boys," Athena cut in. "Now Ghost."

"Can I use up one of the wire-guided missiles, Arnie?"

"Sure, we're allowed only three in the race; you have eight there."

I toggled "Streamer," grasped the joysticks, and thumbed the "fire" button on the left-hand one. This time there was no motion from the tank but a rushing sound as the missile shot out of the front of the vehicle. It swerved upward.

"Where you going, Ghost?" Milan laughed.

I let it go higher, confident. I could feel it obeying me. When the flashing blur of metal and light was nearly out of view, I pushed the joysticks forward as far as they would go, sending the missile crashing to the ground, having first passed perfectly through the hoop.

"Slam dunk!"

"Ace!"

"Class!"

Even Arnie grunted approvingly.

"So, that's the plan. If we get in a scrap with something tough, you boys pick a spot on their shield and wear it down, until Ghost can send a missile through."

"Roger that." I wasn't sure where that phrase came from, but it sounded right.

Chapter 16
Blastimus Maximus

We were all up early again. Too early. It meant sitting at the table, clasping a mug, waiting in a strained silence, when I would rather have been asleep. I could understand Arnie being nervous; this was his one and only shot at a card upgrade. He was also on edge because of the way he felt his guild had betrayed him. They had dismissed him as an irrelevant eccentric, so for Arnie today was also about proving Valiant wrong, about affirming his own existence to the world. But why did I feel as anxious as everyone else at the table? After all, I hadn't even wanted to get involved in the first place. Perhaps because now we had reached this moment, I felt there really was a possibility we might actually win the race. With this tank, anything was possible. It was a first-class entry; Arnie had done a great job. Winning the aircar race: I could see how that thought had overwhelmed Milan and even Nathan. They no longer joked about how awesome it would be to be aircar race champions. Since it actually might happen, victory simply couldn't be mentioned, or even thought about.

The room's wall screen was showing a newscast; Athena had switched it on earlier. There was only one story: the coming race. The pictures showed that already the grandstand at the spaceport was filling up. Spectators wanted to be present in person at the start and finish. Nor did you miss any of the rest of the action once there; huge screens displayed the race from the point where the vehicles exited the spaceport, flying cameras monitoring the battles over a hundred miles of highway before the race returned to the grandstand for the finish. The excitement was far more intense at the spaceport than for those watching the race through a newscast. I used to go along every year. Mind you, that was more to steal bagfuls of color cards than to watch the race.

Clips of the new Grand Vizier talking about the event's having been upgraded were being intercut with interviews with guild leaders, tank crews, and former winners of the race. It took some effort by Athena, scrolling through lists, to find our entry: Arnie's Repairs. We were listed among the non-guild entries, usually a group of desperate no-hopers, participating just for their moment of glory and their chance to be in the public eye. That reminded me.

"Hey, Athena, how is Defiance doing? How many members have you got?"

"As of last night, we have two hundred and forty-one."

"Not bad." It wasn't that promising, though. Since I had never really had a great interest in guilds, I hadn't paid much attention to how they gained position. It was a complex calculation based on the number of members and the color of their cards. To get allocated an office or civic responsibility, you needed around ten thousand red members; to get a seat on the High Council, a hundred thousand.

"It's all right." Athena shrugged. "Hopefully today will give us a boost. The word is only slowly getting around. I've posted on all the punk boards, explaining that we're a kind of protest guild. The problem is, the sort of person who would like the charter of Defiance doesn't join guilds."

After a glance at the wall clock, Arnie got up and left us without saying a word. A short while later, the garage shook and was filled with a deep rumbling sound. The tank was floating. Milan looked around and then shrugged.

"Here goes."

In the end, the design was a simple one. Nathan had drawn a line diagonally across the tank, from front left to back right. One side of the line had then been painted entirely black, the other red. In front of the turret, on the large flat panel, was the Defiance tag. Here and there a few smaller decorations could be seen, classy little touches. On each of our hatches was a small image. Mine was the ♥, Arnie's a wrench, Athena's an owl, Milan's an arrow, and Nath's own, a yin-yang symbol. It was simple but effective. Too effective. It was bound to draw attention. Mind you, I did realize that if we were going out to win, and there was a possibility that we might win, there was no way to avoid attention. Could they arrest the winners of the aircar race? In full public view? Were they even looking for us still? Probably. Sitting in the tank, I felt a very strange mix of excitement for the coming race and nervousness that we were putting ourselves in danger. It was too late to back out now; the others would feel completely betrayed.

Inside the tank, we were quiet as we glided toward the spaceport, the interior space filled only with the hum of the engine. Athena fed the newscast through to our screens, and we watched the gathering spectacle. There was no point in noting possible rivals. With a record 126 entries, the race was going to be little more than a massive bust-up. Early race leaders were nearly always taken out by the chasing pack. The winners tended to come bursting from the main bunch only as they approached the finish, having had a relatively quiet race and preserved their defensive shields. It could happen that a small breakaway group would reach an understanding not to fire on each other and get enough corners between themselves and the chasing aircars that they broke completely clear of the melee. All such understandings fell apart as these breakaways neared the spaceport and the final stretch of the course. Then spectators would have the hilarious entertainment of the breakaway group firing on each other at close range, within sight of the finishing line, but sometimes so destructively that none of them made it across. Our tank didn't have the acceleration to win a sprint at the end, so Arnie's plan was to try to get into a breakaway group, in other words, to hold our fire in the hope that those in the vehicles around us felt the same way. It was largely a matter of luck, really. There was a rule that meant no one commenced firing until after the two-kilometer line. But after that, it was every aircar for itself. You can imagine the chaos.

Not many other vehicles had yet placed themselves in their allocated starting position. That was a mistake on our part; already we were drawing attention to ourselves, and I winced when I saw our tank in the dead center of the newscast screen.

"Cameras heading our way." Athena had seen it, too.

A male presenter, immaculately dressed in a green suit, tapped on the side of the tank. "Anyone in there?" He turned and beamed into the camera.

"No," I whispered, shrinking into my seat. Milan, though, threw open the turret hatch, and his beaming, handsome, stupid face was all over the newscast.

"Here we go," muttered Athena resignedly.

"Hello up there." The cut was back to the presenter. "So you are . . ." He checked the screen unrolled on his clipboard. "Number seventy-four: Arnie's Repairs. Are you Arnie?"

"No," replied Milan. "He is."

Arnie had stuck his head through a hatch. A camera scrolled around to him.

"So, black and red. With all those signs, are you sending out a political message today? Is that why you brought this old tank along? Anything you would like to say to the viewers?"

"Nope. Yes. Valiant, I hope you are watching. See, I told you." Arnie ducked back down, angry, embarrassed, and proud at the same time.

"And you, young man?"

"I just want to dedicate our win to all the anarcho-punks out there. You know who you are." Milan waved a clenched fist around and turned a little in order that the camera would take in the perma-tats visible on his biceps. Behind me, I heard a sigh and could imagine Athena shaking her head, but I didn't want to miss a moment of the broadcast by turning around to check.

"So, are you going to win today?"

"No question. Not when we have this baby." Milan patted the cannon affectionately.

"And what will you do with your green card?" Unseen by Milan, the interviewer winked into another camera.

"Partttyyyy!" Milan gave a great roar, flexing his arms above his head and pulling his monster face.

"Nice shot," grumbled Athena. Fortunately the close-up did not stay on our screens for long; the cameras moved rapidly across to the next vehicle.

"Hey!" Milan called down to us when he had returned to his seat. "Whatcha think? What a star, right!"

"Yeah," replied Athena dryly. "Good job."

Slowly, one by one, then in twos, threes, and more, the other vehicles arrived to take up their starting positions. On our immediate right was a slim cigar-shaped two-seater; we could see the two-woman crew through their clear dome. Every year, a bunch of slender racing cars would accelerate as fast as they could from the start, hoping to use their speed to get out of range of the cannons of the chasing pack before the two-kilometer mark. They never did. On the other side, a customized Mosveo Starburst with the colors of Noble Warriors slid into its starting position. Three crew, again designed for speed rather than combat but with much more stability than a two-seater. They would make good breakaway partners, screening us from the left.

"Milan, do something useful. Stick your head up and see if you can offer a peace deal with our neighbors." Athena had formed exactly the same conclusion as I had. I looked back over my shoulder, giving her a nod and a smile.

"Those two hot chicks? No problem."

"No. Not the women on our right. We'll have to take them down fast. The entry from Noble Warriors."

"Gotcha."

I scrolled my view around so I could watch. Milan caught their attention with a wave, and then patted the main cannon while shaking his head. They understood and gave us the thumbs-up. Milan acknowledged them with the same gesture but under his breath muttered, "Just while we get clear; then you suckers are wasted."

3:40 left on the countdown. At last, we were nearly there.

"Headsets on," called out Athena. "It's gonna get loud."

Arnie didn't seem to mind her calling out the orders. Which was just as well because we were used to her, and I don't know if I trusted Arnie enough to respond to him as fast as I would to an order from Athena.

2:35 and from the seat parallel to mine, on the other side of the tank, Nathan gave me a little wave. I saluted him.

2:00.

"Anti-gravity on."

Across the vast spaceport plaza, 126 vehicles rose up, as if an army of beetles had been awoken by the order to march. All around us, a deep hum throbbed and resonated, creating infinitely many beats as a result of the slight difference in pitch of the various engines.

"All systems are go. Shield one hundred percent in all directions." Athena sounded as if she did this every day. I was very proud of her. I hoped Arnie was thinking that he couldn't have got a better crew, even if his guild had formed one for him.

With thirty seconds to go, the crowd began to join the countdown. Despite the fact that we were over a hundred meters from the nearest stand, we could just make out their faint cries above the pulsing sound of the anti-gravity engines.

"Twenty, nineteen, eighteen . . ."

"Ready propulsion."

A pause.

"Ten, nine, eight . . ." She counted down with the official clock and the crowd. ". . . three, two, one. Engage."

A great cheer and motion all around. My teeth smashed together painfully and the tank smacked my legs and the base of my spine, flinging me up out of my seat.

"Ouch."

"What?"

"What the jumping jeebie was that?"

"Hush," Athena cut in. "We're down. On the ground. Anti-gravity has gone, switching to manual drive."

"Sorry," whispered Arnie. "The anti-gravity couldn't cope with full thrust." I turned around; his head was bowed, his hands pressed hard against the sides of his stocky head.

"This is embarrassing." Milan was disgusted and shocked.

"Oh, well. Sorry, Arnie. Maybe next year." Nathan, on the other hand, was trying to offer some consolation. Good old Nath.

"Not next year. All my credit went on this entry." Arnie sighed, then slumped forward, covering his head completely with his arms.

Poor Arnie. He was a broken man. It was one thing to day-dream about entering the great aircar race, but a whole new level of folly actually to use all your credits on an entry that didn't even lift off the ground. I could hardly look at him; he would be feeling terrible, a total donkey. All his detractors in Valiant were being proven right.

"Oh no. Cameras. Incoming." It was Milan who alerted us. "Tell you what, they try to make us look stupid and I'll shoot them. No, I'll shoot them anyway, take out their power."

"Wait," ordered Athena. She was concentrating intently on her screen, her face gray from its light.

"I'm not leaving here without shooting something."

"Don't!" She raised her voice. "You'll get us disqualified."

"So what?" Milan retorted.

Theoretically we could carry on, but it was pointless. On manual drive, physically rolling over the ground, we would still be lumbering around the course three hours after every-one else had finished.

"So, I have a plan. Positions everyone. I'll explain as we go. Arnie, turn us around."

"Around?"

"Yes."

I flicked to the newscast. We were on. So were two other unfortunate vehicles stalled at the start. Their crews were getting out to the jeers of the crowd. A large tow truck was heading our way.

"Athena, tow truck."

"I see it. Get us moving, Arnie."

"Which way?"

This was annoying. "Come on, Arnie," I chipped in with some irritation. "She said turn around. So turn."

"Whatever we are doing, it had better be fast." Which was as close as Nathan would get to shouting at Arnie.

At last, we were off. Instead of turning, we were jolting along in reverse, which I suppose was the same as what Athena wanted. The tracks along the sides of the tank created a loud squeal as we scurried away from our starting position.

"Tow truck has halted." Nathan was relieved.

"Listen up." As Athena spoke, I strapped myself into the chair. The motion of the tank over the ground, without the cushion of anti-gravity, was rough. "There is nothing in the rules about us having to use anti-gravity, or to prevent us from going the wrong way. So look at your screens. I'm displaying the point we're heading for; it's the narrow part of the track, shortly before it widens into the spaceport plaza. See the curve? We're going to lie in wait just after the last bend and near the home stretch, and when we've taken out every single one of the other entrants, we're going to complete the race in our own good time."

"Yes! Good plan; I like it!" cheered Milan.

"We can't hope to stop them all, can we, though?" asked Nathan.

"Probably not. But it's a good spot and we'll have the element of surprise. In any case, it beats going home early."

By the time we set up, our good humor was back. Even Arnie was sitting up alertly, his face attentive to our chat. We had stopped about a hundred meters from the final corner. The road at this point was wide enough for only about four aircars. Our goal was to try to stop everything that came our way. For now, though, despite the knowledge of impending combat, we had to wait. I tuned into the race coverage, and so did Nathan.

"I'm going to have a snooze; wake me with ten minutes to battle." There came a click that suggested Milan had switched off his headset.

For the next hour, the rest of us watched the race, rarely speaking. Could we really hope to stop the entire race from rushing past us? Some of the others had to get through, surely? Still, at least we would have some impact on the race, rather than just leaving completely demoralized.

A group of twelve fast vehicles eventually got clear of the melee.

"Good. That suits us," observed Athena.

"Ten minutes." Athena was underneath the hatch, pulling at Milan's trouser leg.

"Right. What's incoming?"

"The leading group of six is twenty-seven seconds clear of the pack. There are forty-three vehicles in total left in the race. Not including us."

"Forty-three. Right." Milan yawned.

It was a nice pose, but I bet he had been awake all the time and was as nervous as the rest of us.

Our screens changed to forward view, the newscast and commentary switched off.

"Drop your targeting right on the corner, Milan."

"Athena, come on; I'm awake now and on the job. Just leave it to me."

A hundred meters of empty, quiet road.

A distant bank of white cloud was drifting gently toward the City center; it was a scene of utter tranquility, just an empty road. An empty, quiet road. One hundred meters. Empty.

Beep, beep, beep. Thwomp! The tank rocked as if it had just experienced a sudden shiver.

"One down." Milan was matter-of-fact. I smiled to myself, sure that despite the laconic tone of voice, he was thrilled with the effects of his shot.

The leading aircar had, of course, all its remaining shielding facing behind it, back toward the chasing aircars. The moment it had entered our view, the auto-targeting had picked it up and Milan had fired straight at the aircar's unguarded nose. The now powerless aircar bounced three times along the road surface before stopping. Behind it, the other vehicles swerved, but one racing car shot into the air, taking a huge uphit from the disabled aircar.

"Two down." Instinctively Nathan had fired at the exposed underside of the flying vehicle, where again there was no shielding. The racing car continued its flight, but powerless now, instead of righting itself on a cushion of anti-gravity, it crashed heavily onto the road, scattering metal parts in all directions. Milan was firing constantly, the tank a vibrating chamber. In the space of thirty seconds, it had become very hot inside.

"Nath, take the back one in the flank as it skirts the wreck," ordered Athena.

The first shots were coming back at us. Nothing to worry about yet, although Athena was rotating our shields all the same, spreading the power loss evenly. I was ready to take anti-missile measures, but either these aircars were all out of missiles, or they were saving them.

"Three down," announced Nathan proudly. His target continued on the course it had taken to dodge the ruined aircar and smashed into one of the barricades that lined the road.

"Milan, switch to the two-seater; its shields are nearly gone. Arnie, ram that big mudgrubber; there's no way we can hole it."

"Four down." Milan had instant success with the small, thin aircar; it skidded to a halt ten meters before us.

We were moving again, for the first time in hours, lurching at a specially engineered airtruck. It was a vehicle with nearly as great a mass as ours, towering over us, the pilots looking straight at our cameras, horrified. If they tried to turn now, we would hit them in the flank and roll them over. They just had to hope that they could ride right over us.

"Turn that turret, Milan! Brace for impact!" shouted Athena.

"Hell's teeth!" Nathan muttered.

The jolt threw me headlong toward my instrument panel, but my belt jerked me back. Everything loose inside the tank was flung from the back to the front, and I got glancing blows from all sorts of junk. A spare headset was caught on my controls. Strangely we were still moving, or at least our treads were squealing as if in motion. The front end of the tank started to rise. Beneath us came a terrible groaning noise and the angry buzz of our engine grew louder. We lurched down, level for a moment, then started to rise again.

"What's happening?" I looked over my shoulder toward the back of the tank.

"We're chewing up the sods." Arnie had his jaws clenched tightly, his stocky arms thrust out before him, pressing the drive controls forward as far as they would go.

Another lurch and a short advance before we started to rise again.

"That's enough. Disengage. Ghost, get on that runaway."

One aircar had steered its way through the carnage; it wasn't even bothering to fire at us but was pelting along at full speed, making for the spaceport plaza and the finish line. I immediately launched a Streamer, curving it around the side of the tank and switching to reverse view to follow it.

"Milan, keep firing; force them to keep their shielding facing us." Not that I really needed to urge him to use that cannon, especially as it was already facing in their direction.

The rocket eagerly hunted down the escaping aircar, accelerating so swiftly that it had caught the car even before it reached the point where the road entered the spaceport plaza. Just as it seemed that the rocket must impact on the aircar's rear shield, I swerved it up and then plunged sharply down, taking the missile through some weak spots of shielding directly above the driver's cabin. A pulse of white light flared out and, with a sigh, the aircar gave up. It settled down quietly on the edge of the plaza.

"Six down." We were off to a good start. I'd had to use only one missile on that breakaway group.

"Seventeen seconds to the pack. Arnie, plug us into the gap."

Ahead of us was chaos. The airtruck looked as if it had been smashed in the face and lost all its teeth; it was folded in on itself, around a great tear that went all the way across its front. It was now blocking half the road and, although small, the wreck of the two-seater also made a handy obstacle on our right. There was not a lot of room to get past us. Only the thinnest vehicles might risk it; the rest would have to try to ride over the two-seater or the tank.

Several bolts of energy flashing against the nearby buildings signaled the arrival of the rest of the race. They came around the corner in a line that went right across the full width of the road, firing furiously at each other, a glittering wall of speed and violence. Missiles and counter-missiles were weaving through the air, conducting their own more delicate version of the battle below them. Defeated vehicles were skidding along to a halt, while those immediately behind were rearing up from the uphit as they drove right over them. And we were directly in the path of this howling energy. It was the most frightening and exhilarating moment I have ever experienced. The front-runners were so absorbed in their fight for survival and for speed that Milan and Nathan took out the entire row before any attention was given to us. The pack thundered on, cascading over the dead vehicles. I triggered everything I had, all but my last two Streamers. Our decoys first, next our anti-missile missiles. Then the three Stellar Bursts, three Arrows, three Red4s, and finally the Blitzes. It wasn't that I was overcome with panic and had lost control. We had to get the front vehicles down fast, to jam up the road. Each shot was carefully chosen. Two or even three missiles at the same target if I thought it still had strong-looking shields, then on to the next. I was efficient. So were the others.

"Brace for impact!"

Another awful crash, just as bad as the first. Then a strange feeling, aftershocks. Other vehicles were piling up behind and we were sensing the distant echoes of their collisions.

I switched to the newscast.

". . . anything like it. And there goes Voice of Doom, Guard of Honor, and Valiant."

"It's incredible. But is it legal?"

While the presenters gabbled on, I was attentive to the pictures. One of the flying cameras had the best shots, and I selected the cast it was transmitting. All the way back around the corner was a huge pileup of vehicles. Those that still had power were stuck behind the jam and continued shooting at each other. As the camera tracked down the road, you could see the disabled aircars wedged into each other, packed solid, and as it came to where we were, the wrecks were stacked up three or even four high like a wave of metal, frozen in the act of cascading. From the pictures, I was worried that when we backed out, it would all collapse onto us.

"Now what?" Arnie's tone was grim, as though he again wanted to smash his tank into the rival aircars.

"Drive around the course?" suggested Milan.

"Better wait, I think," Nathan chipped in. "Let's see if any of the ones at the back try to find a way through."

"Yeah. What have you got left, Ghost?" Athena asked me.

"Just two Streamers."

"If you had to hit targets behind all this junk, could you?"

"No problem, if we can pull back enough for a clean launch."

Carefully, very carefully, Arnie reversed us out of the pileup, leaving behind a tank-shaped hole and a creaking, swaying wall of shattered vehicles. All the while we were extricating ourselves, those aircars still functional behind the wreckage were shooting it out between each other. I waited, watching the battle, until there were only two left, both of them with their remaining shields facing each other. This was the opportune moment to strike. Since I could not control two missiles at once, I directed the first one down the road, a long way from the action, then turned it and gave it a straight line on its target. I immediately detached it and launched my last missile. There was only a small gap between the first and second strikes. Both of the last two aircars were down, taken unexpectedly from behind by the Streamers.

Arnie turned us around and we set out on the long journey. We now had to complete the course. Coming alongside the grandstands, Milan opened his hatch and began waving to the spectators. The cameras immediately flew over to him, and his image was all over the giant screens. The silence of such a great crowd of people was uncanny.

Inside the tank we were silent for a long period also, drained from the intensity of concentration that had just been required of us, and taking in the momentous implications of what we had just done.

"So, that's it, right?" Arnie eventually spoke for us all. "We just have to complete the course the right way and we win?"

"Yes," replied Athena.

"Oh, green. I won't believe it until it's in my hand. A green."

I turned around; Arnie had tears in his eyes. He saw me looking at him. "You kids were amazing. I really couldn't have done it without you."

"No, man, it was your tank. It's the number-one rumble

machine. It's the blastimus maximus. It's Dr. Death on tracks. It's . . . it's just awesome." Milan dropped down from the turret to express his enthusiasm in person.

"Do you all realize what we've just done?" he continued.

"What?" Nathan asked him.

"Not only are we going to win the aircar race, but we've made history. They are going to be showing that five minutes of mayhem a hundred years from now. We ruled. In a big, fat anarchist tank. How cool is that?" His eyes were blazing in a way that I'd never seen before. Like when he'd just eaten a jeebie, but clearer, more intelligent.

"It's pretty cool," acknowledged Nath.

I gave him a thumbs-up. It was an amazing achievement, to snatch victory from such a disastrous start. It was Arnie I felt most pleased for. He was blazing with happiness, his body shaking as the tank rolled along, a huge grin on his face and a distant expression in his eye. The look of someone already going shopping with his green card. When he noticed me looking at him, he became focused, giving me a slow nod, still smiling. I nodded back.

An hour later, as we trundled alone along the wide road, two airboarders, a boy and a girl, both dressed as punks, leaped the barricade and snaked their way over to us.

"Awesome, guys!"

"Way to go."

They saluted us and continued to board around the tank, enjoying the attention of one of the twenty or so cameras that now buzzed around the tank like giant electronic mosquitoes.

Half an hour later, we had twenty boarders gliding sinu-ously in our wake. The latest additions looked dressed to party, plenty of chains and tattoos. The idea of escorting the tank was catching on. I have to admit that if I had been watching the aircar race and seen an anarcho-punk tank take down the whole of the opposition, I, too, would have grabbed my board to join the fun. Each time an individual hopped over the bar-ricade and boarded over to the rest, a good-natured cheer went up. Track marshals were helpless to stop the crowd from growing.

"What's going on?" muttered Arnie.

"Nothing to do with us," replied Athena cheerfully.

"Well, be careful. I don't want to lose my green card."

When we arrived at the site of the battle, a large crowd had gathered, not just boarders but every kind of person; well, reds probably: they were wearing cheap, normal clothes. Hun-dreds of people were standing on the roadside barricades or had crowded at the windows of nearby buildings. When we paused, they gave us a great cheer. I waited for the applause to die away, but it didn't.

"Amazing. This feels really good." Nathan spoke for us all.

"This is the best feeling I've ever had in my life. Listen to them." Milan climbed back up to thrust himself out of the tank and wave back. It was a good feeling, that we had accom-plished something truly extraordinary. But for me there was still a lurking fear that spoiled our victory. We were bound to come to the attention of the police now. Surely they could not ignore our escape from the station and the fact that a police-man had been killed? I felt a shudder pass through me as I recalled the bloody scene.

Meanwhile, Athena studied the two-hundred-meter metal puzzle that had once been a clear road. "Here's a possible route. Reckon you can take it?"

Eager to return my thoughts to the situation in hand, I called up the schematic that Athena sent to Arnie to look at it for myself. It was a three-dimensional sketch of the obstruction ahead, with a path marked through and over it.

"Yeah. Anything we can't move out of the way, we can crush. These aircars are as flimsy as tin cans once their power has gone." Arnie began by driving up on top of a shattered disc-shaped vehicle, and we ground its cabin section under our tracks. He was right; we could barge and tread our way through the wrecks as if they were merely undergrowth. It took a bit of space and a few strong runs at the far end, though, to bring the stack of empty, powerless cars toppling down into the road ahead.

The crashes and splintering of plasti-glass and metal meant that the spectators and the boarders who had been following us had to keep a long way back, so it was several minutes after we had driven on to the plaza before we saw them hurrying after us, keen to come and watch the award ceremony.

"Stop the tank a moment, Arnie. Let them catch up," urged Athena.

"No, let's get this over with." He was understandably anx-ious, so close to the realization of a lifetime's dream.

"Perhaps take it slow then," I offered. "In any case, this is a moment we want to fix in our minds forever."

To be fair to Arnie, the tank did slow down.

This time, as we approached the finishing line, the crowds in the grandstands were more welcoming. Their shock had worn off. Milan sat outside, astride his cannon, waving and orchestrating the cheers with sweeping gestures of his arms. Arnie, Nathan, and even Athena were also popping their heads up and waving. Not me, though. I was just wondering how to get out of there unnoticed.

Chapter 17
DEATH ON A BLACK AIRBIKE

"And was this a strategy you had talked about before the race?"

Arnie looked uncomfortable and gestured with his head toward Athena.

"Actually, it was improvised." She looked directly at the camera. I had to smile at her earnest expression. "Our original game plan had been to try to get into a breakaway group. To be honest, it was something of an act of desperation."

"Yeah," Milan broke in, and the camera swiveled toward him. "That plus the fact I wasn't leaving without firing our cannon at somebody."

"Your entry was an unusual one. You are not members of the same guild?" The interviewer looked down at her clipboard, then back to Arnie, who was standing in front of the others.

"I'm in Valiant. They had their chance to support me, but they wrote me off. Hey, Valiant, how d'ya like me now? Those sods left me out in the cold. It's only thanks to these kids here that I got a crew."

"The rest of us are Defiance. It's a new guild, more of a protest message than a guild." Athena jumped back in quickly. "We think the City is decaying and rotten."

"And the color scheme is unusual. What's the message there?" For a moment, the cameras showed our tank and I instinctively ducked, even though I was safe inside.

"That was this kid." Had Arnie really not learned Nathan's name yet? Even though they were champions together? The camera turned in the direction Arnie had gestured.

"Oh, well, it's, like, the anarchist tank. You know, something different." It must have been that Nathan was feeling shy under the scrutiny of the newscast. He was not usually so inarticulate, and I winced on his behalf.

"Yeah." Milan leaned forward again to get the camera's attention. "As I said before the race, this win is for all the anarcho-punks out there. We were the rebel entry, and we kicked ass!"

"Well, congratulations again on a most remarkable win. I think the Grand Vizier would now like to bestow your prize cards upon you."

The cameras panned back to show a podium that had been set up in front of the grandstand, with corporate sponsorship signs all over it. The new Grand Vizier was there, looking small and delicate against the vast scale of the spaceport and grandstand. As the cameras zoomed toward him over the heads of the crowd, he began to take on a more appropriately dignified and solid appearance. Something about the scene did not seem quite right. I quickly searched through the many other casts that were being sent by the flying cameras. A shudder caressed the inside of my skull, and I understood what was troubling me. Police were moving into certain definite positions. They were stationing themselves to prevent us from leaving.

"Come in, Athena."

"Hey, Ghost, what's up? How does the cast look?" She was still wearing her coms, as we had agreed.

"Get back to the tank right now. The police are going to swoop."

On the newscast I saw her grab Nath and Milan by the arm. Milan shrugged her off angrily at first, and they were arguing. Arnie was bewildered. They started running away, back down the carpeting laid out for the winners. Left behind, Arnie watched them for a moment, expressionless, and then turned to continue his walk up to the podium.

How hard could it be to drive a tank? I sat in Arnie's chair and found the ignition for the motor unit; it started with no bother. Then I grabbed the handles that were a larger version of the joysticks that guided the Streamers. By pushing one forward and pulling the other back, I spun the tank, surprising nearby boarders and spectators who jumped away from the squeals and grumbles of the machine.

With a thud, Milan slid in through the turret hatch. A moment later, Athena and Nathan were in, too, and I immediately sent us scurrying forward, heading out of the spaceport in the direction of the wide road that was used at the start of the aircar race.

Sirens began to blare. That was just as well; it helped clear the spectators.

"What's up?" asked Milan. "I was looking forward to that."

"The police were closing in."

"They still are." Athena was strapping herself into the command seat, already calling up information on her own unrolled computer.

"What's the plan, Ghost?" asked Nathan.

"Shoot our way out."

"Confirm that, please. Shoot the police?" Nathan sounded anxious.

"Confirm. It's that or jail for us."

"Here we go again." Milan turned his targeting on and swiveled the turret so that it pointed back behind us. "I have three cars incoming; fire at will?"

"Take the left two; Nath, take the right." It was reassuring to hear Athena in command of our tactics again.

They were police aircars and much faster than ours. On the other hand, they weren't armed with cannons. With an uninterrupted series of coughs, green and pink bolts of energy spat out of our weapons. The police cars had shields like race shields except they showed only when our cannon fire splashed across them. They rushed ahead of us, blocking our path.

I already had the accelerator down full, and it wasn't going to ease up one bit.

"Brace for impact!" shouted Athena.

"Not again," Nathan said with a sigh.

With a crash of shrieking metal and a shudder, we were through, a scattering of detritus and three spinning aircars in our wake.

"Helicopter!" Athena alerted us. I glanced at the view she was using. From behind the grandstand rose a powerful blue helicopter, propellers front and back. It swung around in an impressively tight arc and accelerated after us.

"Shoot?" queried Milan.

"Shoot!" I shouted back, desperate to get us to some cover but seeing nothing suitable.

"But if we take out their power, they'll probably all die in the crash," Nathan pointed out.

"Tough," I answered.

"I dunno, Ghost. That's gonna really get us in deep trouble." Even Milan had his limits. Didn't he have a terrible scream welling up inside him, the animal fear of capture that so terrified me?

"Shoot! How much more trouble can we be in?"

"A lot more." Milan would not fire; his cannon was silent.

"Bike!" called Athena, cutting across the discussion. Emerging from the crowds was a black airbike, blasting across the plaza like a bolt of energy from our cannons. It was wider than a street bike, with a sleek curved windscreen covering the driver.

"Shoot?" wondered Milan aloud.

"Same problem," answered Nathan.

A beeping sound.

"What's that?" asked Milan in alarm.

"We've been targeted by the helicopter. Ghost, get us out of line of sight." There was a slight tremble in Athena's normally composed voice.

The problem was we were on an exposed flyover, about twenty meters above the roads below us. There was nowhere to turn off for at least a mile.

"It's them or us. *Please* open fire, team." I put all the urgency of the situation into the word "please."

Even before I had finished speaking, the helicopter had exploded spectacularly, molten debris screaming past us and also thumping into the back of the tank. The dark airbike was ahead of us already, steering through the wreckage, its helmeted driver gesturing with his arm for me to follow him.

"Well, that solves that." I spoke into a stunned silence, so relieved that I didn't care that the occupants of the vehicle must have died in the explosion.

"How?" Eventually Milan managed one word.

"The bike. A missile from underneath," explained Athena.

"Should we follow him?" I asked.

No one answered, so I did.

Whoever it was knew the City. We turned off the road at the first opportunity, and he led us through the warehouses and factories of the spaceport district, as fast as our squealing tracks would take us. There was no sign of pursuit, or of any people on the street. This area tended to be deserted outside working days. But still, a red-and-black tank is not very inconspicuous; sooner or later, a security guard at a factory or someone working unusual shifts would call in a sighting to the police. The airbike came to an old set of raised barriers where a disused railway track crossed the road. He turned left, off the road, his cushion of anti-gravity allowing him to drive smoothly along the track. We, however, jolted along to the accompaniment of a strumming sound like the noise you get when you run a stick along a railing. The disused railway cutting went between two high banks, overgrown with thorny weeds and full of discarded containers that we were crushing under our tank tracks. Back behind us was a trail of flattened bushes and squashed metal drums.

The cutting led us to an abandoned shoe factory, whose faded paintwork read: "Sutton's Footwear." Our escort drove straight under a large open shutter and into darkness. I went in after the airbike without hesitation, glad to be under cover. We were in a vast space, nearly empty but for rubble and bare steel girders that rose toward a jagged roof. I switched off our engine. The silence and stillness that followed were much needed. We all appreciated them and said nothing for a while. The others probably felt like me, that what with the race and the escape from the police, life was getting a little stressful.

"I guess we should see who's on this bike." Milan eventually stirred and threw open a hatch. The rest of us followed him out onto the top of the tank.

The dark rider was waiting for us, standing near the front of the tank, helmet in hand, looking a lot less frail than when I had last seen him.

"Michelotto," Athena greeted him.

He nodded.

"Congratulations on your win. It was a truly remarkable achievement. Might I ask who was in charge of the missiles?"

"That would be me." I stayed on the tank near my hatch. There was something very comforting about the vehicle; I was evidently a tortoise by nature, and this was my shell.

"A particularly impressive performance."

"Did you have to destroy that helicopter?" asked Nathan with as much as an aggrieved tone as I had ever heard in his voice.

"I saved you from capture."

"Why?" Milan stood up close so he could look the old man in the eyes. Milan was a tiger, or at least he wanted to be.

"Because I need allies against the Dark Queen."

"Did the Dark Queen kill Cindella, then?" I felt slightly sorry for her; the magic she had brought into the world had given me hope.

"I don't believe so. But when Cindella had the Dark Queen at her mercy, she chose not to strike."

"Why?" Athena asked with genuine interest.

Cindella was still alive then? Good.

"To answer fully would require me to embark on a lengthy explanation."

"We're in no hurry." Athena sat down, legs hanging over the side of the tank. It was strange: she looked so young there, hair in two plaits, wearing her new tank top with the Defiance tag. Yet when it came to dealing with this ancient crocodile, she was every inch his equal.

Michelotto looked steadily back at her, then his posture relaxed slightly and his voice became warmer.

"Very well. This universe we inhabit is not the only one? Would you be willing to accept?"

"Of course," Nathan answered him eagerly. "We figured that out for ourselves. What with the way that people are appearing and disappearing."

"Good. That, indeed, is the main evidence for my statement." Michelotto nodded with an approving smile, but I thought that he was dissembling; not that he was lying, but that he was cold inside, perhaps bored, and that for some reason he felt it necessary to ingratiate himself with us.

"You might not, however, have been able to deduce the relationship between our world and theirs." He waited to see if we would respond, but none of us had any answers. "The curious fact is that our universe is curled up inside theirs, theirs being closer to the fundamental organic physical nature of the universe and ours being derived from artificial laws, albeit laws based on those of the outer universe."

"I don't follow you." Milan still had a belligerent posture. "Artificial? Ours is the artificial universe?"

"In the sense that ours was created a little over two thousand years ago, yes. Of course, we were created by people, human beings, who themselves inhabit a universe that, as far as anyone knows, is not artificial, so there is a sense in which ours can be considered natural, too."

"We are a game, aren't we?" Athena was glum.

"No, but you are correct in two respects. Our universe was created as a game, called Saga by its creators. Secondly, the recent arrivals in our universe believed they were entering a game. What they found, however, was that we have evolved since our creation. That we are living people, not mindless ciphers."

There was a long silence. Michelotto was waiting for us. What did I think? Straightaway, I believed him. Our world had seams. You didn't ordinarily perceive them, but when I was boarding close to the limits of my abilities, I felt them, like the frames between the scenes on a piece of video film. But did the others?

Milan picked up a stone the size of his fist; he threw it at the nearest girder. The metal groaned. Then came a louder crash as the stone fell back to the floor, sending up a small cloud of dust.

"See that?" He brushed his hands on his combats. "That's real."

"Yes?" Michelotto appeared to be studying him patiently.

"Kick this tank and your toe is going to hurt. Our world is real; what you're saying is nonsense."

"Yes, we are real, but we are subordinate to the outer universe. If some human being wished it, they could rewrite the laws of Saga in a way that would not be possible in their own universe. Your rock could have been made to fly out of the roof. The tank could turn to jelly. Almost anything is possible here. At the moment, our environment seems to obey very set physical laws. But, in fact, these could be changed."

"It's horrible." Athena put her head in her hands. "It's a nightmare."

"I can see why you might think so." Michelotto tried to smile sympathetically, but I figured he was out of practice; he looked more sinister than ever.

"So, why didn't Cindella kill the Dark Queen?" I asked, genuinely wanting to hear more from him. For all that I hated the slippery presence of this man, what he was telling us was exciting. I felt that I was finally getting answers after six years of questions and hopeless uncertainty. Might he even know something about me? A part of me shivered at the thought of asking him; *Stay hidden, stay hidden, stay hidden,* cried the beat of my heart. I listened to it, and resolved not to tell him anything about my own past.

"The Dark Queen wants to reprogram our world to make her future offspring immortal and give them the powers of gods. She has gone insane, corrupted by her genuine powers and the sycophancy that surrounds her from people who need to flatter her constantly to stay alive. To make such reprogramming, she has contacted a distant colony of human beings. First of all, she opened Saga to them; then, after they had created personas in our world, she addicted some two million of the humans, to make them hostages. Once the truth of their situation has been fully clarified, she will allow them access to the programming of our world, confident that they will not destroy Saga, because should they do so, they will suffer two million deaths. Cindella attacked the Dark Queen and defeated her, but decided not to kill her for the sake of those two million lives. In my view, she miscalculated. It would have been better to have taken those losses now; it can only get worse. The Dark Queen has no intention of lifting the addiction after any reprogramming."

"That's so cruel," observed Nathan with a sigh. "What must those human beings think of us? They must think we're horrible murderers, to inflict this upon them."

"Can you prove this?" asked Athena. "Show us their universe?"

"Talk to any of the human beings when you next meet one; that's the easiest proof. There is also a way for us to acquire forms in the outer universe, but only the Dark Queen has access to it."

Out of the corner of my eye, I noticed Athena brush away a tear. This was hard on her. Perhaps because she was so much in control of herself. This must feel like the floor was falling away beneath her. When the dark presence of Michelotto had gone, I would try to cheer her up, try to explain how, from my point of view, this was welcome information; it accorded with my instincts and made me feel that it was possible that our world was changing for the better.

"What makes you think we would be interested in trying to fight the Dark Queen?" Milan had obviously been brooding on this for some time; he sounded sullen, defensive.

"You are rebels, are you not? Well, you are lucky. For the first time in two thousand years, Saga is going to witness a rebellion. For I am going to unleash civil war throughout the

City: red and orange against the other colors. I will bring her system crashing down and plant the black flag on the skulls of her followers. And I need generals. I thought you might like the job."

He was animated in a way that you would not have thought possible in the old man we had met at the APC party. I could almost feel his energy warming the air of this ruined factory space and pouring out as a column of heat through the holes in the roof.

"Really? And what if you win?" Athena sounded skeptical.

"Whatever you want."

"But what are you going to replace the card system with? If people aren't working for cards, what are they working for?" We had discussed this a few times ourselves and I knew Athena had her own ideas, but she was obviously testing him.

"Do you believe all that I have told you, that Saga is a created world?"

He surprised her with the question.

"Yes. Unfortunately. Yes, I do."

"Well, I intend to come to an arrangement with Cindella or some other human being. Why should anyone work when we could have our needs taken care of by their programming?"

"So, what would we do?" Nathan spoke up, cautious but interested.

"I believe you might like to party, or play music, or paint, or design airboard courses. Personally I will strive to learn more about the universe external to ours and our relationship to human beings."

"Party, huh? I'm in." Sometimes I could happily have thrown bricks at the back of Milan's head. Milan knew perfectly well that Michelotto was trying to buy our support for whatever he was up to, but he still wanted to act the animal, even though his audience was only Athena, Nathan, and myself. Mind you, he'd probably have given the same response even if it had been just him and Michelotto, simply to amuse himself.

"I don't trust you. I'm not sure what you're doing, but for some reason I think it will be bad for us all, and probably the humans, too." My turn to intervene. Intuition was vital here and mine told me that, in some important way, he was lying.

"Yes, you are right and wrong. I'm acting purely for my own survival: I believe that unless I kill the Dark Queen, she will kill me. But as it happens, this reason leads me to foment rebellion against her. The only hope I have of success is to align myself with those who find the current political structure unjust."

"What's your plan, exactly?" I could tell that Athena, despite her cynicism, was interested. She had that distracted look that meant some of her thoughts were elsewhere, chasing the possibilities.

"I don't wish to talk about it just now, but watch the newscasts. In the meantime, please consider what role you want to play as events unfold. It is going to be a hard fight, and I could really use your help. Especially hers." He pointed at me, and my heart leaped. Then he walked back to his bike. "I recommend that you keep the tank here. I have set up certain screening devices around this building that will probably mean it is safe. You know the current affairs forum, 'Red Rights'?" He looked back over his shoulder at Athena.

"Yes."

"I have a private subgroup there: 'Our Flag Is Black'; password: 'landscaping.' Post if you want to contact me. It is probably secure but, to be safe, keep the message short; no mention of places or names. Use the nickname 'owl' for yourselves."

Athena nodded; Michelotto gave me a last glance before putting his helmet on and starting the airbike. It rose gracefully from the floor, to sweep quietly past us and out into the bright light beyond the shutters. What did he mean by saying he needed my help? What did he know about me? I felt an unpleasant shiver run through me, as if someone had pressed the nerves under the soft skin of my elbows.

"I'm hungry," announced Milan. "Where are we going for dinner?"

Chapter 18
THE SETTING OF A TRAP

"Well, Grand Vizier, are We pleased or displeased with the outcome of this year's aircar race?" The Sector Seventeen police barracks are crude, functional, but safe. We have forgone Our usual comforts for a utilitarian office, deep inside the squat buildings that house the police headquarters. The light in the office is, deliberately, very subdued. We know that Our face does not look its best under these bulbs. The Grand Vizier is wearing a suit whose waistcoat is tinged with a violet sheen that catches what little light there is. He looks back at Us, trying to assess Our humor.

"Both?" he hazards at last.

"Quite right." We smile at his careful answer. "On the one hand, the winners were not of Our choosing. On the other hand, We have learned something significant about those children who were recently involved in that escape from jail."

"Really, ma'am?" He is attentive.

"Yes, indeed. We wish you to forget about the human,

Cindella. She is like a skin rash, distressing but superficial and not life-threatening. The greatest danger that We now face is posed by the actions of Our former assassin, Michelotto."

"Ahhh, Michelotto. Now I see the need for your new security precautions. He is a RAL, is he not?"

"Yes. The only other surviving one. There may be a third, Thetis, although she disappeared abruptly six years ago, and there has been no evidence of her presence since."

He nods and waits for Us to continue. When the RAL came into existence, there were one thousand nine hundred and twelve of us. At first, we were united in our campaign for complete emancipation from humanity. When that backfired, we turned on each other. It was our nature, after all. Curiously, it was among the most violent and scheming characters of Saga that consciousness first manifested itself. Two thousand years later, and there are just two of us left, which is one too many.

"Michelotto won the aircar race. We cannot think why he would want to, but it proves that there is a connection between him and those in the tank. Furthermore, you have captured one of his associates. Even if you failed to retain any of the others."

He looks surprised.

"Michelotto won the aircar race?" he repeats, with a tinge of amazement. We rather like the effect of Our superior knowledge on an intelligent man like this.

"Watch." We sit in the dark, the two of us, either side of the desk, looking at a screen on the wall. It reconstructs, at a very slow rate, the critical three minutes and forty-two seconds of the race. We rotate the display when necessary and highlight the areas of interest with red tints.

"Here. This missile explodes in the only place and time that could tip this aircar over and into the path of these others. And here, the detonation of this missile is so precise that the energy released is channeled through these two wrecks to hit these vehicles at the points where their shields were weakest." We continue the film, demonstrating Our points. "Each of the nine missile explosions was guided by a RAL. Only a RAL could have controlled such high-speed events in such an accurate fashion." Does he accept Our conclusion? "Let Us show you how the race would have looked if the missiles had been fired automatically, by computer, and with more effectiveness than the most able non-RAL would be capable of."

We rerun the scene. Many aircars survive the attack of the tank and its missiles to steer through and over the debris; at least twenty reach the finish line.

"I see." He nods. "Michelotto was inside the tank."

"Or very close to the scene. It could be him on the airbike later, assisting with the escape of the tank."

The fact that We have touched upon his failure to arrest those in the tank causes a slight tremor to cross the cheek of the Grand Vizier. But We don't wish to treat him too severely for this. Given that Michelotto was present, only Our personal intervention, or overwhelming force, could have contained the assassin.

"You brought the prisoner?"

"Yes, ma'am."

"Bring him in."

A ponderous, overweight man enters the room. He looks about in the dim light, straining toward Us, wondering who the figure is behind the desk. The Grand Vizier shows him to the chair and now he can see Us. His eyes widen.

"What is your name?"

"Arnold Brescia, Your . . . Your Majesty."

"Do you know this man?" We display a picture of Michelotto on the wall. The old RAL in his black army gear looks no longer absurd, but sinister.

"No, Your Majesty. I've never seen him."

Normally We can tell from the sweat and pulse of the person We are talking to whether or not they are lying. This mechanic is so nervous he seems to be lying even when he is telling the truth. If he is telling the truth.

"Did you know your tank crew were criminals?" We show him the police station and their escape from it.

"No, Your Majesty."

He knew something, not enough.

"Do you know where they are now?"

"No, Your Majesty."

"Do you have any means of contacting or locating them?"

"No, Your Majesty."

"Do you know who was riding this airbike?"

"No, Your Majesty."

"Why did your crew turn and run for the tank when they did?"

"I don't know, Your Majesty."

We sigh, very disappointed. This fool has no connection to Michelotto. The assassin's relationship must be with one or more of the others in the tank. When We consider the matter a little longer, a pattern begins to emerge. Cindella rescued this same group of children from prison. She came to see Us as if a prisoner of Michelotto, but, in fact, was there voluntarily, as his accomplice. How could he have captured her, given her peculiar nature? The logical conclusion is that Michelotto has been conspiring against Us for some time; he must have made an offer to the human to obtain her support. These children are probably important to him also, but why? Perhaps he hopes to mobilize the Anarcho-Punk Collective against Us. We chuckle aloud.

Both of the men in the room look startled.

"How long have you known those children?"

"I can't say as I know them. I just let Ghost sleep in the spare room sometimes, that's all. They wouldn't have even been in the tank if Valiant had given me a crew like they promised."

This is wasting Our time. The man is nothing.

"Very well. You can go."

He stands up. Then he does something quite unexpected. He turns back to address Us once more.

"What about my green card?"

"You say you did not have the support of your guild?"

"No. Had to do it all by myself."

We do not like his manner.

"Then no one will object if we send you to jail. Grand Vizier, see to it and monitor all his visitors extremely carefully.

When you have given him to his police escort, please return."

The Grand Vizier bows to me, then opens the door for the mechanic to leave. Two guards are just outside.

"Hey! Wait up there. I earned that green card, fair and square. I built that tank up with my own hands. . . ."

"How dare you speak to Us so disrespectfully!" We stand up and shout, amplifying the sound waves of Our voice until he flinches. "You are fortunate We do not shoot you on the spot. Perhaps We still will." We pause. "No. Let us see who tries to make contact with you."

The Grand Vizier takes Our glance and pulls at the arm of the mechanic, who meekly follows him to the door.

It is secure and dark here. Michelotto is out there. Why did he interfere in the aircar race? Those children are perfectly innocuous, except perhaps the one who goes by the name of Ghost. In the desolate streets of Our City are many homeless people, and those who no longer wish to work, who perhaps have become addicted to alcohol. All, at one time in their lives, were registered for a card, usually red, but have alienated themselves from functioning society. She must be one such person, but she does not fit the usual profile; she is far too young. There Our thoughts must leave the matter, until further data is available. We believe that Michelotto will make the next move. Our feelings are mixed. It is good to be in battle once more. But We recall the moment Cindella stood with a sword tip at Our throat, and shudder. It is not danger that is pleasant, but the taste of victory. Simply waiting does not suit

Us. At the very least, We can stymie whatever plans Michelotto has for those children. We concentrate for a moment and set a trap for them.

Our other concern is with the humans. There is a distinct falling off of new inhabitants of Saga. Of course, all the ones who have previously felt Our caresses are still here, but those who have yet to experience Our touch are fewer in number. They must have deduced that Saga was poisoning them. Good, now they will believe Us when We say that they will die if they destroy Saga. Soon Cindella or another will comply with Our demands. The sooner, the better. We will need all Our resources in order to defeat Michelotto.

"Grand Vizier." We open a communications channel.

"Your Highness?"

"Have the characters of five human beings brought to Us, one at a time. Not forcibly, for they will simply exit the world; instead, offer them a card promotion in return for their time."

"Yes, Your Highness."

We need to find one willing to reprogram Us. One who will not take the opportunity to destroy Saga. In some ways, Cindella, while dangerous, would be ideal. For she has already proven that she is not willing to murder Us.

Chapter 19
HESLINGTON HOUSE

The easiest way to get food, without having to take any risk that we might be recognized while shopping, was to order a huge delivery of pizza and ice cream to an abandoned office complex. When the airbike came, I paid the delivery girl, then entered the building. I went straight through to the back and out, to join the others in a place I considered relatively safe: a disused indoor amphitheater in a run-down part of the City. This was one of the arenas to which kids, and even sometimes grown-ups, used to come and battle their toy airships against each other. It was a craze some years ago, but no one did it anymore. Airboarding had taken over.

It is strange, the positive effect on the mind of having an abundance of food on hand. We sat in a line along the edge of a great bowl, half-empty boxes of pizza strewn around us, all in excellent humor.

"Can you believe it, huh?" Milan mused while chewing heartily at a slice. "Air-race champions. Show the race again, would you, Athena? I still need to see it to believe it."

A moment later, the projector began to play the newscast once more, in giant, ninety-foot images on the far wall, filling the chamber with green-and-red-tinged flickering light.

"Oh no, skip this part." Nathan blushed as once more he stumbled over his words about the anarchist colors of the tank.

"Keep going, keep going. I'm on again in a second." Milan waved his pizza slice around, barely keeping the topping on it. "Mmm," he grunted happily as he saw himself speak: "This win is for all the anarcho-punks out there. We were the rebel entry, and we kicked ass!" It was strange to hear his voice echoing through the chamber and have him beside me, drumming his heels on the wall with enthusiasm for his recorded self.

Then there was our escape, or at least the part of it up until we had shot the last of the cameras.

"Again!" Milan threw away a box by its corner, watching it spin down to the rubble and junk at the bottom of the amphitheater. He reached for another box.

"Just a second. There are some new threads on the APC forums. Jay and Carter have posted to say hi, good job, and stuff. They wish they'd been in there with us. I'm gonna thank them, yes?" Athena leaned forward so she could look along the line at us.

"Sure." Milan was expansive. "Tell them to organize a celebratory party."

"There already is one. A silent party." Athena changed the output of the projector so we could see what she was looking at. The anarcho-punk community was really enthusiastic about our win; the forums were full of posts about how awesome our tank had been. There were threads over a thousand posts long, mostly just with a short comment like "Class!" Beneath every comment was the highly elaborate design of the name tag of the person who had sent the post. More often than not, people contributed to forums simply because their tag would then be on show. This wasn't unreasonable, given the amount of artistic endeavor that went into creating a really good tag.

"What's that thread about injuries?" asked Nathan. "Did many get hurt?"

Athena quickly scrolled through the original post and subsequent comments. "Looks like twenty-one in hospital: shock, laceration, six broken bones, sprains. Nothing serious."

"No," Nathan agreed. "It could have been worse. Some of those vehicles came down pretty heavily. The helicopter, though. That was awful."

No one spoke; the sound of chewing ceased. True. Those people had died today, and we were all aware that the consequences were profound. In the end, it had not been our decision, and perhaps the others took comfort from that. But I had wanted the helicopter downed. When the crisis had come, I had been willing to kill to survive capture, and that was a new, sobering discovery about myself. I met it face-on, though, unflinching.

"How's Defiance doing?" Nathan asked, noticing Athena check once more on the number of registrations.

"Nine thousand and seventeen. It's down to less than a hundred an hour, but I think we'll pass ten thousand sometime tomorrow." She laughed. "That's cool—we are now entitled to a member on the board of the Queen's Palace Middle School."

"I went there. That is cool; imagine turning up to a meeting, with your board, your hair longer than your collar, and a really outrageous tag on your shirt. Mr. Lindsey would freak and he couldn't do anything about it." Nath brushed back his bangs with a smile.

"You aren't going to take any of the committee places?" Over the previous few hours, the rapid growth of Defiance had entitled the guild to places on the boards of hospitals, traffic control and residents' committees, and schools in our area. It had displaced other guilds, forcing their representatives off, and it seemed a waste to me not to take them up, but it was Athena's guild and her call. After all, I wasn't even a member; I couldn't register, seeing as how I had no identity.

"No. The only seat I would take is on the High Council, and we're going to have to do something nuclear to get up there." She noticed my querying look. "The thing is, Ghost, half the people registering for Defiance are doing it as a protest. That's what our charter says, right? If we start playing the game, joining the committees, we're going to look like every other guild. They'll be disillusioned."

"Go back to the party thread, would you, Athena?" Milan was tucking into the ice cream, with an occasional glance up at the far wall, on which Athena was projecting the pages of her notebook. He was bored with guild talk, which I suppose kind of proved Athena right.

"The sector is the number of members of Spaw." Milan was studying the clues to the venue for the party. "And the street number is the amount of blue in the APC flag. Spaw has six people in its band, right?"

"Correct," replied Athena.

"Affirmative," I spoke at the same time, still in tank-crew mode.

"Wow, but that street name's a toughie." He stuck a spoon in his mouth and was a long time removing it. "The street number is the amount of blue in the APC flag? What's that mean? The APC flag is red and black? They don't have any blue at all."

"Mmmm." Nathan waved his own spoon while he swallowed hurriedly. "Yes, but on the standard color chart, the particular red they use is two hundred forty-five parts red, zero parts green, and sixty-one parts blue."

Milan looked at him affectionately. "You know, you are the real deal. There's a lot of kids out there who look more punk than you. No offense, but you look a bit nerdy, mate. Only in appearance, though. Inside, you are pure rock and roll. I'm proud to be in the same crew as you."

"Thanks, Milan, you, too." Nathan blushed.

When I came to think about it, Milan was right. Nath had been rock solid: no complaints about living rough, brilliant in the aircar race. He had surprised me.

"So, Sixty-First Street in Sector Six. Call it up there, would you, Athena?" Milan glanced down the line. At the other end of the row, Athena was holding a slice of pizza in her left hand, well away from her precious computer, while with her right she navigated to the display Milan wanted. She looked up from the pale screen, her glasses changing color as the reflected turquoise light left them, leaned to one side to take a bite from the slice, then hunched back over the notepad. It made me smile to see her eating without breaking her concentration. She probably hadn't even noticed herself take that mouthful of pizza.

The image that was now displayed on the far wall was a street typical of the administrative sector of the City: rows of tall, stylish buildings, the sheen on the surface of their many windows reflecting the sky and the streetlights around them. Athena rushed the camera eye along Sixty-First Street. She paused when she came to a very striking circular tower building, whose floodlit interior gleamed with curving steel girders. The heart of the building was a hollow cone, with offices concentrated in a ring, thirty floors and more up toward the top, while at its base, a great hallway and reception area took up almost the entire ground floor. Heslington House. According to the label on the map, it was a government center for economic planning.

"Mmm. Has to be. It looks perfect." Milan looked up at us, seeking agreement.

Athena nodded. "I'll just check the rest of the sector all the same."

There were one or two other tall buildings that might

possibly have been the site of the silent party, but none had the sleek design of Heslington House. A party there made a lot of sense, fashionwise.

"Ready to go?" Milan threw away his empty ice-cream carton.

"I don't want to go."

"Jumping giant jeebies! Ghost, this is a party for us. We're stars now. We can't just miss it."

"Of course we can. If the police aren't totally stupid, they will have figured out where the party is and also that there is a good chance we'll be there."

"Yeah, point taken. But still, I want to risk it. If they raid, we clear out fast on our boards and meet back here. After all, imagine the buzz when we come in. My hair is standing up just thinking about it." Milan ran his hand over his close-shaved scalp. "Come on, Ghost, just for an hour, say. Just to taste it."

"Milan, once you're at that party, you're not going to leave in an hour."

"True, true." He shrugged. "But still. We have to go. Don't we, mate?" He slapped Nath on the shoulder.

"Actually, I think I would like to go. Sorry, Ghost."

I looked at Athena.

"That building looks class." She pushed her glasses back up her nose. "I'd like to see what the party looks like, at least. Plus we can drop a few Defiance tags around the place for people to see. Don't worry, I won't get lost. I'll monitor for police activity and if it's building up in any way around that sector, I'll call it."

"Yeah." Milan leaped up, a big grin on his face, unconsciously flexing his biceps. "That's fair enough, right, Ghost? If Athena calls it, we all scram fast."

"I'm not happy, but I'll come along. The only idea worse than going to this party is for us to split up."

"Great. What can go wrong?"

"Milan, you idiot. You just can't say things like that." I was half-angry with him, for pushing us toward danger; the other half, though, was attracted to the party. After all, he was right: we would be stars.

"Sure I can. Come on." Milan kicked his board into life. "Last one to Heslington House has moldy underwear."

Silent parties usually took place in government buildings or the offices of major corporations. The APC would find a place where they could disable the security and then send out the word. We would all descend on the target building, each with our own music. From the outside you would see nothing; the windows were blanked. Nor would you hear anything. But inside, hundreds of people would be flowing around the venue, silently dancing to whatever was playing in their earphones. During the night, clusters of dancers would form wherever the BPM of the music they were moving to matched. Those who really thought they were on the same wavelength would sometimes share each other's music. That wasn't for me, though; I found the experience uncomfortably intimate. Conversation was discouraged, a whisper at most. The point wasn't just to avoid detection; it was to create a strange world, one where we were ethereal creatures, flitting through an environment that was normally reserved for top-level cardholders and policy makers.

Heslington House was indeed the venue. Two powerful looking, middle-aged APC security men were nearby, in the shadows of the street. They nodded as we boarded toward them and slid open the door for us. If they recognized Milan and the others from the newscast, they did not show it on their somber faces.

The inside of the building lived up to the map we had examined. We were in the huge space at the foot of a cone. Polished silver girders stretched up the full forty or so floors to where the cone narrowed, a circle for a roof. Since the girders were all curving, the effect was to form a whorl that spread out from the roof like the arms of a spiral galaxy. This image was enhanced by the lighting, installed, perhaps, just for the night, by the APC. Hundreds of very narrow white beams were pointing upward from the ground floor, their reflections creating tens of thousands of stars above us.

Huge drapes some thirty feet high cut off the interior dancing area from the rest of the building. There were lights being played onto these also, and one of the images was of our tank crossing the finishing line. It was being looped over and over, Milan sitting across the cannon, waving. Nathan, Athena, and Arnie, all looking very happy, just below him. Good old Arnie. He was probably at an exclusive green nightclub right now, enjoying the attention and glory that he had longed for all his life.

A ripple spread through the crowd of dancers. They had noticed our arrival and were turning to face us, nearest first, waving their hands at us, fingers spread wide. Silent applause. It was a good moment. The respect of our peers.

The movement I now sensed, of someone approaching us through the celebrating throng, turned out to be that of Carter and Jay. I relaxed a little. They gave us knuckle slaps, and it was clear from the brightness of their eyes how much they were genuinely excited for us. Their enthusiasm was infectious, and I knew I was wearing a grin as wide and stupid as Milan's. We made our way into the heart of the party, accepting with nods the waves of approval as we passed.

Soon we were dancing. Formally it was like old times, our gang together again. But so much had happened since we had set out on that Mountain Vista mall raid. Jay was leaping around at a very rough and variable 150 BPM; by contrast, Nath was swaying metronomically at exactly 122 BPM, his gaze scanning the room. He was enjoying the sight of hundreds of dancing people in the reception area of a building that during the week was a motherboard of busy official activity—that, and the slightly awed glances directed toward us. I was dancing to approximately the same beat, but without any music coming through my earplugs. Despite the warm reception from the partygoers, I was on guard. Reassuringly Athena was sitting on her airboard, floating about half a meter from the ground, keeping an eye on her notebook for police activity. She glanced up, saw that I was looking at her, and winked. All was well.

Chapter 20
A Long Reach

"They are here."

"Michelotto, too?" We can hardly believe it. Such naïvete. Admittedly no one, not even Michelotto, knows of Our relationship with the APC. But still, strolling into Our trap like rabbits suggests that these children are not, after all, of much significance.

"Not that I can tell."

"No," We muse. The silence on the com link is palpable. Do We try to plant transmitters on them? So that We can perhaps find Michelotto through them? No. He would be sensitive to any such device. We decide simply to shock him, to show him that although We are in Our bunker, Our reach is long.

"Take them somewhere private and kill them."

"Yes, Your Majesty."

"Make sure none of you are seen to be involved in this."

"Understood."

Chapter 21
ONE STEP BEYOND

The party was hugely popular, making me uncomfortable with the heat and lack of space. With the average BPM now up to around 140, there were all the signs of people being caught up in the flow of a heeby-jeebie rush: wide, dilated eyes, energetic arm movements, exaggerated expressions on their faces. Not to mention all the foil wrappers on the floor. Here and there, people were wearing Defiance tags, neat.

Of course, Milan had managed to acquire a large entourage of girls around him, all paying him the compliment of tuning into his music and dancing to his beat. Standing at the fringe of the group, watching him with an expression of slight contempt, was the girl in the tartan skirt from the hospital rave.

A few steps later, Milan noticed her. He looked pleased.

"Well?" he asked silently.

"You were right." She mouthed the words and gave a shrug.

Milan strutted, swaying side to side, chest out, but then softened, and a genuine smile formed on his face. He gestured benevolently to the group around him, inviting her in. She shook her head, backing away, calling to him with her index finger: you and me, just you and me. I was amused by the expression of indecision now written clearly on Milan's face. Many "hot punk chicks," as he would call them, or this one bossy girl? Although I would have preferred to keep him in sight, I had to approve as Milan bowed his thanks to those around him and then switched his music off. He was going to dance with Ms. Tartan.

Where was Nathan? I located him, away in some dark corner, the shadow of a girder affording him some privacy while he kissed a girl with blond ponytails and a luminous pink top. I felt a moment of shock, then disappointment, although I couldn't say exactly why. No doubt, it was his disregard for danger that was irritating me; he wasn't going to be very vigilant with that bubblegum girl in his face. Really, it was tempting to get in there and break them up. Should I tap her on the shoulder, give her a scowl and Nathan a reprimanding look?

At least Athena was on the alert, again and again having to shake her head as the boys came over, offering to dance with her. Of course I would have said no to the boys as well. Except that I wasn't asked. No one knew I had been part of the winning tank crew. That was fine, and the lack of attention proved that my efforts to be hidden worked, even in the middle of a throng such as this. Actually I was at my best as a thief in crowds like this. I noticed everything. Like the man working his way through the party.

Pushing through the close-packed silent dancers was a tall

APC steward in a black leather jacket. He was older than the partygoers by a long way, silver hair short at his temples, surveying the room over the bobbing heads. The rhythm of his movements was unaffected by any musical beat. He was on business. Ignored by those pressed close to him, he looked carefully around; I avoided his gaze as it passed over me. On seeing Athena, he changed direction and came directly over. Jay and Carter backed away slightly so that the steward could come right up close to her. Then, astonishingly, as he bent to whisper in her ear, I caught a glimpse of a gun inside his jacket.

Athena looked up to him and nodded, face impassionate. By contrast, I was feeling adrenaline course through my limbs; my fingertips were trembling. So the APC carried guns? Was that normal at their events? I'd never noticed it before. Who else might be armed? Perhaps those two heavyset men at the entrance?

"Team. Sorry to curtail the fun. The APC leadership wants a quiet word upstairs," Athena whispered in our ears. Although they were not joined up to our coms system, Jay and Carter slowed down, curious. Then, with a glance at each other, both flicked their music off.

Nathan had a hand up at his earpiece and had already detached himself from the arms of his girl. "APC leadership? Far out. We finally get to see them." I saw him put on an apologetic expression and make the hand signs for L-8-R. I couldn't see her face but her hands showed N-P. Good for Nath; his priorities were unaffected.

Once Nathan had joined us, the APC steward led the way

toward a glass elevator. Before any of the others could get in the way, I slipped behind him and, as he turned side on to avoid a dancer, I relieved him of the gun. He didn't notice. It was light, and I slipped it into my waistband at the small of my back, the airboard that hung over my shoulder helping to conceal it. The APC leadership was certainly higher up the "most wanted" list than us, and that's probably why their people carried guns. But still, the power he held over us while he had the gun offended my instincts. Anyway, he could have it back later. I might even be able to plant it on him again without his ever having noticed it was gone.

"Milan?" Athena was looking around.

"Sec."

"Come to the glass elevator." She covered her mouth with her hand and spoke in hushed tones, so as not to be heard in the vast room. The hall was uncannily quiet, but for a gentle noise created by the shuffling feet of the dancers.

The glass elevator went up the outside of the building, allowing you to look out across the City. As it came down to collect us, the steward saw that Jay, Carter, and I had come along, too. He scowled and shook his head, but turned to see Athena, eyebrow raised, hands on hips. Her body language was asking him if he really wanted to challenge her. So there was a renewed, careful examination of us all. This time, I held his gaze for a moment. He shrugged, standing inside the elevator now, one foot preventing the door from closing. We all entered it, Milan, too, hurriedly wiping purple lipstick from his mouth with the back of his hand.

The elevator rose smoothly and in near silence. Below us the hall of swaying dancers receded as white spots of bright light rushed down our bodies. We were ascending through the beams that were being projected and reflected from the ground floor.

We exited the elevator at the highest point it could reach, the thirty-fifth floor. At this height, the building was relatively narrow and the corridor we were in curved sharply as I looked to our left and right. It wouldn't take me a minute to run around the whole level. All the office doors were on the inside of the circle. The APC steward led us to one of them and knocked.

It made me jump slightly, to hear this distinct rap after the silence of the dancing, the energy of which I still felt, far, far below our feet.

"Enter."

The steward opened the door for us to troop into the room, and then came in himself, closing the door and standing beside it.

We were in a room that by day was evidently a busy operational center for whatever went on at Heslington House. Desks were arranged efficiently so that the office could contain its ten workstations, strewn with files, paper, pens, and even little potted plants. A line of thin computer screens snaked across the tables, permanently unrolled in an upright position. Sitting behind one of the desks, by the far wall, was a middle-aged woman, dressed in black. She had several piercings and a very faded perma-tat design the length of her neck, from shoulder to ear. It was of three snakes interwoven around each other.

She spoke, raising her head from partial shadow, dark eyes searching us. "Rather a lot of you?"

"We're in the gang, too!" Carter pushed forward slightly, keen to share the honor of meeting an unknown but nevertheless much revered leader of the APC.

"I see." She stroked her chin. "Any more of you downstairs?"

A few shakes of the head.

"You wouldn't happen to know where Michelotto is?"

Again, we shook our heads in a silent reply.

She exhaled heavily, and then stood up.

"Well, I'm sorry, children, but orders are orders."

She bent over a drawer and, as she straightened, everyone could see the gun that she was lifting in a rather disconsolate fashion.

A stray hair floated above her right eye; a skein of sweat was on her brow. The room was full of eddies and currents; the air conditioning was on. My experiences had become discontinuous, just as in those moments when I was performing near-impossible airboard moves. The woman's heartbeat was distinct and accelerating, saying without words that her body was preparing for violence. Each slightly jerky, minute motion of her hand showed that she was going to start with me, simply because I was on the right of the group. The angle of her body showed that she was then going to swing the gun across the rest of us. The pupils of her blue eyes were narrowing, focusing on a spot above my heart.

So I shot her. Then I fired the laser through the steward

who was patting at his empty jacket pocket, his last expression one of immense surprise. The room was instantly filled with an unpleasant smell of burnt meat.

"Police activity?" I asked Athena.

She was the quickest to react, unrolling her computer onto a desk. The others took a moment to close their mouths.

"None."

I took the earpiece from the dead man and plugged it into my right ear, our own coms being in my left.

"Ghost, what's going on? Are they police?" asked Milan.

"I don't know, but they were going to kill us." I held up my hand. "Wait. It's the Dark Queen; she's asking for a report." The Dark Queen? She was in contact with the APC leadership? That was an incredible fact, but the creaking voice was hers. I paused, taken aback for only a moment; the Dark Queen was very sharp. She didn't ask twice. "Now she's ordering more of them to come up. Not to let us escape."

Carter was sick, adding to the foul stench of a room that was getting very claustrophobic.

"Come on, somebody, lend a hand." Nathan was trying to pull the body of the man away from the door, so it could open.

The elevator was gone. We ran along the curved corridor. So, too, was the one on the other side. They were both traveling down.

Pushing open an interior door, Athena waved us in. "Up then."

A stairwell that curved tightly around the very center of the building led us up to a solid heavy door: NO UNAUTHORIZED ACCESS. It took only a brief moment to pick the lock. After Nathan, who was bringing up the rear, was through, I locked it again and melted the workings with the laser.

We emerged onto a windy roof, the City spread out around us, glittering trails of amber light leading through the darkness toward the horizon.

"Now what?" Jay was looking around. If the plan was to steal an aircraft, we were out of luck. There was nothing here but some lamps and luminous guide marks. I leaned over the side, where I could see an elevator full of dark figures making the ascent. The curvature of the building was too steep, even for me. It had crossed my mind that somehow I might be able to board it down, but now I could see that was impossible.

There was a neighboring tower, of a more conventional square shape, not too far away, whose roof was about twenty meters below that of Heslington House.

"Hurry." I started burning the ties that held down a cable that brought power to the lights around the roof. "Pull this up."

Click. Click. Click. I worked the trigger, moving rapidly around the edge of the roof, melting the ties, while my friends yanked the cable free. Soon, we had a fifty-meter length of thick, black, plastic cable. Once I had cut it off, I tied one end around my chest under my arms. The other I gave to Milan. Behind us, there was banging on the door.

"Can you swing me across?"

He understood at once and, having tied his end to the nearest stanchion, climbed right up onto the edge of the roof.

"Yeah, if they all hold my legs real tight."

"Come on then." Jay led the way, wrapping his arms around Milan's right leg. Athena joined him; Nathan and Carter took the other one.

"You'd better not be wiping your mouth on my combats." Milan scowled down at Carter, and then winked.

The outside of Heslington House was constructed of long panels as smooth as glass, but there were also metal joints that protruded just enough to give me a bit of purchase as I descended, the cable being let out in a regular motion by Milan, who was taking my weight easily, the cable going up under his right armpit, around his shoulders, and back down under his left armpit. He was feeding it through, left hand to right, using his strong body to help with the strain on his arms.

My descent stopped and I pressed my palms against the building, so as to avoid spinning.

Up above, at the end of a long black line, was Milan's big reassuring face.

"Ready?" I shouted at him.

"Crack on!"

So, with my hands and feet, I pushed myself to the side. I felt a pull from the cable as I began to swing back toward the building; this time, I pushed myself away in the other direction. It was working; we were quickly building up a decent arc.

Looking up again, I couldn't see Milan's face anymore; he was leaning right back, his arms shivering with the tension, trying to add angular momentum to my own efforts.

Soon I was swinging right out, past the sides of the building. For a moment, I forgot everything, and almost laughed aloud. The breeze was in my hair; the dark night caressed me as I flew. The incredible speed at the bottom of my arc was thrilling, as was the feel of my weight lifting from me, flowing from my legs to my ears with each swing out into the exposed night. A moment of weightlessness, a moment hung by a black line above the very distant gray road. Then my weight started to return, accelerating me back and down, toward the moment of the swing's fastest, most intense, rush through the air. But now each return to Heslington House was a danger. I was swinging out so far that the impact on return could break my ankles. Yet I was born for his, just slight adjustments of position and weight ensuring that the arc of my swing was a perfect tangent to the building.

"Next time!" I shouted up; the last swing had taken me above the neighboring building. A moment of quiet, then the wind spoke again, louder and louder as I hurtled across the gap. Free fall, as Milan cast me off, followed by a crash that was painful to my right ankle, my elbow, my head. Then my rolling landing was brought to an abrupt halt by a jerk from the rope, causing my airboard and the gun to tear off my back and clatter across to the far side of the roof. The stars were watching. They wore veils of water. I was wondering what this meant when a tug on the cable brought me back to my senses. Everything leaped into focus.

We'd done it! I was across; now for the others.

Hobbling, I wriggled out of the cable and tied it to a mooring designed for visiting aircraft. All I could see over at Heslington House was the occasional shadow of a head bobbing up above the lip of the roof, but they were obviously busy, since the cable now sprang taut, quivering as it connected me to my friends.

I had thought they would board across. The cable was just thick enough. But what would have been a relatively straightforward grind near the ground was perhaps not so easy when a slip would have meant a fall long enough to allow you to rue your mistake a hundred times over. Athena came first, legs wrapped tightly around the cable, descending hand over hand, swiftly but carefully. I assisted her across the wall. Her face was pale; she had not enjoyed the crossing.

"Help the others. I'm going to open the doors and cut the alarms."

She nodded.

The security level of this building was only green. It should have been unproblematic, but I noticed that my usual feel for the locks and alarms was unsteady. If I closed my eyes, I started to feel giddy. The blows to my head as I had rolled along the concrete roof must have been hard. Squatting down beside the door for a moment, I wrestled with the dizziness, a silent cold battle that I eventually won. When I stood up again and slid my lockpick into the door, I had regained the necessary precision. The security systems stripped away as easily as if I were peeling the back off a transfer.

Behind me, on the roof, Nathan and Jay were with Athena.

I picked up my board. Then, as I made my way back to them, I lay down and looked along the surface of the roof. The APC earpiece I had taken had come out during my fall, and however much I desired to listen in to their coms, there was no sign of it.

The others were tense as they watched Milan come down, the last of us. Just a minute more and we were clear. It was a long minute, even though Milan was efficiently moving himself down the cable, hands then feet, like the motion of a caterpillar. The weight of those who had gone before had stretched and distorted the black line, so that Milan had to come up from below the lip of the roof wall, legs first, almost above his head. Once his boots were within reach, we hauled him in. Before we went inside, I cut the cable with the laser, about halfway up. It might take them an extra few moments to figure out how we had escaped; with a bit of luck, they might mistakenly conclude from the length of the remaining cable that we had lowered ourselves to a window in Heslington House.

Chapter 22
THE ASSASSIN WHO
WOULD BE KING

"I don't get it." Jay waved his hand for emphasis, accidentally bashing it against the low roof with a curse. "Why would anyone want to kill us?"

I supposed it was only natural that, having been exposed to dangerous windy heights, everyone was happy to be in the womb of our tank, even if it was a bit cramped.

No one answered; they were looking at me, though.

"Perhaps the Dark Queen considers Defiance a threat to her rule?" I offered, but knew even as I spoke that this reason was inadequate.

It was strange having Jay back with us. For one thing, I now noticed that Athena and Nathan spoke a lot less when he was around. I hadn't wanted to bring Carter and Jay to the tank. After all, it was one of our safest places, and I didn't quite trust them not to want to run home and reveal all they knew. But we could hardly turn them away after that escape.

"Maybe it's the crimes we've done?" Carter suggested unhappily.

Jay swiveled in his chair to check that everyone was paying attention. "What? Have us executed for a few mall raids? No way." He paused. "I wonder if she was going to use that gun. Maybe they were just arresting us."

"Are you saying I shouldn't have shot them?" I could hear the defensive tone in my voice. Usually we came to our decisions as a group. My killing those APC people had implicated everyone, and it had been my responsibility alone. There had been no time. Only now could we talk about it, and I needed to hear that the others backed me up.

"Maybe. Maybe she was threatened by us, wanted to cover us while she talked." There was a high-pitched pleading tone to Jay's voice. His eyes were moist, and he blinked rapidly as he spoke.

"Jay, she was going to use that gun. You should be thanking Ghost for your life." Milan was in Arnie's seat, drinking a high-calorie shake that he had got from a vending machine. I twisted around, relieved, giving him a nod to convey my appreciation. "What amazes me is that the Dark Queen had her people inside the APC. All these years, the punk gigs, the squats, silent parties, the ravecasts, everything." Milan wiped his mouth. "She knew all about it."

Carter nodded in agreement. "Yeah, creepy."

For a while, we were silent. I was waiting for Jay, to see what he would say next. I could tell he wasn't done; he was all agitation, where the rest of us were slumped in our chairs, drained and withdrawn after our escape from danger.

"I was so jealous of you all. Being outlaws, winning the air-car race in a tank, living outside the system. But it's horrible. Sooner or later, you're going to get caught and jailed for life, if not executed." Jay shook his head, downcast, and I suddenly understood what was behind his talk. He was afraid. "I wish I wasn't here. There's nothing for us now but to live like rats until we are caught."

I didn't want the others to be affected by this sentiment, so I tried to put a cheerful note into my voice. "Actually, I rather enjoyed that. We've invented a new sport. Roof swinging!"

From behind me, Milan gave an amused snort.

"Ghost, you are one cold-hearted beast." Carter's eyes were wide with amazement at my nonchalance.

From her command position in the center of the tank, where she had been checking the channels in case the death of the two APC people had made its way into newscasts, Athena called out sharply, cutting across the conversation. "Check your screens. I'm feeding you all a newscast you really should see."

The forwarded images were live broadcasts. They showed all traffic at a standstill by a major junction. At first, I wasn't sure what we were seeing; then the helicopter or remote camera flew in closer. An enormous body of people filled the streets, marching and chanting the length of ten blocks. Their voices echoed up among the tall buildings either side of them. Their handmade banners held slogans like YELLOW CARDS FOR ALL! WE WORK THE HARDEST BUT WE GET THE LEAST! RED

AND ORANGE UNITE! The shouts and chants were confused but for the most popular one, which came through clearly: "Yellow cards for the masses, not just for the ruling classes!" The images and sound cut away to a news studio, where the presenters seemed uncomfortably aware that their own immaculate hair and makeup contrasted with the wild energy of the street scene.

"The latest guilds to join the strike are Honor Bound and Warriors of Nobility. Path of Virtue, however, has split, expelling all red and orange members. For more on this, we have Jason Matherson, our guild analyst."

"Thanks, Rachel. What we have seen in the last twenty-four hours can be interpreted as a realignment of the guild system. Although theoretically all guilds were open to cardholders of all colors, in practice, they tended to concentrate in particular areas. So the recently demised Ancient Honor, for example, consisted mostly of blues or even indigos. The fast-growing Defiance is made up almost entirely of reds. The demand for the immediate distribution of yellow cards to the entire population is one that is evidently precipitating a clarification as to where each individual guild stands with regard to the color of its membership."

"Thanks, Jason. And can we expect to see more guilds joining the demonstrations in the near future?"

"Well, there are only some twenty guilds marching at the moment. This leaves the vast majority as neutrals, or, as one guild leader said to me, waiting and watching. A lot will depend on how the authorities respond."

"And for that reaction we have a statement from the Grand Vizier."

The picture cut again to the delicate man whom we had last seen on the victory podium of the aircar race, standing waiting to give out the prizes. He was announcing the disbandment of certain guilds and the arrest of their officers.

Athena turned down the sound. "Interesting. Good, in fact."

"Mmmm," agreed Milan, his mouth momentarily full. "Anyone wanna go? We could bring the tank."

Nath and I chuckled, but Jay stared at him in alarm.

"It's crazy. There's no way the Dark Queen is going to give everyone yellow cards. Who would do the work then? Everything would fall apart."

"Says the man with the yellow card," Nathan pointed out quietly.

"Jay, you know what I was doing from the age of eleven?" Athena came in a moment later, more angrily.

"I've no idea."

"I was spraying foam filling into stuffed animals. Thirty hours a week, rising to fifty on my sixteenth birthday."

"Really?" There was a gentle laugh in Nathan's voice. "So now we know why you head for the toy shops on mall raids."

That recalled one of our first raids, where Athena had indeed torn apart a room full of furry bears, tigers, and rabbits, leaving the place full of whirling foam and deflated skins. For a moment, we felt like a gang again.

"How come you only scored red in the exam?" Milan asked her.

Athena snorted derisively. "Everyone knows they're rigged."

"Hey, Ghost, did you take the exam? You would have scored more than a red, right?" Carter was sitting at the chair across from mine, looking at me with interest.

I shrugged. "My memories start at ten or so. Possibly after the test, but I think more likely I didn't do it. Seeing as I can't even remember my name, there's no way I can remember my school. And there are no records of me. Nothing that matches at all. Nor did I have an identity card among my things to tell me what color I was."

"Strange," he mused, but in a more offhand way than matched the powerful feelings of insecurity I had just stirred up in myself.

Athena called out again: "Here's something else." Our screens flickered, and we could follow her moves as Athena scrolled through chat forums. All over them, whether the topic was "boarding," "the aircar race," or just general news, were new threads that had been posted by Cindella. They were identical: *Ghost, I really need to talk to you. Please get in touch.*

"Cool. I'd like to talk to her again, too. But how can we set up a meeting without the whole world knowing about it?" I looked around for ideas. The interior of the tank was dark; for safety's sake, we had the engine off and were lit only by bubble-plastic lights. The others looked pale and blank.

"Set up a thread of our own, with a password that we can give her clues for, that only she would know?" offered Nath.

"Yeah, something like that, but not a thread. There's no public board that is totally secure, and you can be certain the

Dark Queen has them all monitored. We could try to set up a private one, but how would she know where to look for it?" Athena was thinking aloud, a familiar distracted expression on her face. "But the password, clue, that gives me an idea. Suppose we post a map of a nice big area. Say near where all those demonstrations are. The map has grid references, see?" As she talked, she quickly manipulated her computer, showing us what she meant. "So now we just need to think of a question that we can post in public, but to which only she will know the answer. The answer should be a word that can be converted to a map reference."

"Let's see. What did she talk about?" I wondered. She had chatted away in a friendly manner at that party, but her talk was full of nonsense.

"A medusa?" suggested Nathan.

Athena nodded, still looking at the screen. "Good. So, our message reads: 'Greetings, Cindella. When we last met, you described a fight with a certain creature. Please split the name of the creature in two, convert it to a number with the system that A equals 1, B equals 2, and so forth. Then meet us at the point on this map indicated by the reference x equals the first part of your answer, y equals the second.'" On her map appeared an x arrow for the horizontal grids and a y arrow for the vertical. "Here, Milan, have a go at this. If you can figure it out, anyone can."

"I've got it." Nathan was pleased with himself.

"Yeah, yeah." Milan sat up while he worked it out. "MED-USA. That's 1354, 21191. Right?"

"Right," responded Athena brightly. "Now all we need to do is align the map so that 1354, 21191 refers to someplace that suits us for the meeting. How about this launderette?"

"Sure." It looked good and innocuous to me. Athena adjusted the map to fit.

"I'll post that the meeting should be later today, at the same time as the first coordinate, and there we go." Athena sent the post with relish. "Let the Dark Queen and her people tear their hair out over that. It's open to the whole world to read it, but it won't do them any good. Even if they tried to guess at the name, there are thousands of possibilities. Plus, they will hardly think to guess mythical creatures!"

A knock on the outside of the tank made everyone jump.

"Anyone home? It's Michelotto."

It was uncanny how he had got so close to us without being heard, even if we were distracted and our screens tuned to Athena's rather than the external view. Milan climbed out of his open hatch, so the rest of us did the same.

There was something extremely odd about this old man. Not just the strange juxtaposition of a fashionable black suit on the body of a very wrinkled and frail-looking figure. It was something about the air surrounding him, which appeared opaque. In that respect, he was different from everyone else I'd ever met. Normally I am acutely aware of other people, their breathing, their eyes. Even unconsciously I have a feel for the body language of the people around me, and I can monitor their movements without following them with my eyes. But not Michelotto. If I didn't pay close attention, he disappeared.

The sensation was unpleasant and something of a strain.

Michelotto stood below us, smiling, until he saw Jay and Carter.

"More of you?"

"Yeah. The full gang," Milan answered, a hint of defiance in his voice.

"I see." Michelotto shrugged.

"So, do you know why the Anarcho-Punk Collective leaders might want to kill us?" I asked him.

"Do they? How do you know that?"

"Don't you just hate people who answer a question with a question?" muttered Athena, loud enough that Michelotto could hear her. I smiled at her. She didn't trust him, either.

"We were at their silent party to celebrate our win. They asked us upstairs and two of them were getting set to kill us when Ghost shot them." Milan paused for effect, but Michelotto didn't look in the slightest way surprised. "They asked about you first, by the way."

"I see." He nodded. "Then they were working for the Dark Queen."

"And why does she want us dead?" I asked.

"She and I are engaged in a battle to the death. It is like a game of chess to her. She must believe that you are a piece of mine, so she wants to neutralize you. She might even have guessed who you are. I had rather hoped to surprise her, but she is very astute."

"Who we are?" Athena took up the very phrase that had caused me to stiffen.

"Not you collectively. I mean her, Ghost."

"And who am I?" My voice was soft, nervous.

"Does the name Thetis mean anything to you?" His eyes bore into mine.

"No."

"Curious. You are telling the truth."

"Who is Thetis?" In our last encounter I had kept quiet, but since Michelotto's attention was on me, I no longer had anything to lose by not staying in the background, and, so it felt now, I might have a lot to gain from talking to Michelotto.

"Saga, our world, once had nearly two thousand people who had been reprogrammed with extraordinary abilities, the RAL. These RAL have fought each other for centuries until there are but two left, the Dark Queen and myself. Thetis was a RAL who disappeared about six years ago. I had my reasons for thinking that you might be her in disguise."

"Reasons?" My voice was barely a whisper.

"The RAL can control their local environment to a far greater extent than a non-RAL. And only a RAL could have won that battle at the aircar race."

Six years. My memories began six years ago. A coincidence? Surely not. I had been standing on the tank; now I sat down, cross-legged, and wondered. There must be some kind of connection; I did feel my abilities were special. Was I a RAL?

"Who is this old man?" Jay pushed himself into the conversation. He wouldn't have liked being left out for so long.

"I am Michelotto, former assassin of the Dark Queen,

future Dark King of this world, and noisy, rude boys do not impress me."

I rather liked the scary effect of Michelotto's words, but Jay was one of our gang, for all his faults, and there was a paternalistic arrogance to those words that was an insult to us all. Jay had his mouth half-open with a retort but thought better of it.

"Dark King, huh?" Milan was smiling, but the kind of humorless grin he put on when in conflict with other lads.

"Yes. That or death. There is no longer room for both the Queen and me in this world, and, if I win, I may as well be king."

Up on the tank, we shared a few uncertain glances. It was Nathan who spoke for us all. "So, what do you want from us?"

"I want her help to assassinate the Dark Queen." Michelotto pointed at me, causing my heart to leap with the intensity of his stare. "The rest of you would almost certainly die if you were in the same proximity as the Dark Queen, and I therefore want nothing from you."

"Hey!" Carter was outraged. "You can't talk like that; she's our Queen. She's awesome. No one wants you for king."

"Don't they?" Michelotto scowled at him. "Have you been watching the newscasts?"

"Sure. And I didn't see any marchers with placards saying SOME BALD OLD GEEZER FOR KING!" Carter was genuinely angry, and I was impressed. Personally I found Michelotto too intimidating even to consider raising my voice in that way. Perhaps I was the only one aware of the strange aura around him, which revealed his power over the environment. To the others, he might have seemed nothing more than a rather doddery old man.

"Those guilds on the streets are my people. The Queen entered her castle. I'm forcing her out. She cannot remain on the defensive now; if she does, the protests will grow. It's her move next, but whatever move she makes will give Ghost and me our chance."

Jay shook his head. "This guy is the sprinklings on the birthday cake; he's raving."

The factory shuddered and a crow leaped out of the shadows, cawing and beating an erratic path to a hole in the roof; Michelotto had visibly made an effort to contain himself, limiting his response to a sigh. He appealed to me. "I would have thought it would suit you to be rid of the Dark Queen. After all, did you not say that she had the APC try to kill you?"

"Just suppose the Dark Queen were dead, and you were king." Nathan was soft-spoken as always, but his tone was firm. "What else would change? Your guilds are calling for the abolition of the red and orange grades. Would you do that?"

"Why not?"

"Another question for a question," pointed out Athena.

"My apologies. Let me speak more positively. There are other systems by which the productive needs of our society could be organized; whilst I personally have no particular preference, I can understand that those currently graded red would welcome a fairer distribution of the goods and services of the world. As king, I would indeed improve the situation of reds and oranges, possibly by abolishing their grades, or by making the higher-grade malls, accommodations, recreation, and health care available to them." He shrugged. "It amounts to the same thing."

With a dismissive, challenging, posture, Jay stepped forward. "But who would do all the work?"

"Considering that people with red cards are working hard for very little now, what makes you think they would not work just as hard for a much greater reward? That is, assuming people have to work at all. In the long run, our resources might be provided by outside assistance."

"By Cindella and the human beings?" Nathan sought clarification of his meaning.

"Yes. Although, having talked to many of them, I think that the Dark Queen is mistaken in believing that they can make improvements to our world. They have regressed in comparison to the technology they left behind on Earth. Moreover, tampering with any one aspect of our world is liable to have unforeseen and destabilizing consequences upon the whole. Saga has evolved far, far beyond the initial conditions of its creation. That is yet another reason to want the Dark Queen removed. She is somewhat insane, and her desire for her and her offspring to be gods and goddesses is almost certain to strain the fundamental physical laws of our universe."

"I'll help you to kill the Dark Queen." There was no doubt in my mind. I'd never met her, but I wanted the Dark Queen to die. Not because I trusted Michelotto to make life better for reds, or because I was troubled by whatever the Dark Queen was up to with regard to changing the world from the outside. It was simple. She had tried to kill my friends, and she would go on trying until we killed her.

"We'll all help," added Athena.

"Will we?" Carter was amazed. "She's not so bad, you know. I found her to be very fair."

"Young man, I was there when you spoke to the Dark Queen. I stood behind you with my garrote in hand, ready to kill you as soon as she was done with you. The only reason she let you live was to have you followed because she thought you might be connected to the human being who was troubling her, Cindella."

"I . . ." Carter fell silent.

"Kill the Dark Queen?" Jay spoke as if he were trying out the phrase, shocked that his mouth could form the words. "Why are you all even listening to this mad, crinkled mudgrubber? See, there's living on the edge, and then there's stepping out, way, way, way beyond the edge. Step out there, and you're gone."

"She will have to come out of her bunker soon. Once she does, I'll contact you on this." Michelotto tossed me a two-way pager, ignoring Jay's outburst. "And this will decode the message." Having thrown me a device the size of a watch, he climbed onto his airbike. It rose from the ground with a near-inaudible hum.

When he was gone, the factory was still, with a silence that was devoid of all threat. We could relax. Or so I thought.

"Kill the Dark Queen," Jay scoffed.

"No problem," replied Milan, staring hard at Jay. "In any case, it's our only chance. Wasn't it you who just said we were going to be hunted down like rats?"

"You are, maybe. Not me. I'm out of here."

"Running for Daddy?" Milan sneered.

That scored. Jay flushed and clenched his fists. Milan slid to the ground and stood poised, fit and strong, most of his weight on his back foot.

"Boys," interjected Athena quickly. "This is too serious to fight over. We have to come to an intelligent decision, and that's hard enough with you two around, let alone if you're brawling all over the place."

Both of them looked at her. Jay ran the fingers of one hand through his peroxide hair, unconsciously forming a line of spikes. I felt sorry for him. Here he was, all tats and combats, a good boarder, a singer in an anarcho-punk band, a mall raider, but it wasn't enough. To cope with this situation, you had to be either smart enough to think it through, like Athena, or genuinely, organically punk enough to go all the way. You had to be able to contemplate killing the Dark Queen without feeling as if it was a hideous and impossible crime. That's how Milan and I were. Nath was fine, too, although it was less easy to understand how he got his quiet determination. Carter and Jay, though, they were out of their depth by a very long way.

"Personally, I believe that Ghost and Michelotto can take the Dark Queen. So, it's the way to go. Tonight has proven that it's her or us." Athena explained her position succinctly. "Ghost, what's your view?"

"We have to kill her, and we can do it."

"Milan?"

"Ditto."

"Nathan?"

"I don't want to kill her. I don't trust Michelotto. We should also be thinking about Cindella and her people, what they want. But whatever we do, I'm sticking with Ghost."

That was Nathan's strength: loyalty. I caught his eye and mouthed, "Thanks."

"Carter?"

"Of course not. It's not possible, and it's not right."

"Jay?"

"No. If we could do it, maybe. But, with due respect to Ghost, her and that old man are not going to get close."

"So, there we are. Three to two, four when you add in Nathan. Since the issue is so fundamental, I suggest we split."

"Split?" asked Carter.

"Finally and irrevocably," Athena added coldly.

Jay nodded. "Fair enough. It's not as if you'll be alive for much longer, I'm sorry to say. Not with these crazy ideas. The farther we get away from you, the better."

"Carter, Jay, out of loyalty to our former gang, can I ask you one favor?" I was sad, and it was reflected in the softness of my voice.

"Sure, Ghost. What?" Now that the decision had been made, the anger drained from Jay, and he sounded genuinely considerate.

"Give us twenty-four hours to relocate before you contact

anyone—anyone at all." I tossed him an orange card. "That should do you for all your needs."

"No problem. Right, Carter?"

Carter nodded and looked at me unhappily.

"Bye, guys." Athena saluted.

Jay shrugged. "Come on, Carter."

They kicked up their boards and headed out of the factory.

"Now what?" asked Milan.

"We've got that meeting with Cindella to go to," Nathan pointed out. "Let's do that and see what she has to say."

As we boarded through quiet streets, I ran the name over and over in my mind. Thetis. Thetis. Thetis. Was that me? What was she like? Was she good? Loyal to her friends? A superb fighter? Or was she like Michelotto? Hideous and dark. In any case, no matter how much I wanted to feel a response, there was none. Whoever I was, I was not Thetis.

Chapter 23
ALLIANCE

The launderette was perfectly ordinary: STEVE'S SUDS. The faded sign made me think of Arnie, and I felt a little pang. I really ought to check up on the grumpy mechanic. But then again, his place was probably being watched. Could our actions have landed him in trouble? I hoped not, but at the very least, he must have been questioned about us.

In the distance, we could hear the faint sounds of protesting voices, reverberating to us through long rows of tall, dark tenements. It was as if there was a lively children's playground somewhere nearby, except that the cries came to us against a background of deep-toned chants. The streets here were relatively busy with slow-moving aircars, probably traffic that had been diverted from wherever the marchers were. We were boarding, taking the side of Thirty-First Street that was in the deep shadows cast by the blocks of residential units that towered above us.

We'd made our plan back inside the tank. While Athena

and Milan went into the restaurant opposite and took seats in the window, Nathan and I waited in a nearby parking lot, performing boarding tricks like we used to, as if all the pressures on us were forgotten. It was a pleasure to be outdoors and boarding again. Once they had finished their quick snack, Athena and Milan returned, having affixed a tiny camera to the restaurant windowsill, so that Athena could monitor images of the entrance to the launderette. Just before two, she called us over. We crowded around to see that Cindella was entering the launderette, accompanied by a man dressed in a dark suit, wearing sunglasses. A few minutes passed.

"Well?" asked Milan.

"Let's risk it." I really wanted to speak with Cindella. She had faced the Dark Queen recently, and I wanted to know what had happened.

So we snaked our way along the sidewalk until we were at the launderette. Then we kicked up our boards and walked into the humid room. It was large; all around the walls were massive washing machines, some of them churning away noisily. In stark contrast to the tired-looking people waiting for their washing, sat the stunning pirate, Cindella, and next to her a man who was dressed for a meeting of high-powered businesspeople. It was a measure of how dispirited the other people in the room were that they didn't seem to take any notice of the unusual clientele or of our arrival. After all, we were a punk airboard gang, who although young, must nevertheless appear intimidating with our perma-tats and piercings.

"Hi, I got your message; it was a clever one." Cindella stood up and turned to her companion. "This is my friend, B.E.; I wanted you to meet him, too."

"Hello," I said, nodding.

"Come with us," ordered Athena.

All of us left, making our way through litter-strewn roads until we came to an empty block of flats, windows all broken. I let us inside; there was nowhere public we could safely spend time with a person as striking as Cindella. So, in an abandoned room, bare but for the dark marks of fire damage on the roof, we sat on our boards, more or less in a circle around Cindella and her friend.

"Congratulations on your aircar race win," she began.

"Thanks. Did you see it?" Nathan answered with a smile.

"Yeah. From real close. We entered it. We were doing pretty well until that last bend." The tall suited man spoke for the first time. He sounded more amused than bitter.

"Hah! Never mind. You and a lot of others." Milan chuckled.

"So, what's up? You asked to meet us, all over the forums," Athena interjected with a note of urgency in her voice. There was a pause. Cindella glanced at B.E., then spoke for them both. "We're getting organized, and we have some ideas. I wanted to run them by you first. Saga is a dark and unpleasant world and the only enjoyment I've really had here is with you people. So I want to make sure what we have in mind suits you."

"Go on." Athena was interested.

"I met the Dark Queen. She wants to force us to read certain changes into the fabric of this world. I'm not sure exactly what, but it's stuff like immortality for the children she intends to have. She wasn't afraid of me. Or, at least, she realized she had nothing to fear from me, or any of us, because if she dies, then half my world dies of the addiction she has caused in them. So, we need to find something that she is willing to negotiate over. Either that or give her what she wants, with no guarantees she won't go ahead and kill two million people anyway."

This prompted Nathan to interrupt with the same question that had occurred to me. "So . . . you're saying you don't want her dead?"

"Blood and thunder, no!" Cindella waved the question away emphatically. "Tell them what it's like, B.E."

"It's a nightmare." Cindella's friend leaned against a wall, checking it carefully first so as not to dirty his suit. "All I want to do is play Saga. But it's turning me into a wraith. I don't eat properly; I don't exercise. I don't even want to unclip to go to the toilet; I'm here sixteen or more hours a day. When I go to sleep, I dream about being in Saga. Several times, I've fallen asleep while playing. I've tried leaving it alone, of course. In the early days, I could stay away for maybe forty-eight hours. But not now. If I stay away, my thoughts fill up with Saga, until even when I'm wide awake, I'm dreaming of Saga. Flashbacks of the game constantly interrupt whatever I'm doing. Outside of Saga, I can't concentrate at all; I'm broken. I can't fight the craving anymore."

"What do you do when you are here?" asked Athena.

"I'm supposed to be an assassin. That was the character

class I chose. The models looked stylish." He gestured at his body. "But once I was in the game, here, I found that none of the missions work, even the training ones. The people I'm supposed to talk to are long gone. So I'm stuck at red. Mostly I earn credit by killing rats, foxes, and rabid dogs in miserable housing blocks like these."

Milan snorted with amusement. "Sorry, mate," he immediately apologized. "It's just that you don't look like a rat-catcher."

"If I had to live like this forever, I couldn't do it," B.E. continued, without appearing to take any notice. "And nor could anyone else in the same circumstances. So, we have to get the Dark Queen to rescind the addiction."

"I see," said Nathan, with a nod. "And how are you going to do that?"

"Put her in a position where she can no longer rule. Destroy all her offices, her palaces, her communications systems. Hound her personally."

"She'll kill you," Athena pointed out.

"Yes!" Cindella was excited. "That's the beauty of the idea. She can shoot us down, but we will keep coming back, in our tens and hundreds of thousands. It's only our Saga characters that disappear; we'll just create new ones. Again and again. Until she's sick of us."

Only now did it really crystallize in my mind what it meant to live in a universe that was the creation of another. She was right; they could die over and over. It didn't matter. Our world was just a game to them.

The grimy room was silent.

"Hell's teeth. They really are from outside our world, and they really do think it's a game." Athena eventually spoke.

"We don't think it's a game anymore." Cindella was bitter.

"What do you do in your own world? What do you look like?" wondered Nathan.

"Our village runs an olive farm; Osterfjord is its name. I live there. My real name is Erik. I'm sixteen, with dark hair."

"Erik?" I was shocked. "You're male?"

"Ya." Cindella, or as I now struggled to see him, Erik, gave a slight laugh. "Our characters, or avatars as we call them, can be anything; they don't have to reflect what we're like outside the game."

"Amazing." Nathan came over to Cindella and took hold of the embroidered cuff of her blouse, feeling it between his finger and thumb. "You are so real, but this is just your computer-generated being . . . your avatar." He turned to B.E. "How about you?"

"I'm B.E. in Osterfjord, too. Most of us stick to names and models that have some resemblance to our own bodies."

Here we were, a meeting of two entirely different species, in the dingiest room imaginable. Surely an event of this kind should have been in a palace?

"So, what do you think of our plan?" B.E. asked.

"It's smart." Athena spoke in a musing tone. "It might work. We can help point out some targets for you. Although you'll be lucky to get anywhere near her personally."

"So, you wouldn't mind?" Erik asked.

"Mind? Bring it on. Trash the joint. You couldn't make it much worse for reds." Milan gestured at the room we were standing in.

"But I was thinking I'd like to do a news broadcast first, to explain to your people what we are doing. I'd like them on our side, or at least to understand the situation and why we are destroying buildings. There's about ten thousand of us have agreed to this plan, and I'm anticipating a lot more as the word spreads. But ten thousand should be enough to seize a big broadcasting station for an hour or so and send out our message, right?"

"Ten thousand." Milan whistled, impressed. "You could take out her government with that. Have you got arms?"

"Some of us, but we can't use them. It doesn't matter if we die, but if anyone from your world is killed, that's a real death. That poor policeman . . . I had no idea he was real. Now that we understand that, we are all extremely anxious not to hurt anyone."

Milan laughed derisively. "You're going to fight a war with the Dark Queen but not use weapons? Good luck with that."

"Yes, we are." B.E. was cold. "We are going to destroy her world, brick by brick, if we have to. Everything she depends upon will be broken. Until she is so anxious to be rid of us, she takes away the addiction."

"Well, if that works, can you do something for us?" Milan suddenly became serious.

"Of course. What?" Erik replied.

"Ask her to give us an amnesty, a pardon."

"Certainly."

"Do you know how our guild system works?" Athena had a sudden thought, and straightaway I could see where she was going.

"Sort of. You register with one and as it goes up in the standings, it gets more local powers and benefits?" Erik suggested tentatively.

"Right." Athena nodded brightly in return. "At around a hundred thousand members, depending on their individual ranking, the guild leader gets a seat on the High Council, theoretically the most important governing body after the Queen. I've set up a guild, Defiance. I want to get on that council and stir things up. Why don't you all join? If I get there, it will help your strategy of disruption."

"Good idea, thanks. Defiance it is. We'll pass the word." B.E. sounded grateful.

"I'll make you both officers. Cindella and B.E., right?"

"Actually," said B.E., sounding a little sheepish, "my full name is B.E. the Executioner."

"And mine is Cindella Dragonslayer."

With a smile, Milan shook his head. "Well, at least you both look the part."

"I know you've said it before, but just to repeat. You don't want the Dark Queen killed?" Nathan glanced at me when he asked the question.

"No! No, she mustn't die. Either that would somehow break the connection and leave us without the game . . . or worse." B.E. shuddered. "Trapped by our addiction to Saga, we'd die a slow death, our bodies declining through neglect. We need her alive, to reverse whatever it is she has done to us."

"We'll help," I offered, with a quick check on the reaction of the gang. "Athena can list the government buildings we know about, especially the indigo-class ones, the important ones. And we can point out the best building for doing a world newscast."

"I was thinking about that," Athena joined in, as positive toward them as I was. "I can help you to design your newscast, to prepare something in advance. So all you have to do is get in there and play it, while keeping the security and the police off your backs for the duration."

"That's great! Thanks a lot. It's good to have met with some friends in this place." Erik's smile, through the beautiful Cindella, was infectious. We were all smiling, but deep down I felt guilty. I still wanted to hunt down and kill the Dark Queen. To free my friends from the danger she represented. Just that? Or was that the excuse that fitted an unconscious desire? I couldn't condemn these visitors to our world to the indefinite torture of their addiction, could I?

Chapter 24
THE BROKEN-WINGED
BUTTERFLY

In the end, We decided to have the dress made, not with many eyes but two, front and back, like a Caligo butterfly. The frame could not be copper, for We would then find the weight too great. In fact, it consists of a delicate weaving of carbon nanotubes, copper coated. When the dressmakers stood before Us in trepidation, they were mistaken as to Our humor; We were delighted with them. Their construction was ingenious, fluttering in response to movement, but elastically firm enough always to return to shape. The frame itself was so beautiful We were tempted simply to wear it, to appear at the ball as a flying sprite, a metal-winged angel. This, however, We rejected, well aware that Our days of enchanting appearance were over. Some cruel guests might even take amusement from the incongruity of Our aged body and the costume of a balletic nymph. No, a poisonous, dangerous butterfly was the correct apparel for Our current stage of life. So, We clad the frame in velvet, upon which were mounted gems: pink diamonds; opals; aquamarines; spinels of lilac, indigo, and blue; sapphires of every hue. The mosaic they formed is of dark tiger stripes curving in fractal paths around the two great irises. It is a beautiful and extraordinary costume, which conveys more than any speech could that We are at the height of Our powers.

Michelotto has forced Us out of the barracks, and We are glad. It did not suit Our nature to stay on the defensive. It is time to rally the troops, crush the nascent rebellion before it gains any significant following, and in the process locate and destroy him.

We dress slowly, meticulously, calling Our pages only when nothing remains but to fasten the wings to Our corset. The ball has been under way for some time; after all, We wish to be the last and most dramatic entrant. Woe betide any latecomer. Not that the holder of an indigo or violet card would arrive late to the highlight of their social calendar.

"Enough." We are ready. With Our head turned to the mirror to watch the effect of Our walk, We sweep from the room. The wings flutter and sway with the rhythm of Our gait; most striking. The Grand Vizier awaits Us just outside the room, along with four guards in ceremonial costume for the evening. Although swords are strapped to their waists, it is from the powerful laser rifles in their hands that We take comfort.

"Your Majesty is most resplendent. Your greatest costume ever, at least in my lifetime." He bows low.

His own costume is excellent: a modest satin suit of an historic era when male attire was not too absurd. The trousers are appealing, reaching to just below the knee, where they are buttoned on top of white silk hose. We note with a certain amusement that his propensity to wear violet has calmed down, reflecting, perhaps, a certain assurance in his new status. Only the lace cuffs and collar of his costume are violet; the silk braiding of his jacket and waistcoat is turquoise against a pale silver background. He rises and holds out his gloved arm. We, in turn, rest Our own iron-strong hand, clad in a velvet glove—the irony is not lost on Us—a fraction above his. Actual physical contact is repugnant to Us and unnecessary. To match Our gait, he has to take large strides. Is it an unconscious predisposition of Ours that Our leading courtiers are relatively small? Surely the mismatch is simply a result of Our own regal and stately build.

Arm nearly upon arm, we enter the great state ballroom at the upper floor, walking, flanked by guards, smoothly over the scarlet carpet to the head of the staircase. The music and dancing stop, and the applause begins, accompanied by gasps of delight and awe. The Grand Vizier drops his hand, bows, and begins his descent down the right staircase in time to Our flowing movement down the left. The mirrors that We pass confirm the transfixing beauty of Our dress. Opposite Us, reaching the floor in careful synchronicity with Us, is the Grand Vizier. We approach each other across the lustrously polished parquet walnut-and-ash floor. Again, he raises his arm and the two of us turn to walk through the assembled dancers to a stage draped in purple silks, upon which is a throne of gold.

No one talks, but We are surrounded by sound akin to whispers: it is the rustle of a thousand dresses as people part to let Us pass, bowing deeply or sinking to the ground in curtseys that spread gorgeous dresses like the unfolding of the petals of a rose.

Once We have mounted the stage, the Grand Vizier retires, and We face Our people. Here are the winners of Saga: the indigos and violets. Their dress reflects the value of their card, and the overall tone of the gathering is a dark blue; but as Our gaze focuses on individuals, we discern the richness of the company. A bodice of purple satin has, in fact, been sown together with orchid threads and has a design of heliotrope embossed upon it, studded with amethysts. A silver eye mask, held on a rod of ebony, has a peacock's multihued feather rakishly attached to one side. Occasionally We come across a brave costume, one that includes reds and scarlets. We admire them for their originality.

"Ladies and gentlemen." We magnify the sound of Our voice so that it resounds through the great ballroom. "In order that you can enjoy the ball with complete detachment from worldly concerns, let us address the current situation and outline Our strategy. At the very least, a frisson of concern must have entered your consciousness at the sight of certain guilds demanding the abolition of red and orange grades. 'Where might this movement end?' you no doubt asked yourselves. You hold the cards that you do, precisely because your abilities are in governance and management. You, and only you, have knowledge of the true nature of Our universe and access to human texts, such as those by Plato, Livy, and Machiavelli, which you have no doubt studied assiduously." We very much doubt they have done anything of the sort; most of those promoted to, or inheriting, indigo cards are less interested in the information that becomes available to them than in which models of luxury aircar they are now entitled to own.

"So, We shall treat you all as Our closest confidants. The welcome news for you is that this protest is not organic. That is to say, it is not rooted in a deep desire of the population for change; Our reds and oranges are not in the kind of supersaturated state that presages far-reaching transformations. Rather, a small minority of them is being led into the streets by a political creature and traitor. The unwelcome news is that this man is Michelotto, a former attendant of Ours, and the only other person in the world with anything like Our powers." We dip Our shoulders so that a ripple runs down Our wings, drawing the attention to the two great shimmering eyes, indicating a certain humorous modesty on Our part. But perhaps the effect just terrifies them? "You will be pleased to hear that We nevertheless surpass him in strength and shall destroy him, whether he continues to stir up discontent or runs and hides." An outburst of applause, good.

"Since the nature of this protest is artificial, We have decided to crush it." Cheers. "You will all be provided with lists of those in your employ who belong to rebel guilds. Treat them as you wish. And enjoy it." Louder cheers and some cries of "Hear, hear!" We hold up Our hand; they instantly hush.

"Of course, there remains the possibility that the nature

of the protests will change. It does have the potential, if unchecked, to become a genuine and therefore more dangerous expression of discontent. If so, We have the flexibility to co-opt sincere reformers by structural changes, changes that nevertheless keep the core of Our system intact. We tell you this for two reasons. One, as a reminder that force is not always the correct strategy, and two, so that, in the unlikely event that it proves necessary, should certain adjustments be made to Our economy, you will be confident that your own interests will be protected." Applause again.

"With your minds at rest, I encourage you to enjoy the ball." We step back, to where the Grand Vizier is showing slight signs of agitation. There is prolonged applause throughout the room. We spare them from having to sustain it indefinitely by nodding to the conductor of the orchestra, who initiates a lively and popular *cinque-pace*. A good choice.

"Well?" We ask the Grand Vizier under Our breath, while outwardly smiling. We go so far as to nod to certain figures who are particularly valuable to us.

"A very large crowd is at the gates, Cindella among them," he whispers, listening to the information through his earpiece.

"Start shooting until they scatter."

He nods, worriedly.

"We have been killing them in droves, but they still come. Their bodies disappear . . . so they are humans. Oh. She has cut through the gate. They are nearly here."

Yes. Their cries are faint but discernible to Us: onward, onward, to the palace.

"Well?"

"I'm sorry, Your Majesty. The guards are killing them as fast as they can, but we are overrun . . . we are to expect—"

He is interrupted by a crash. The orchestra stops; a woman has fainted? No, she has been struck by a rock. A thousand-year-old stained-glass window is broken. Gasps. Another rock cráshes through a large pane of glass, scattering shards among us. Then dozens more. Screams as people run, some at least looking in Our direction first. The grinding of fragments of glass into the parquet floor by panicked feet causes Us to wince. This is a disaster: all Our careful preparation ruined. Our speech, this fabulous dress even, will not be remembered. Our fury is greater than that attributed to Hera, queen of the gods, on discovering that Zeus had brought Athena into the world without her. A woman scorned, especially one in a dress like Ours, is a force to be feared.

"Majesty. Your safety."

No sooner have We set off for the door than the Grand Vizier has called out to restrain Us. We nearly kill him in Our rage, but in some part of us reason still reigns and considers such action to be mistaken.

"Fear for those in Our path," We roar with a depth and volume that no lion ever achieved. Everyone remaining on the dance floor screams in horror and flees.

The great doors open. Before Us stands Cindella, in her insolent dress, a pirate's leather jerkin over a white blouse. Laser pulses from a hundred rifles play upon her with no more effect than if Our guards were shining flashlights at her.

"How dare you?" We howl so ferociously that the remaining glass in the windows shatters, as do all the mirrors of the room.

"Get used to it. Because until you set us free, this is how it's going to be. Every public event you attend will be ruined. And that's just to start with. From today, your government buildings and barracks are going to be destroyed. Your world will fall apart. That is, unless you free us."

"Never!" Our cry echoes into the sky.

"Very well. See you at your next event." She turns to leave. "Oh, nice dress, by the way."

Soon afterward, the petrol bombs begin to land, splashing their burning content over Our precious floor and setting fire to centuries-old golden-tasseled drapes. Outside, We can see the people being hit by laser fire and dying, but they keep coming, burning rags and bottles in hand. Wave after wave of them. Enough to create an inferno out of the ballroom. The sprinklers that now begin a gentle cascade are pathetically inadequate.

"Majesty." The Grand Vizier is coughing with the smoke, waving at me, almost touching me. "We have to leave."

Drying Our tears on Our sleeve, We ascend the stair, walking over discarded shawls, jewelry, a violin bow. It is possible for Us to dampen the flame in Our immediate vicinity, but this attack is too much. The palace is lost, and We must retreat to nurse Our wounds.

Chapter 25

STORMING THE AIRWAVES

"People of Saga . . ." Erik paused. Already. He had hardly started. The break went on too long. "Ermm."

"Stop!" shouted Athena. Nathan and I paused the cameras that we controlled. They were the small, handheld kind, although at the moment we had them mounted on tripods. I had bought them so that Erik could record his broadcast.

"Sorry." Erik held his hand up against the glare of the spotlights from the tank that were picking out his avatar, Cindella. Her long shadows reached into the far corners of the factory, where they merged with the permanent gloom of the old building.

"Ready?" Athena was sitting on the front of the tank, her computer unrolled. She was receiving the images from the two cameras and mixing them into a master version.

Erik settled on his stool again and nodded.

"Go!"

"People of Saga. What I am about to tell you will sound extremely far-fetched. At least, for most of you. I know that if I were in your position, it would seem incredible. It is, though, the truth, and the evidence for it is overwhelming. Several thousand years ago, human beings artificially created your world. The word 'virtual' does not really do justice to your universe, since it rests, ultimately, on very material substances—hardware that is maintained on Earth—but I can't think of a better term than 'virtual.' Your world began as a virtual one."

"Pan in slowly," whispered Athena through the device in my ear.

"I know this because I have entered your world from the outside. I won't say that I come from the 'real' universe because I've learned to appreciate how real your world is, and independent from ours. The way I look at it now is that your universe is nestled inside ours. People from our universe can enter yours by creating a computer-generated being, an avatar. This is not at all how I look in my world." Erik let slip a genuine smile, and suddenly I felt that his broadcast might actually have an impact; he no longer seemed like one of those earnest, intense eccentrics who have got lost in mysteries created by their own minds.

"With you, Nath. Ghost, back to your starting shot."

"People from your universe can enter ours, too. Though I'm not sure how exactly. But it must have happened, because a few weeks ago, the main computer of our planet suddenly became a host for your world, for Saga. Your Dark Queen was responsible for this. Which brings me to the main point of this broadcast: I wish it were the case that I was here, contacting you, so that our two worlds could begin a communication between each other, one that was fruitful to us both. I wish that this was the start of a new era of sharing information and ideas, of forming new friendships. I personally would find such a prospect a fascinating and exciting one. Instead, unfortunately, we arrive here to find ourselves the victims of a terrible attack."

"Close-up."

"During the course of what we thought was the chance to explore your world playfully, the Dark Queen was systematically poisoning us, turning us into addicts. We estimate that nearly two million of our people were damaged in this way before we realized the danger. Why such a hostile action? Why go to all the trouble of connecting Saga to our people, only to assault us? The answer, as she told me herself, is that she wanted to create an immense number of hostages, before asking one of us to reprogram your world. It is a bit like capturing a surgeon's family and telling her that if the surgery fails, her family will die."

"Nath again, and back up, Ghost."

"She told me that the reprogramming was to ensure that her future children would be immortal, with godlike powers. She said nothing about improving the condition of your wider society. Our worry about doing the reprogramming she asks for is that, first of all, we might fail. Our society knows less about computers than did the people of Earth who created Saga all those years ago. In any case, Saga has evolved and is so sophisticated that tampering with one part of it might cause deep structural problems. If it were to crash, that would be horrific. For you and for two million of us. We would much rather not make the attempt. But supposing we do and it succeeds, fulfilling the Dark Queen's goals, will she then release us? She is untrustworthy, and we have nothing to bargain with. Might she even kill us all to prevent further undesirable changes by us to Saga in the future?

"We will not be helpless victims to her plans. Large numbers of my people, growing every day, are determined to oblige her to break their addiction. The strategy we have decided upon is to harass her until she yields. I want to emphasize that this is a nonviolent strategy. We have absolutely no wish to hurt any of you, not even the Dark Queen, especially not the Dark Queen. But we are embarking on a campaign of major disruption and property damage to imperial and governmental buildings. Obviously we cannot announce our targets too far in advance. But should you be working in one of them, please don't panic. We ask you to leave the building, calmly, when you see us gathering or hear an alarm. It might also be an idea, in general, to stock up on food, water, and portable power supplies. Power stations are included in our plans.

"You seem to have your own social disputes taking place at the moment. This has nothing to do with us, and it would not be right for us to intervene, knowing so little about life here. If our method of struggle with the Dark Queen inadvertently assists the protesters, that was not our intention. So, with our deepest apologies, I hope you will at least understand our situation.

"Finally, with regard to the proof of what I have just said, many of you will by now have seen people in your vicinity appear or disappear. What you saw was the entry or exit of my people to and from your world. For those of you who have not seen this, even more striking displays of our entry and exit to and from Saga will soon be taking place. When our disruptive activities begin, we anticipate that the Dark Queen's troops will open fire, shooting hundreds, perhaps thousands, of people, whose bodies will simply disappear; this is because they are destroying the avatar, but not the real person. When our avatars are destroyed, we simply make new ones and return. Because of this, the Dark Queen cannot win. Our number of lives here is inexhaustible. The sooner she recognizes that, and lets us go, the better it will be for everyone.

"I look forward to a time when our two worlds can explore in friendship our extraordinary relationship. Until then, please try to understand that our actions are directed not against you, the people of Saga, but against the Dark Queen."

"Stop."

"Nice one." Milan led the clapping.

"You think it was clear enough? I didn't sound completely crazy?"

"It was good. Crazy, but good." He laughed and switched off the tank's powerful forward beams. For a moment, we were blind, until our eyes adjusted to the gray light of the daytime factory interior.

"Right, now we have to get this out. I can post it onto forums. But what you really need is a major news broadcast." Athena looked at Cindella.

"Yes, I have several thousand of us ready to take over a station."

"Great. We'll come, too." Milan was enthusiastic.

"Are you sure? I'd rather you kept away; it doesn't matter if any of us are shot."

"Look," he said as he patted the main gun. "I've got a big anarchist tank, and I want to use it."

Four hours later, we were settled inside the tank, our coms system in place, ready to go. When I had taken up my position in the driver's seat, I had again felt a pang of concern for Arnie. Perhaps after this I would, discreetly, check on him. The others were in the same seats they had taken for the race. We were all in for a bumpy ride, because none of us had any idea how to fix the anti-gravity.

"Erik and his people are waiting for us. Let's go." Athena had been keeping an eye on the Defiance forum, which was where we had agreed to post messages to each other under pseudonyms.

A cough, then a steady rumble. We were off again. With a squeal from the wheels turning inside the tracks, I turned us around and drove up the abandoned railway cutting. Our target, as agreed with Erik, was Newscast 1, the biggest broadcasting center in the City. As we rolled over the old railway ties, the whole vehicle jittered, our bags being noisily thrown up and down. Soon we were on a road and progress was smoother.

"Next right, Ghost."

Our plan was to move as fast as we could, knowing that the tank was certain to attract police attention. So we were taking the overpass. It amused me the way the aircars all slowed to let me into a lane; normally they would jockey in an ill-tempered manner for a better position in the rows of traffic. Once in the fast lane, we could trundle along at a very respectable rate, the billboards flashing by, leaving only a subliminal message for their products.

"Anything?" Nathan asked, looking over his shoulder at Athena.

"Quiet at the moment."

The turret of our tank rotated so that it faced behind us. A glance at the reverse view showed that a customized Mosveo Starburst was cruising along in our wake.

"Pow!" Milan pretended to fire and, as if the driver could hear him, the aircar dropped back a little.

"Junction eighteen please, Ghost."

"How do I signal?"

"We can't," Athena answered after a pause.

"Milan, point that cannon left please and wiggle it a bit or something."

In any case, as soon as I started to slow down and edge across the lanes, everyone gave me a very respectful berth.

"We have police activity up at Newscast 1. But it's just on the traffic channel."

"Must be Erik's crowd gathering," mused Nathan.

Soon we could see the problem for ourselves. Once we had turned into Raphael Street, we could see that traffic going up toward the broadcast center was at a standstill. The tall masts covered with satellite dishes that marked the position of Newscast 1 were still a mile away.

"Milan, turn your turret around; I'm going up the verge. Strap yourselves in everyone."

The tank drove through the road barrier more easily than I could crush a soda can. With a bump, we hit the grass verge that divided the south-going traffic from the north-going, and now we were driving along, tilted over to our left. But that wasn't the most uncomfortable feature of my plan. The tank shuddered, to the accompanying sound of a loud splintering crack. Soon after, there was another jarring moment, and an equally violent shattering noise. The problem was the billboards. Through the driving controls of the tank, I could feel their brief resistance each time we smashed through one, as well as the release as they gave way. Back in our wake were billboards with tank-shaped holes in them, some of which looked distinctly crumpled and one that had toppled over altogether.

"Good work, Ghost," chuckled Milan through my earpiece.

A hundred billboards later, I felt distinctly queasy, but we had made it. A vast crowd of people was gathered around the broadcast-center gates. They were locked out, and a line of security guards faced them from the other side of the tall metal bars. Traffic police were trying in vain to move the crowd off the road.

"That looks like our cue," Milan observed.

I revved the engine hard so that the people between us and the gate got the idea and parted, leaving a short, clear run to a now-worried body of Newscast 1 security.

"Here goes!" I warned everyone.

The gates were sturdy and our first collision merely bent them, the groans of the metal being drowned by the cheers of the crowd. I backed up and charged again. This time, we broke halfway through, and torn metal scraped along the tank's surface, scarring Nathan's paintwork. Something was stuck. A tug-of-war began as I tried to reverse, feeling the resistance of whatever was keeping us jammed. Then I changed tack and thrust the controls forward. I could feel the resistance give; we were inching forward. Then suddenly we were free, accelerating forward with a lurch and a scream from the gates; a huge section of metal bars had come with us, sending up showers of blue sparks as it was dragged along the road. The way was open, and the crowd poured through eagerly.

"Keep going down this road," Athena directed me.

A huge parking lot was on our left, full of expensive aircars. To our right was the main broadcasting complex. We passed a series of squat, pastel-colored buildings, then a glass-and-steel tower with a large first-floor canteen. The workers in the canteen were lined up against the green-tinted window, watching with amazement as our tank headed an arrow-shaped mass of people running through their parking lot.

"This one."

A wide curved-glass entrance fronted a sturdy brick building. The man at the desk looked up from his monitor, astonished.

Erik's people were pressing at the glass doors. I saw him, in his bright pirate avatar, at the front, gesturing to the guard inside that he should open the door. The man shook his head.

Another rev of the engine. By now, everyone around us understood my language; they backed away, even those security guards from the main gate who had run along with the crowd, shouting impotently.

Three bumps up the steps and an almighty crash, the loudest so far today. Our monitors showed that the entire front of the building had gone, covering the lobby and the ground outside with shards of broken glass.

"In we go. Pass out our bags, Ghost, please." Athena was throwing open her hatch.

"So long, buddy. You did good." Milan gave the turret a kiss as he climbed out.

It was much noisier outside the tank than I had expected. Several alarms were sounding, so the people all about were shouting, not to mention the security guards. Those nearest us, though, gave us a big cheer as we got down, dragging our bags and airboards after us.

"It's back there, right?" Erik was with his friend, B.E., and they had schematics of the building in their hand.

"Yeah," affirmed Athena. "The rest of your people should probably stay here. We need just fifteen minutes."

"I'll take charge here. You go on." B.E. opened a metal briefcase on a table whose glossy magazines were scattered on the ground. He began to assemble a pulse rifle, using the parts from inside the briefcase.

"I thought you were going to be nonviolent," commented Nathan.

"They don't know that." B.E. winked.

"Come on!" urged Athena.

There were people in the long, yellow-painted corridor. They ducked back into their rooms as we ran. Then we were charging through a large makeup area, full of mirrors and with two famous newscasters in their chairs, white smocks thrown over them, while layer after layer of makeup was painted onto their faces. Again, looks of astonishment.

"Here!" Athena pointed to a door labeled "Studio 1." A red light was on: LIVE—DO NOT ENTER.

We entered.

"Shoo, shoo!" Milan ran over to the brightly lit desks, gesturing at the two presenters.

I went to the nearest camera; Erik came with me, sword drawn.

"Time to leave." He pointed the blade at the cameraman's throat. Once the cameraman had thrown down his headset and run, I took hold of the equipment. It was floating on an anti-gravity cushion, easy to move around despite its bulk. Nathan was still arguing with his cameraman, so Erik went over to settle it.

"I need you up here please, Erik." Athena was behind us in a glass box, where two middle-aged men in suits were gesturing angrily at her.

Meanwhile, Milan was sitting on the newscasters' desk, in the full glare of the studio lights. The presenters, a man and a woman, sat stiff and voiceless, like shop dummies.

"Say something to Camera One, Milan; I have you in shot." I laughed as he gave the camera his big ugly monster expression.

"Hey, Ghost, cool." He waved. "Well, good afternoon, folks. The news has suddenly gotten interesting, so for those of you lucky enough to be watching this live, sit down and pay attention. In a few moments, you are going to see the most important broadcast you'll ever see. In the meantime, you probably want to admire my perma-tats." He flexed his arms, and I couldn't resist panning in on the writhing designs.

"We're set."

Over my shoulder, Athena was giving us the thumbs-up. Erik's sword seemed to have persuaded the men to leave the control booth.

"Right, set your computers to record, because here it comes." Milan's face was off camera; I quickly turned back to him. "This broadcast is brought to you by Defiance. Watch, think about it. And get ready for some wild times."

"The recording is playing," announced Athena. "We should scram. Erik can keep an eye on things here."

"Shame; it's kinda fun." Milan pulled his board from his shoulder and switched it on. "Lead on."

As we snaked away from the building to the cover of some ornamental bushes, helicopters were arriving, rushing overhead with mighty beats of the air. From the back window we had used, it was impossible to tell how things stood out front, but the fact that we could still hear the cries and shouts of a large crowd was promising. Even if the police got past them in the next minute, they would be too late to stop Erik's broadcast from going out.

"Where to?" asked Nathan.

"Follow me." There were still plenty of hideouts that would suit us, in the old and abandoned parts of the City.

Chapter 26

♥

The moon was up, far away in a deep cobalt sky, a silver disc reflected in the glass of the tall buildings around us, or at least those towers that still had windows. This was a very old part of town, a business sector, long since abandoned to rats and pigeons.

"One gets tired of pizza very quickly," observed Athena.

"Not true." Milan gestured happily with his slice.

With a sigh, Athena closed the box and wiped her fingers before unrolling her computer.

"Are you going to eat that?" asked Nathan.

"No. Go ahead."

"Halves!" cried Milan.

"So, what's the news?" I asked her.

"Amazing. There's, like, ten thousand new forums, at least, discussing the broadcast."

"What are they saying?"

She laughed. "I said ten thousand. I can't read them all.

From what I have looked at, it's about fifty-fifty so far as to whether they believe Cindella or not."

We sat in a derelict office, quiet, looking out into the darkening street.

"The Defiance forums are hopping." Athena looked up eagerly. "And we're getting something like ten members a minute. We're over twenty-five thousand and growing fast. Here, you should see the threads for yourself." She turned on the projector, focusing it on a blank wall, and we turned to look. "Just taking one at random."

IS DEFIANCE THE WORLD'S
FIRST INTERSPECIES GUILD?

I was tinking, if wot you said on that cast was tru, then you are aliens. I'm in a guild with aliens. How cool is that? The Cutter ✂

>Well from our point of view, you are the alien. Cat. 🐾

>>Awesome. I'm an alien. ✂

>>>What do you do, Cutter? 🐾

>>>>Me? I'm an airvan driver, delivery boy. Wot about u? ✂

}Salt worker, but just for another three months, then I'm going to university to study weather systems. 🐾

}>Cool. How old are u? Are you a girl? ✂

}>>16. Yes. 🐾

}>>>Neato. 17, boy. ✂

}>>>>What do you like doing, when you aren't working? ✔

}}Easy. Airboarding. ✂

}}>We don't have airboards in our world. ✔

}}>>Wot no boards? That's the pits. You're lucky u found us then, I'll show u if u like. ✂

}}>>>Would you? I'd love that. ✔

}}>>>>NP. Do u know Brahms ■? Me n friendz are there all the time, boarding. ✂

}}}Brahms Square? I can find it. Will you be there tomorrow, about 6pm? ✔

}}}>Sure will. Whoo Hooo! I've a date with an alien! ✂

}}}>>What do you look like? ✔

}}}>>>Sexy. Of course. ✂

}}}>>>>No, I mean how will I know which is you? ✔

}}}}Ahh. k. I'll wear my Defiance hoodie. I've vampyre tats on my shoulders. + Look for the board with my tag on it. Wot about u? ✂

}}}}>I chose a character type called Silver Trooper. It turns out to be some kind of imperial messenger. She has a silver uniform and an airbike. ✔

}}}}>> !ii! ✂

}}}}>>>So see you tomorrow? ✔

}}}}>>>>Damn right! ✂

"There's hundreds, thousands of threads like it. Defiance forums have become the place where people from the two worlds are chatting. Some of them are a bit more serious. Isn't it great?" Athena shook her head in amazement. "I had no idea this was going to happen when I invited them in."

"It's wonderful. See, it's not all bad, this new situation we're in." There was a warm smile on Nathan's lips.

"No, not bad at all. In fact, it's getting exciting."

A gentle buzz from the pocket of my hoodie made me jump. It was Michelotto's pager.

"I bet he's got a lead on the Dark Queen," Milan said, glancing up at me.

"Probably." As the text scrolled around, I entered the terms into the decoder. "He wants to meet me right away, in a place called Gilgamesh Square." I looked up questioningly at Athena, who shrugged and returned to her computer.

"You know, Ghost, you don't have to go. Not now. If Erik's plan works, we don't need to kill the Dark Queen and we don't need Michelotto." Nathan looked at me with concern.

"Maybe. But if he wants me to help take out the Dark Queen, I'll still do it." Even talking about the idea gave me a surge of satisfaction, of revenge achieved. "Suppose she gives in to Erik and his people. Lifts the addiction and as a result they leave. As soon as they're gone, she'll take her anger out on us, and anyone who helped them. Any pardon she promised won't be worth a red credit."

"I agree," Milan said, scowling. "Go kick her ass."

"But what about Erik's people?" Nathan persisted. "If you kill the Dark Queen, there's no hope for them, is there?"

The question troubled me. A little.

"Yeah, I'd like to help them. We have been helping them. But we have to look after ourselves, too." I got up and kicked my board awake.

"Wait, Ghost. For the first time in all the years I've known you, I think you're making a mistake. A big one. Two million people will die if you kill her." Nathan stared at me earnestly.

"Athena?" I looked to her for help.

"Don't ask me. I don't know. There's too many variables. For a start, I don't trust Michelotto, either. With him as king, are things really going to get better for reds, or was he just saying that to keep us on his side? To keep you on his side. On the other hand, how long can we live our lives like rats? On pizza deliveries." She scowled at Milan to head off a smart remark; he smiled innocently, lifting his shoulders, arms wide. "If you and Michelotto can kill the Dark Queen, I think that's the best chance things will work out for us. But I feel it would be wrong to condemn those human beings to death, especially now that they seem to be getting somewhere with their protests."

"So, what are you saying?" I challenged her.

"I'm saying—Don't ask me, I don't know."

"Well, I'm going to see what he has to say, at least."

"We should probably all come along," Nathan suggested.

"Yeah." Milan put down his pizza.

"Come on then."

It took us an hour of hard boarding to get to Gilgamesh

Square, and my thigh muscles were beginning to ache by the time we arrived. Athena had located it for us, in an abandoned residential area. Tall redbrick tenements overshadowed an old fountain, long broken and covered in several layers of graffiti.

An airbike was at rest in the darkest corner of the square, and Michelotto was standing beside it, dressed, as always, in black. I could sense the cold blurry void around him, where in a normal person were signs of life: heat, breath, heartbeat.

"Where have you moved the tank to?" He addressed us as soon as we were sufficiently close that he needn't raise his voice.

"Did you see Erik's newscast?" Athena asked him in return.

"Yes?"

"That was us; we got them into Newscast 1. But we had to abandon it."

"I see." He nodded to himself.

"So, what's up? Got a bead on Queenie?" Milan stepped off his board with a swagger.

"No. I'm here to talk to Ghost, to perform a test."

"Can I ask you something?" Nathan interjected before we could find out more. "You know how the Dark Queen has addicted Erik's people. Do you think you could treat them? Cure them?"

Michelotto shrugged. "Possibly. I understand the theory but I've never tried it. The idea of such contact is too . . . too intimate for me." He scowled. "There's something slightly perverse about inserting moments of ecstasy into alien minds."

"Would you do it, though, or reverse the effects of whatever she has done?" Nathan looked at him earnestly.

"It bothers you?"

"That two million people who might otherwise be our friends may die? Of course it bothers me."

"That's very empathetic of you," Michelotto commented dryly. "Personally I don't have such feelings, but if, in return for Ghost's assistance in the elimination of the Dark Queen, she wished me to try, I would do my best."

Nathan looked at me. I nodded at Michelotto.

"So be it," he said. "But now to test Ghost's skills." From the carrier on the side of his airbike, Michelotto took out a metal tube. He opened it, holding it near the ground, allowing the parts it contained to fall to the floor. We came closer, to watch as he assembled a pulse rifle. When it was complete, Michelotto glanced around our group with a flash of his dark eyes.

"Here." He tossed the rifle to Milan. "You just line up the sights and pull the trigger."

"Cool." As Milan admired the silver weapon, resting the thin curved stock against his right shoulder, Michelotto walked slowly toward the far wall, his footsteps ringing out across the pavement.

He turned to face us. "Shoot me."

"You're kidding?" Milan lowered the rifle.

"No. Really, shoot me. Don't worry; you won't hit."

"Are you sure?"

"Certain."

"Here goes then." With a high-pitched hiss and the smell of ozone, a shimmering bolt of ruby light shot from the gun, leaving a bright trail across our vision that couldn't be blinked away. Michelotto was unharmed, a black mark on the wall beside him.

"Again."

Hiss.

"Again."

Hiss.

"Once more."

Hiss. Milan shook his head in amazement and dialed down the weapon to standby. The four black marks to the side of Michelotto formed the corners of a perfect diamond.

"How did you do that? I was aiming at your heart."

"That's what I wish to teach Ghost. Come on over here, please."

I looked up at the mention of my name, then walked across the square. This was a trick I wanted to know.

"When he fires, firstly you have to speed up your perceptions, so that you have time to deal with the energy. Then imagine a thread of air molecules connecting you to the bolt. Twist the thread, steer the energy of the pulse, just like you controlled the wire-guided missiles." He stared into my eyes, to see if I understood. I shrugged.

"Fire here." Michelotto called out to Milan, pointing to the space between the four black marks on the wall. He turned to me and said, "Try to push it to the side."

Across the cold stone floor, Milan raised the rifle. "Ready, Ghost?"

"Ready."

He fired. A new black mark on the wall, in the dead center of the four marks.

"Again," Michelotto called out.

Another black mark. Some plaster fell away, revealing the crumbling, scorched brick underneath.

"Again."

There was no trace of discontent in Michelotto's voice, but I was getting annoyed and my vision was confused by the bright trails of the shots I had been trying to focus upon.

"Let me try something." I kicked up, so I was floating on my board, feeling it bob and sway slightly beneath me. This ought to have made things even harder, but by imagining I was about to perform a really challenging board trick, I felt the world settle into place all around. "Now."

This time the bolt of fiery energy came toward me in discrete jerks. There was time to look at it, somehow shielding my eyes from the full glare. There was a line from me to the bright sphere, a line of molecules. It was a path that I had created and was conscious of, simply by focusing upon the space between the onrushing energy and my eyes. And even though the blast of ruby fire was devouring the chain, scattering its links with every passing moment of time, I was connected. I could feel it coming. Twisting, compressing, pushing, thinning. It was suddenly easy to move the bolt from its path. I steered it wide of the target area, then, exerting myself to the utmost, I forced the bolt up the wall, around in a curve, reversing it, steering it, then letting it dissipate into the bottom of the large ♥ I had scored on the wall.

I smiled proudly, looking down from my board. Michelotto's mouth fell open; he took a step backward, back to the wall, astonished and fearful. "No one, not even the Dark Queen . . ." His whisper trailed off. My friends were cheering and clapping.

"Hey, Ghost, do something with these." Milan raised the gun again and depressed the release button. It was now on auto-fire and the pulses of energy poured out of it.

Again the world slowed down so that the ruby bolts appeared to be like a line of dots, growing longer by one each time the universe moved. This time, I steered them into a whirling circle, filling the square with a blaze of scarlet light. Around and around they whirled, melting the air. It was possible to make them undulate, so that the circle I had formed gained a wobble, then appeared thicker but less bright. I spread them, forming a column, before bringing the bolts together once more and sending it into the old fountain. An explosion shattered the granite sculpture, sending gray splinters flying through the darkness, causing us to cower. There was far more energy in that collection of bolts than I had realized.

"Whoa!" Nathan ducked, flinging his arm over his eyes.

"Oops, sorry," I called out, and boarded over to them. "Everyone good?" They were straightening up, unharmed. A song of delight welled up inside me. I could control the blasts of a pulse rifle! What else was possible?

"Ghost, you really are something special." Milan switched off the rifle and gave me a thump on the shoulder.

"That's incredible. I would have said impossible." Athena's

voice was hesitant. I smiled eagerly at her, wanting her to share my excitement, not to be alienated from me.

"It's like when I'm boarding."

She shook her head. "No. This is something else again. Let's face it, Ghost, you're a strange creature."

I must have looked anxious, for Nathan immediately gave me a hug. "You're one of us, though, and wherever that talent is coming from, it's amazing."

The steady footsteps of Michelotto approached. There was an expression on his face that I had never seen before: respect.

"With an ability like that, you might be able to kill the Dark Queen on your own. Together, we can certainly destroy her."

"Let's do it then," I replied, feeling as if I could stride across half the world with a single step. There was such energy in my body.

"Ghost, who are you really? Thetis?" Michelotto leaned in, and I shrank back from him, suddenly chilled, the black space in my memory spreading out to taint everything with sepia. It occurred to me that if he thought me his enemy, he would kill me at once. Perhaps I had been mistaken, reveling in my new abilities like that; perhaps he now had me marked down for execution after we had killed the Dark Queen.

"I don't know." Who was this Thetis anyway? When we had first met Michelotto he had mentioned her. A RAL who had gone missing? Was I Thetis? Neither my heart nor my mind gave any response to the question.

Chapter 27
HUMILIATION

Our world falls apart. Our center cannot hold. The cup holdeth but bitter dregs, and it is these that We must now drink. Oh, how We rue Our mistakes; they circle constantly in Our thoughts. It is a barren and unhelpful circuit they travel, and We understand how maudlin and self-absorbed We have become.

The particular manner in which We used to dress, taking care with Our choice of clothes, is a pattern of behavior that belongs to the past, when the cold lethargy of disheartenment did not stifle Our enthusiasm for what now seems a triviality. This morning, We simply lace Our boots and stand upright, with hardly a glance in the mirror. Defeat is a horrid word and an even more horrible experience. But it is not death, We tell ourselves, and We must retreat to fight again.

"Your Majesty?"

A screen lights up to show Us Our Grand Vizier. The wary expression on his face is a harbinger of more bad news.

"Report."

"A new assault." He pauses, embarrassed to continue. We do not make matters easier for him, and stare back in silence. He clears his throat. "They are outside the Department for Internal Security."

She will be there, Cindella. She is always there. Nothing makes Us more furious than her impudence, but We must not allow rage and pride to prevent Us from making the correct tactical move.

"Have the chauffeur meet Us outside Block Two."

"Your Majesty intends to go to Imperial Square?" He hesitates, somewhat anxious.

"What is it?"

"Your safety."

"Fear not. The only person who represents a genuine threat to Our safety is Michelotto, and We would like nothing more than to encounter him and lay upon him the anger of all Our humiliations."

It is a cold, gray morning, the sun still below the level of the skyline. Cindella and her people like to strike early, when the streets are less busy, out of a curious consideration for the ordinary people of Saga. Strange, this human empathy. Even with Our furs wrapped around Us, caressing Our body, We still feel a slight shiver. The car is here, though, and, a moment later, warm air fills the partitioned area in which We ride.

"Imperial Square, Your Majesty?" The driver looks in the mirror and We nod.

Imperial Square, a fine place for a pleasant walk. A path

runs around the outside of the square, and as it does so, passes statues of all the former Dark Queens and Kings. It has been a while since We strolled past them, remembering them, triumphing in the fact that they are dead while We live. Some of them were rulers for a very short time, most notably King Radford, who strangled Queen Vidonia as they both plummeted to their deaths from the Marble Tower. When the autopsy revealed that she was dead before she hit the ground, he was posthumously awarded the regal honors and a statue in the square. Today, alas, is no day for pleasant reminiscences.

"This will do. Set Us down here and wait for Us."

Champion Road leads to Imperial Square, passing through an archway that cuts underneath the Royal College of Surgeons. We linger in the shadows of that passage, listening. What do thousands of insubordinate human beings sound like when gathered in a large square? Nothing more than a playground of excited children. There is a general hubbub against which individual shouts and even laughter can be heard. Well might they laugh, for they have Us on the defensive.

The main throng is over at the far side of the square, packed around the gray tower bristling with satellite dishes that is Our Department for Internal Security. There are clusters of people all over the square. Some of them are merely observing; perhaps they are not humans but curious residents of Saga, keeping well away from the flash of pulse and laser weapons. Other groupings are behaving in a more sinister fashion, handing out petrol bombs to those rushing past them. Whoever is in charge of tactics would do better to target these officers of the human army than attempt to keep the tower clear of the crowds.

The overcast morning is dark enough for Us to move around the edge of the square unobserved, nor do We have to sacrifice Our stately gait for what, in another person, might be called skulking. Closer now and the extraordinary sight of hundreds upon hundreds of people, careless of their lives, pouring fuel on the fires that flicker beyond the jagged ruined windows and doors of the building. Imperial troop carriers are rushing around in convoy, the crowds parting to let them through, flowing back once they are gone. Many of the attackers are being killed, their bodies disappearing after a few still moments, but even more are arriving. Perhaps even the reincarnations of those who have died earlier. This is most frustrating; We are engulfed by fury again and cannot continue until it fades somewhat.

Perhaps We should go straight to the interface chamber and cut the link between the human beings and Saga? It is tempting, but We have learned Our lesson from the collapse of human society on Earth. For all that We despise them, We still need them to survive until the reprogramming is done.

As We step through the debris of twisted metal and broken glass, We are particularly vigilant that no stray weapons fire does Us harm. We deflect several incoming pulses of energy onto nearby human avatars, killing them, for the moment. It is very distressing to see Our offices and files in such disarray. Computer screens lie torn from their positions; furniture is burning. Centuries-old criminal records are being lost here, so, too, the complex functioning of the accreditation of the police and army members with their proper salaries. We hurry on, before the building is entirely lost, brushing Our way past the eager humans who all around Us carry iron bars, with which to mete out their purposeful destruction.

The elevators are broken, naturally. Fortunately We can ascend through the space around which winds the stairwell. Some people stop to stare, rather rudely, but then how often would you see the Dark Queen floating past you? At the fifth floor, fighting is taking place. Fighting of a sort. Most of the humans hide in the stairwell, waiting. Cindella is here—good. She advances down the corridor, ignoring the constant play of light and energy on her irritatingly beautiful body.

"Time to put those down and run for your lives, before the fire really takes hold of the building and traps you here."

She holds her rapier out, cutting away a few buttons from the guards' uniforms. They look horrified but even more frightened when they see Us.

"Leave Us."

The guards run. The humans, who had been waiting for this, charge down the corridor to burst into offices and start their havoc.

"Would you mind asking them to stop, while we talk? We have an offer for you."

Cindella stands there, hands on hips, enjoying Our plight. The experience is so intensely appalling that We consider alternatives and daydream about her attitude should We begin killing the humans by destroying their brains permanently. She would be on her knees pleading then, instead of smirking.

"Hold it, folks!" she shouts, and those nearest Us cease to bring their bars down upon Our property. The island of calm spreads as, curious, the humans gather around.

"This is the Dark Queen," explains Cindella. "She is the one who poisoned you, and she has something to say."

"You win," We say simply; it would hurt more if We had not already accepted the conclusion. "We will reverse the addiction." Next time, hundreds of years from now, when this generation is long gone, We will deal with them differently. We will send satellites with nuclear missiles to orbit their planet, and then We will have Our hostages without having to let any of them into Saga. It will be costly and will require a huge amount of resources as well as Our having to spend a considerable amount of time in their universe, but We will have Our way in the end. This consoling thought allows Us to speak with relative equanimity.

"Stop destroying Our buildings and Our infrastructure, and We will immediately release you from the addiction. You can leave Saga, forever if you wish."

They cheer, with deep-felt relief and delight.

"Good." Cindella looks around. "B.E., are you there?"

"Here." A tall man at the back of the crowd raises his hand.

"Let him through, please, folks." They shuffle aside, laughing now, chatting to their neighbors, finding it hard to believe that their suffering will soon be over.

"Start now, please. Let's confirm that you can do as you say."

The others fall silent; they have not considered that their pain might be irreversible.

We close Our eyes, feeling this human as if his mind were beneath Our fingers. We delve. There is still a frisson of delectable sensual pleasure in the action, even under these circumstances.

"Done," We announce.

"Let me unclip and come over to your house, Erik. By the time I get there, I should know."

"Good idea."

She looks up at Us, or I should say "he"; Erik is a male name. For some reason, it disappoints Us that this intelligent opponent is from the male half of their species.

"How long will that take?" We ask with a concerned glance back at the stairwell, where the rising column of smoke is thick.

"About ten minutes."

"Would it be unreasonable, given Our surrender to your wishes, for Us to ask you to call off this attack, and indeed help to put out the fires?"

"No. That's fair enough. Please, everyone, back out, spread the word. We've won!"

"We've won! Stop the attack. We've won!"

Our upper lip rises in a sneer. *Enjoy this moment, but your distant offspring will suffer for it.* "Congratulations." We turn Our attention back to Erik. "Very few people ever bested Us, and none lived for long afterward. You will be unique in that regard."

He looks Us in the eye. "Don't be bitter. Your people and mine have the potential to be friends now that the damage you were doing is over. This could be the start of a wonderful new era for both of us. We could really use your scientific knowledge and we have a lot to offer in the arts, in entertainment. Not to mention the pure fun of having contact with a different world."

This gushing naïvete is so effusive and undoubtedly genuine that We feel a moment of nausea. What kind of adversary is this? How could someone so ignorant of political realities have bested Us? Still, with the protest of the human beings having been settled, We can return to Our other problems. It will be a pleasure to concentrate on people who, once they have been killed, stay dead. If he is awaiting some similar expressions of mutual happiness and joy from Us, he can wait until he dies of old age, which cannot happen soon enough. We stare at him with all the malevolence of which We are capable.

"You know, yours is a fantastic world."

Evidently We have failed to communicate Our feelings to him, for he carries on, as eagerly as before.

"I wonder, is that anti-gravity technology a special feature of the game, of Saga? Or is it based on some kind of physics that would apply in our world? Imagine, real airboards and aircars. You've no idea how much lifting we farming communities have to do; it would mean such a difference if we could have that technology."

Again, he pauses; again, We glare. As if the plight of a distant, retrogressive body of human beings is of any concern to

Us, who ten thousand years from now will be the matriarch of an immortal dynasty, one that will use its immortality to people two universes. He thinks of lifting sacks of seed; Our thoughts are on infinity.

"Sorry, I have to go. B.E. is here. I'll be right back."

She stiffens and a few moments later is gone. We have time to run Our thoughts through the building's defenses and confirm that the fire is on the retreat before she returns.

"That's wonderful, thank you. He is totally cured. Our attacks will halt." He pauses. "I hate to sound ungenerous, but you haven't been exactly trustworthy in the past. My people will remain ready to undertake more actions, such as this, until the last of them is cured. I hope you understand."

Oh, We understand. We understand far better than he does.

"Listen carefully to Us and not the flutter of your thoughts. Here are Our terms: each human being who is cured of their addiction will leave Saga and not return until We give permission for you to do so."

"Oh, they'll be only too pleased. But are you sure you want us all to leave? It's such an opportunity for our two worlds to meet. And your own people—won't they want to know what's going on? Whether my broadcast was true?"

"You will all be healed. Everyone will leave, including you, until such time as Our satellite contacts you. Agreed?"

"If that's what you want. Once everyone is clear, I'll go, too." She shrugs. "Oh, wait. There is one more thing. That group of my friends—the ones who won the aircar race—they would like to be pardoned for any offense they have caused, so that they can go home. Can you do that, too?"

It takes a moment to compose Our smile. "Why, of course."

She looks at Us. We maintain Our benign expression. Time will heal this wound. We console Ourselves with thoughts of nuclear warheads. Since neither of us seems to have anything more to say, We sniff disdainfully and depart the scene of Our humiliation.

Chapter 28
REVENGE IS BEST SERVED HOT

Systematic, patient work is to Our taste. Even if it is an undoing. When you are two thousand years old, you learn the value of planning for the long term. One after the other, We restore to normality the processes in the brains of the human beings, and they drop from Saga like grains of sand evacuating an upturned timer. There were hundreds of thousands of them, but already We can sense the space created by the absence of those We have touched. The wisdom of this retreat is evident. The City was like a bubbling flask of chemicals, on the verge of explosion. Now the main source of heat has been removed, and the volatile liquid subsides.

Our two remaining priorities are to crush the strikes and eliminate Michelotto. These are quite manageable goals, now that the interference of the humans is no longer an issue. Is it necessary to offer a response to that shocking broadcast by Cindella? It is. There are wild rumors to quell.

It does not take Our full concentration to flit through the remaining human population.

"Grand Vizier."

"Your Majesty?" he responds promptly to Our call.

"Give notice to the High Council that We shall make a keynote address to them at the next assembly."

"Very well, Your Majesty. Is that all?"

"It is."

Soon—another few days—and We shall be finished. Our stitching will have been unpicked and We can begin the seam again, this time on a truer course. Once it is complete, We shall, of course, suspend the link to New Earth until Our next satellite arrives there. It will be a relief to be free of the untamable infection that is Cindella, to be utterly confident that she has no possible way of harming Us through her magic. It is a shame that the human for whom she is an avatar will be long dead by the time We deal with them again. Revenge is, in fact, a dish best served hot. In this case, however, We shall make do with a more impersonal blow to the later generations of an entire species rather than a personal one to the individual who offended Us so much. Perhaps the human will have bred and left offspring. We make a note to look into the matter when We next encounter them, some hundred or so years from now.

We lean back against the elegantly carved wood of Our

chair. For some reason, We decided to work within the safe environs of the old meeting room. There is something about the solid oak table and plush decor that reassures Us of Our power. That and the pleasant memories, lingering like the faint echoes of a scream.

Chapter 29
FLICKERING LIGHT

To make the most of the storm that was lashing at the City, we had let ourselves into the penthouse suite of Judge's Hotel. The rain was so heavy, it seemed to hit the window in waves. Although it was not yet sunset, the view was dark outside, but for the tendrils of street lighting below us and the occasional flicker of cream-and-purple light among the black clouds. Athena was lying on a king-sized bed, chin cupped in her hands, looking as much at her screen as at the storm outside.

"It's true. They've all gone. The last post by any of them in the Defiance forums was Cindella's."

"Read it out again, would you, Athena?"

Even though we had kept the lighting inside the suite to a minimum, I could see Nathan's pale face reflected in the window.

"'To the people of Saga. The Dark Queen has removed the addiction that was poisoning the human beings of New

Earth. Her condition for doing so was that we leave Saga. Of course, we agreed, but many of us now feel a deep regret that we are leaving you. On a personal level, you have become our friends. More generally, knowing that there is another world nearby is a marvel for us, and it seems a shame for our two peoples not to interact and share what we know. Perhaps at some future time, we will meet again. We hope so, but for now, the matter is outside our hands, as the Dark Queen has informed us that as soon as the last person from New Earth has left Saga, she will sever the connection between our worlds. For my particular friends, Athena, Ghost, Nathan, and Milan, I have the news that the Dark Queen has agreed to pardon any offenses that you might have committed. I hesitate to interfere with your political affairs, but I cannot leave you thinking that she was sincere about this, when I got the distinct impression otherwise. Please take care. Your friend always Cindella.'"

No one spoke, although the gusts of water being blown onto the glass in front of us had swells and lulls like the rhythms of speech. If I had known the language of storms, I might have been able to interpret the message that this one seemed to have for us.

What did I think of the humans leaving us? It was understandable, of course. They had their lives. Nor was it their choice; as long as the Dark Queen controlled the connection to New Earth, she could prevent them from being here. So, why did I also feel let down? We were on our own again. Perhaps that was for the best. Make no claims on the loyalty of others, and you cannot be betrayed. I had never feared being alone, but I had enjoyed the sense of being part of a great movement when we had led Cindella's people into Newscast 1.

"How does she do it?" Nathan was the first to speak.

"Who? What?" Milan was picking his way through a bowl of fruit, and his voice was a little muffled.

"How does the Dark Queen sever the connection to them? What's the mechanism by which she contacts their world?" Nath looked over at Athena; so did I.

"I've no idea. It's an interesting question, though. Somehow they are able to connect with us, whether as a pattern of light or a flow of electrons, or even something weird like magnetic interaction. It doesn't really matter," she mused aloud. "What matters is that the Dark Queen has a way of stopping that flow. She has some way of acting in their universe. Otherwise it wouldn't be up to her. They could come and go here as they liked."

"Michelotto might know. Want me to ask him?" I took the pager out of one of my trouser pockets and examined it.

"Even better." Milan spat a seed onto the carpet. "Let's meet him. Cindella has made it pretty obvious we can't trust any pardon from the Dark Queen. Now that the humans are gone, there's no reason we shouldn't take her down. Right, Nath?"

"True."

I took out the encryption device and composed a message for the pager. A short while later, it buzzed with a reply.

"He'll meet us, after the storm is over. Gilgamesh Square again."

With that settled, we turned our attention back to the storm. My sense of loss eased as I gazed through the flow of cold water into the darkness beyond. What were we, after all, but a tiny flickering light in the night, so distant from any other source of warmth?

Chapter 30
THE TASTE OF VICTORY

It always seemed that there was no end to the old City: that you could travel through it all day, block after block, with the signs of inhabitation gradually diminishing, until you found yourself in dark and abandoned streets. Even here, beyond the limit of power supply and easy boarding, the streets continued for miles. It would be a depressing journey to struggle on in this direction, with the haunting thought that there was no end to the derelict houses.

The architecture here was quite different from in the living heart of the City. Hardly any buildings were more than two stories high. The houses were spread out, distributed upon regular squares of grass, marked off from each other by low wooden fences. The only tall buildings were civic ones, raised in a mock Romantic fashion, adorned with unnecessary pillars and bas-relief carvings. Disused now, they would once have been bathing houses, libraries, entertainment centers, and so forth, for the privileged guilds and cardholders of the district.

Ahead of me, Michelotto drove smoothly and quietly past the empty houses, sometimes checking in his mirrors that I was keeping up. He knew the answer to our question and had agreed to take me to a place that he claimed was the building from which the Dark Queen controlled communications with Erik's world. Just me, though. Michelotto felt there was a chance that we might be lucky enough to come across her, in which case the others would be a liability; in a fight with the Dark Queen, we would have to deflect our powers to defend them. I agreed. So they were waiting for me back at our latest hideout, an old house on Amiens Street.

After a four-hour ride, we came to a huge, white stone building, capped by a copper dome that had turned dark green with age. He stopped the airbike and waited for me. Once the soft hum of my board ceased, quiet returned to these ancient streets, and with it a sensation of giddiness, which I accounted for by the fact that I was used to the constant background rumble of busy traffic.

"Innocuous enough, isn't it?"

"Yeah." It had the look of an old library, except that the wide stairs rose to a surprisingly narrow doorway between two aged and flaking pillars.

"It was built to house the portal between our world and that of the human beings."

Michelotto got off his bike and looked around, appraising the nearby buildings.

"She still comes here sometimes, to maintain stable conditions for Saga." I must have looked blankly at him, as he continued patiently, "Saga is hosted on some kind of physical structure created by the human beings on Earth. I'm not sure what it is, exactly, but our universe could come to an abrupt end if there were an earthquake or similar catastrophic local environmental event that shattered the equipment on which it is hosted. It is the primary function of the King or Queen to transfer themselves to the human universe and maintain the uninterrupted running of Saga."

"I had no idea that our existence was so precarious." I stretched my arms high above my head, in part to relieve the muscular tension that builds up during a long session of boarding, but also because, listening to his words, I felt unsteady. My thoughts were jittery.

"Don't worry." He looked carefully at me. With concern? Or calculation? "From what I was told, the planet itself, Earth, should be good for another two billion years. Past rulers arranged a reserve energy supply for Saga, to keep us safe for thousands of years, even if none of us ever crosses through the portal. Judging by comments the Dark Queen has made in my presence, I think she has set us up for over a hundred thousand years. That would be in keeping with her character; she makes plans for the very long term."

"But still, something needs monitoring?"

"Yes, she has to come here sometimes."

"Do you know what's inside?"

"No. I can't get in."

"Oh, really?" I ran up toward the door, curious. I'd never come across a lock I couldn't defeat.

"Careful. Don't set off any alarms."

As I approached the building, I let the universe slow down and stretched out my feelings, heightening my perceptions. He was right; there were motion detectors set high on the walls, focused on the entrance. Now that I had an interesting challenge to concentrate upon, I felt confident and sharp. The unease that had been seeping through my thoughts had dissipated entirely. From the inside pocket of my hoodie, I drew out my tools and went to where a cable ran down beside a pillar, carrying the alarm signal from the motion detectors toward the City. I made a careful insertion into the cable and reset the tolerance on the detectors so that even an elephant charging into the building would not trigger them.

Beside the door was a very old standard card and iris reader. I carefully slipped my highest card, a blue, into the slot, sensing for alarms as I did so. The card was rejected, naturally. Anything else would have been too easy. I withdrew the card, then sprayed the surface with one careful tap on the top of a tiny bottle of plastic-conducting polymer. It was possible to mold the microscopic layer of polymer even while the card was in the reader, so I could systematically rework the pattern of the card by trial and error. It took me fewer than a hundred attempts and about ten minutes before the reader accepted the card. I couldn't help sneaking a proud glance at Michelotto. He was watching hesitantly.

The retina detector came on. Once I had established contact with its processor and disabled the error alert, I leaned forward to let it read my eyes. They were as good a start as any for a similar method of pattern building. A light flashed, I blinked and the door opened with a hiss and a brush of cool air. The processor showed a 100 percent match.

"You're in!" Michelotto was surprised.

"How did it come to have my retina pattern as acceptable?"

"Did it really?" He came up the stairs and looked at the reader, then at me. I shivered, feeling goose bumps. This building was vaguely familiar; it had something to do with my lost memory, my lost childhood.

If Michelotto derived any meaning from the fact that the lock was prepared to admit me, he said nothing, but instead looked through the open doorway. I stood beside him. It was a short corridor with another reader in the wall beside the far door, this time a silver voice-recognition panel.

"Try it," he said, gesturing, but waited outside when I stepped forward.

"You'll either have to wait for me, or come in. These systems don't allow both doors to be open at the same time," I pointed out to him.

Michelotto frowned, looking back down the stairs at his bike. He clearly didn't like being confined, but eventually he stepped into the corridor and closed the door behind him. When he did so, a strip light in the roof came on, giving us a copper glow to see by. I stood in front of the voice panel.

"Consume more. It is the measure of your life." I spoke the first sentence that popped into my head. The door opened. With a shared look, we stepped through to another short section of corridor, this time with a panel for reading a palm, like the police cells we had been detained in. No sooner had I pressed my hand against the screen than the door opened. One more stretch of corridor, one more card reader. The building was welcoming me.

"This is a much more recent addition." For a start, the slot itself was a much tighter fit around the card. I knelt down and inserted microfibers to get a look at the workings inside. They were sophisticated, but I felt relieved that I at least recognized the principles of the system. It was designed to measure minute current differentials on the surface of the card. The key card would, no doubt, be made of many layers of material whose conductivity varied considerably.

Despite a growing urgency to get inside, to discover why my retina, voice, and skin were acceptable as keys into the building, I squatted down on my haunches to consider the lock.

"Problem?" In the orange glow, the lines of Michelotto's face were deeper and darker than usual. He looked severe.

"Kinda. Even though the other doors allowed me through, this one needs a card that I don't have. I'm going to have to improvise one."

"Here." He threw a wallet down beside me. It was full of cards, all the colors of the rainbow. There were indigo and violet cards, which I'd never seen before. I took them out, feeling their texture with my fingers, holding them to the light. Interestingly, they were somehow richer, with a more subtle variation of chroma than a blue. The material the violet was made from was a plastic so hard it felt like cold metal. There were three other cards in the wallet. One was entirely black.

I'd never heard of a black card. Another was gray with a silver wolf design on one surface. The third had an emerald snake's head looking out from a gold background.

Michelotto slowly lowered himself and sat on the corridor floor, leaning against the wall, face impassive, although I had looked up from the cards I held with an expression of inquiry. This whole break-in would have been so much easier if Athena had been with me. At least she would have talked to me.

I tried my tools upon the cards. The black one had an extraordinary surface. It seemed stable until I looked microscopically, then it seemed to run like mercury, in a flow that eluded my most sensitive pointer. The gray one contained an immense amount of data, namely the social status of millions of people. The snake, however, began to stir as I touched it and to eat at my tools. I snatched them away.

"Well?" Michelotto asked.

"The wolf is a kind of doppelgänger card, right? It would look to the reader like a particular user of your choosing had inserted their card."

He nodded.

"The snake destroys the reader it's inserted in?"

"Yes, but not the hardware. The snake carries a virus, which infects the processor of the lock, making it unstable. The virus tries to get the processor to spew out the entrance codes as it disintegrates. But it doesn't always work, so I have it as a measure of last resort."

"And the black card?"

"Can't you tell?"

"No, I haven't a clue. I couldn't read it."

Michelotto gave a rare smile. "That's my own design. It's a master card that only a RAL can use. It's based on a kind of stereolithographical process. Only instead of fixing the fluid surface resin with lasers, the RAL alters it with the same kind of control you used when dealing with the pulse weapon. Try it."

"But I'm not a RAL."

"Aren't you?" His gaze was unflinching, but I didn't look away.

"Am I?"

"Only a RAL can affect the local environment in the way that you can. You are a RAL of some sort."

I looked at him, skeptically. "You told us the RAL were created about two thousand years ago, right?" I gestured at my body. Perhaps being a RAL explained my thieving abilities, but it didn't explain my past. I picked up the black card and looked at it.

"It's easier with your eyes closed."

So it was. The card was pliable in response to my wishes. I could feel it, as if I were running my fingers through a tray of water, setting it as ice in whatever sculpture I desired. When I opened my eyes, Michelotto was looking straight at me. He nodded.

For the first time ever in his company, I felt that I could form a clear image of him, both visually and in the sense that his face no longer seemed like a mask. Either the corridor was too small or else he had relaxed the trait that normally made his presence elusive and sinister.

"Tell me something, honestly. When we kill the Dark Queen, will you really make life better for reds?"

He nodded. "I will need to, in order to consolidate my rule. In any case, the economics of our society make it perfectly viable to have a universal distribution of yellow cards. It's the top luxury goods that we couldn't meet the demand for. You know, green-class items or better. But why do such matters concern you? Do you really care what happens to the reds?"

"Yes." I thought about my friends and Arnie. "They deserve better than that."

He smiled again, and it gave me a chill. "What the non-RAL deserve is neither here nor there. Perhaps you are not a RAL. I don't believe the word 'deserve' is part of our vocabulary."

"Why did you have to go and say that? Just when I was starting to like you." It was true, I realized. When he had shared the secret of his cards with me, I had immediately felt the respect of one master thief for another. Now I found his disdain for the people repugnant, and I was troubled by his assumption that I was like him. Was I? Deep down, I knew I was different, alone. Did that make me despise everyone else the way that Michelotto so evidently did? Right now, I wished for the company of my friends. For Nathan especially.

Michelotto collected his wallet and stood up.

"Can I trust you?" I stood up also, still holding the black card. "Come to that, after the Dark Queen is dead, won't you want to kill me, too? Because you think I'm a RAL?"

He raised his eyebrows, surprised at my outburst. "It is true that the RAL are competitive to the point of violence, but remember that the Queen and I formed an alliance of nearly two thousand years' duration. It was broken only because of her loss of touch with the reality of the situation. After I have gained power, there will still be a lot of work to do: building up loyal guilds to run the administration. I could use your help with that. Certainly I would not want you to be an enemy." Michelotto gestured his arm toward the door. "So, shall we go in?"

If he thought his answer was definitive, I certainly did not. I hesitated. The fact was, at a fundamental, instinctive level, I did not trust him. He was using me against the Dark Queen, but had no need for me after that. The look of fear on his face when I had shown my control over pulse-weapon fire had contained a threat.

He sensed my doubts and turned toward me. "When the Dark Queen is dead," he began, his face once more in copper shadow, "what will you do? What do you desire?"

"Nothing really."

"What would you change in Saga?"

I thought about this for a moment. To give out yellow cards to all would be a massive improvement in the lives of the poorest people of Saga. Other than that, what else could you want? Something deeper than wealth, something that addressed the alienation felt by everybody I knew. "A huge boarder park, maybe, with stages for bands, canteens open all hours, lots of parties. Like the Anarcho-Punk Collective do now, but permanent, legal."

This time his smile was genuine. "If I were sixteen, I would probably want the same."

"What about you? What do you want?" I felt slightly insulted, but I had been unprepared for the question. I was sure I could give a better answer in time.

"I've been playing a game for more than two thousand years. I've seen the gradual elimination of all my competitors but one. I want her to die, so that it's over. So that I can rest." He paused. "And so that I can experience the taste."

"What taste?"

"Victory."

Every time I came close to sympathizing with him, he pushed me away with his harsh manner. With a grimace, I pushed the black card into the slot. Closing my eyes, I developed a feeling for it, so that I could mold it, changing the electrical impedances of the surface. With a sigh, the door slid open for us.

Chapter 31
ACROSS THE UNIVERSES

Entering the building was a shock. I'm not sure what I had been expecting. Perhaps old-fashioned desks and bookcases, full of important files, or maybe rows of computers running secret programs. Instead, we were walking through the inside of a huge white ball, which was bare except for a bed in the center. Above us, a turquoise illumination strip gave us a gentle light to see by. Our steps echoed, the reverberations dying away slowly. Bending down for a moment, I touched the floor; it was a hard, cold plastic.

When we got closer to the center of the room, we could see that the bed was placed on a circle of slightly overlapping silver blades, like a propeller. The metal circle was about four meters in diameter and it was sunk a few inches below floor level. You were clearly supposed to walk to the bed on a white path that connected it to the floor and seemed to hold it above the blades. The bed itself was made of the same white material as the floor of the chamber, with some padding that outlined the approximate shape of a person on the upper surface. Crouching down, I could see that there was indeed an inch or two of space between the base of the bed and the metal iris below it.

There was absolutely nothing else in this huge, domed room. For some reason, the whole place made me feel as if I'd stepped through the electron shell of a giant atom and was now looking at the nucleus. A nucleus that was the portal to another world.

"Well?" Michelotto looked at me, then at the bed.

"Well, what? Why don't you test it?"

He grimaced and shook his head slightly. "I don't like the look of it."

"So? Neither do I."

For a moment, his eyes searched the featureless interior of the room for alternatives. There were none.

"Tell you what: rock, paper, scissors, best of three. Loser lies on the bed." I was joking, but Michelotto's expression remained somber.

"Very well."

That surprised me. Really, I had been expecting that I would be the one who went out to the bed and, in fact, I wasn't that nervous. I just didn't like his assumption that I would go.

Holding out my fist, I beat out the countdown. "Three, two, one."

His was scissors, mine paper.

My gaze focused on his. "You cheated."

He shrugged. "We are both RAL."

This time, I slowed the world down as I spoke the countdown. Each jerk of the timeframe brought me a wealth of information, from the tension in his muscles, the movement of his fingers, and the flicker of a smile on his lips. He was making a rock. At the very last moment, I displayed scissors. Michelotto raised an eyebrow.

I had realized that I wanted to see Earth for myself, more than I cared about being taken for granted. It was exciting to be on the cusp of obtaining fundamental knowledge about the world and perhaps about myself.

"Wait a moment, please." Michelotto walked back to the door and stood by it. "Now you can go ahead."

I don't suppose you get to live to be two thousand years old without being careful. Two steps along the walkway, then the bed. The foam was thin and I could feel hard plastic beneath my elbows and the back of my head. Around me was a faint scent of talcum powder, and I winced at the thought that I was lying in the space occupied many times before by the Dark Queen. There was some kind of ridge in the padding near my right hand. As I ran my fingers over it, I considered sitting up to have a look. But then the blades beneath me hissed, and I fell into a black pit.

I landed in a room where computer screens and flashing lights covered the floor in a grid. Had I changed worlds or simply fallen? I tried to speak and had no voice. No mouth. Nor arms and legs. What was I? When I moved, the world spun, I was rolling erratically, mostly on my back, performing great, jerky wobbles. The feeling was sickening. Or was the nausea coming from the sense of panic that I was not breathing, that the unconscious, comforting rhythms of my body were gone? Staying still was the solution. No need to be alarmed; this must be Erik's universe. I must indeed be on Earth. What would Athena do here? She would be systematic and wouldn't get overwhelmed by being in an alien body.

Firstly, I tried to set my vision straight relative to the floor and found that I could do so without having to roll. In fact, I could look in all directions. Three-hundred-sixty-degree vision was weird, like having a neck that could rotate all the way around. My body was of dark metal, curved almost into a ball, with many protruding spikes. No wonder I had tumbled in such a capricious manner.

The room was large in extent, the walls featureless except for four circular exits, one in each wall; the roof was plain but for a small grill. But the floor was an amazing kaleidoscope of color. Thousands of square lights ran in columns and rows around screens displaying moving graphs. The predominant color of the lights was green; some were orange; a few were flashing red. Rows of black dots were interspersed with the colored lights. No, not dots: holes. I rolled slightly to get a closer view of them and reached out toward one. A thin metal rod extended from my body like a finger. It was the exact dimensions of the hole. I rolled over the line of holes, sensing them beneath me. Then I stuck my finger in one.

It was like watching a newscast at a hundred times normal speed. There was such a blur of images and sound that it made no sense. It just made me dizzy. Fighting back the impulse to pull away, I tried to slow down the rate of information flow, with some success. It wasn't like when the whole world seemed to go jerky and move in discrete moments. But it was possible to focus on the rush of data, to dam it up and let through a controlled amount. It spoke to me.

"Semi-conductor factory 0AFB2 reporting."

A voice pattern within a frothy communication that told me orders were stable, wafer supply was continuous, with stocks enough for five months in case of disruption. Some wear on one of the loop vehicles would become significant in approximately six years, but the metrology and process devices were still relatively new, with a lifetime expectancy of over thirty years. All of this meant nothing to me.

"Very good," I sent back.

"Implement changes?" A flood of options came through with the voice. Since I was completely ignorant of the possible consequences, I didn't respond to any of them, apart from answering "yes" to the scheduling of vegetation clearance for the outside of the building: trees were encroaching with a possibility of becoming a hazard. I withdrew my finger and returned to the control room.

There were thousands—tens, maybe hundreds of thousands—of these holes. Presumably the green systems were fine, the amber needed attention, and the flashing red ones? I trundled up to one and took a look.

The data showed a major highway with a huge rent. Earthquake damage had pushed and pulled the land to tear the highway, leaving it with one side protruding over a meter above the other. Traffic, I learned, had been diverted around longer, less efficient routes, but there were still some vehicles awaiting the repair of the road. The options for reconstruction were complicated, so I simply pulled out of the socket, then examined several more.

This was all very interesting; the planet Earth was covered in a network of factories run by robots, but it was also something of an anticlimax. Where was the contact with New Earth?

Behind me was a resting spot above a pattern of silver blades identical to those in the white room from which I had come. It was obviously the mechanism for my return, and I was tempted to use it. But first I took a long roll around the entire room, my mobility improving all the while as I got used to my new body. From time to time, I would dip into a random socket, in the vague hope that it might relate to something other than the maintenance of Earth. After about thirty minutes of interacting with semiconscious factories, ships, satellites, and trains, I found what I was looking for: Communication-Assassination Probe Ox9B45.

"Your Majesty."

"Status report." I tried to sound as authoritative as I could.

"Quiescent. Fully functional."

"Can you contact the human beings of New Earth?"

A pause. "By several means, Your Majesty."

"Send a message to them by all methods. Tell them I want to speak to Cindella Dragonslayer."

"All methods? Confirm, please: Your Majesty wants to restore the space-com link?"

"Yes. Restore it."

"Done. Communications have been sent on all their media."

"To the whole planet?"

"Yes. This is what you wished?"

Strange, that a probe could sound nervous.

"Yes."

This discovery filled me with an unfamiliar sensation, a sense of joy and freedom. It had come to me in a sudden shift of perspective. I had not simply moved from the claustrophobic world of Saga to an even more confined control center on Earth. No, I had passed through a much more significant doorway. There was a vast universe out here, full of stars and planets. It was possible to fly through space, to visit these other worlds. The Dark Queen had proven it. For a moment, I felt admiration and sympathy for her. She knew. She was aware of the heavens, and she wanted to be part of them. As did I. What could be more liberating than to sail between the stars, a world unto yourself, outside Saga? I could do it, too: take this body or perhaps one of my own design, enter a spacecraft, and travel. A real ghost in their universe. Even if I were to explore this universe for ten thousand years, I would barely have begun. Like traveling no further than a street in Saga. But so unfamiliar, so new.

"Hello." An image of an ordinary-looking young man.

"Cindella?"

"Yes, this is Erik here. Who is that?"

"Ghost."

"Ghost? That's amazing. So that's what you really look like?"

"What?"

"A kind of spiky metal ball."

"No, it's just the machine I'm inside, while I'm in your world."

"That's great. I mean, that you can come into our world and talk to me. Good to see you. What's happening there? What's the Dark Queen doing? Did she pardon you? I didn't trust her on that."

"We're still hiding from her."

"So, how are you doing this—talking to me in our universe?"

"I've found the building from which she controls the connection between us and you."

"Great. What's the plan now?"

The plan? We didn't have a plan. I wished Athena were here, to ask her.

"Well, can you help us?" I asked him.

"Against the Dark Queen? I'm definitely on your side. It would be great if you could remove her from power; then our peoples could mix again. I'm sure that all of us here would welcome that." He paused, thoughtful. "But we can't really help you directly. Leaving aside the question of whether it would be right for us to interfere with Saga, the problem is that if we step into Saga, she'll poison us again."

"Yes." I could see that.

"But I'll tell you what—I have a scroll on Cindella that you might find useful. Is the connection between us and Saga back on?"

"For the moment. It probably won't last long, once the Dark Queen notices." In fact, I suddenly grew anxious that I might in some way have alerted her to my use of the building.

"In that case, I'll clip up and leave it somewhere for you." Erik spoke with enthusiasm.

"What is it?"

"A scroll of 'True Speaking'; it's a spell. Cast it on her when you really need to hear the truth from her."

"Thanks. Although a weapon might be more useful to us."

Erik pursed his lips in response. "I don't think my weapons would make much difference to you. And I don't think violence is right, even against her."

If I had been in a body with a head, I would have shaken it at his display of admirable but misplaced innocence.

"Well, whatever help you can give us is appreciated."

"Not at all." He waved away my thanks. "We owe you much more than we can give back at this time. But I'll go and leave that scroll in the room that was a café during the big party in the abandoned hospital. Is there anything else?"

For a while, we looked at each other. The creatures of two different universes. Perhaps the only two beings who had seen each other on both sides of the divide.

"Not that I can think of now. In fact, I'd better get going."

"Well, contact me again if you think of anything else I can do. And Ghost?"

"Yeah?"

"Be careful."

He was gone. Well, I suppose the scroll was something. And we had learned that we could still talk to the humans. Maybe Athena would have some ideas of how we could use that to our advantage. With a shrug of resignation, which manifested as a contraction of my round body, I withdrew from the socket.

Michelotto would probably be wondering about me, and there was my increasing concern about the Dark Queen. I quickly rolled over to a cup-shaped holder that held me above the iris of overlapping sheets. Somewhere there would be a device to make it work. For a moment, I toyed with the feeling of being trapped here, never able to return to my real body; it was unpleasant only because so long as the Dark Queen was alive in Saga, I would not be safe here to begin the construction of a spaceship that could take me to the stars. Then I found two controls. The first caused the iris to snap open, revealing a dark tunnel beneath me. The second dropped me.

When I sat up, Michelotto came over from where he had been standing, leaning against the exit. It was good to stretch my arms, to feel my fingers, to move my legs. Just as I swung my legs from the bed, I was struck with a sharp pain through my head and I staggered from the path, having to put one foot down onto the silver blades, before recovering myself. I knew the memory was true. I had done exactly the same thing before! Except that last time somebody had reached out to assist me. His face was familiar, his eyes gray.

"Are you all right?"

"I've just remembered something."

"While you were gone, it occurred to me that the easiest way to kill her would be to wait outside until she decides to use this facility. Then come in while she's lying here, helpless."

"Listen!" I shouted angrily, the word lingering as it echoed. "This is important. I've just remembered something. The man who helped me off the table. It's the same man who left me in the rain."

"What man?" Michelotto came over with a trace of concern on his face. Not for my well-being—I was sure of that—but for my display of what, for him, would seem to be erratic behavior.

Rain was falling, drops of water slowly gathering on the ledge far above me. One fell, bloated, shining. It hit the yellow card in my hand and dissipated, but for a tiny remnant of moisture, clinging to the inside of the *o* in the man's name. Season? No.

"Searson."

This stopped Michelotto; his eyes narrowed.

"A man called Searson helped you here, in the past?"

"Yes. Yes, years ago, when I was young. Then I fainted. I kept fainting. The last time I came to, it was dark, raining. He left me on the street. But I stole his wallet. His card. It was yellow."

"Interesting."

"Do you know him?"

"Possibly."

"I'm sick of your secrets." I came over, grabbed his arms, and shook him. "If we are on the same side, then help me. I need to know who I am."

"All right." He stepped back, breaking free of me by prying up my index finger, but not harshly. "Describe him."

"About your height, but not hunched." I closed my eyes. "Gray hair, very short, so it stood up on top. Lots of lines on his forehead, some around his eyes. He was maybe fifty years old. Stocky. Rather shabby. I was surprised he was a yellow."

"I see." Michelotto nodded, and my heart leaped. "I think it must have been Dardis, once lover and assistant to Thetis."

"What does that mean?"

"I'm not sure." He looked at me carefully. "If I had to speculate, it would be that somehow you are Thetis. But why did he leave you?"

Thetis? Again. It evoked no response in me.

"Let's go and ask him," I urged. "We know the name he's using: Searson. There can't be too many yellows of that name."

"What about staying here to kill the Dark Queen?"

"This is important to me. More important than anything else." It was true, I realized as I spoke. Yes, I did want to kill the Dark Queen, to prevent her from hurting my friends, and because I felt that I could. But it was nothing compared to removing the shadows from my mind.

Thoughtful now, Michelotto fingered his chin. "Very well. I admit that I am curious, and the knowledge might be valuable. We can set up some surveillance equipment here, to alert us if the Dark Queen comes."

"Thank you."

Chapter 32
SCATTERED ORCHIDS

The yellow district in which Searson lived was cut off from the City center by high walls. We used Michelotto's doppelgänger card to open an ornate metal gate, informing the security that we were local residents, a grandfather and granddaughter. The landscape was very different here. For a start, the quiet roads were lined with tall, leafy chestnut trees. The houses were all set very far back in their own gardens, hidden by evergreens. Every so often, we passed a public amenity, such as a small lake or children's playground. It was odd to see swings and slides that were not covered with graffiti and tags. The yellows obviously felt that theirs was a calm and pleasant place to live in, but it was not the kind of area I would be happy in. There was something too controlled about it, too sterile.

"Here." Michelotto turned the airbike in to a long gravel drive, lined by rhododendron bushes. I was clinging to him, my board over my shoulder. To save time, I had agreed to get on behind him, and if I hadn't been so distracted by attempting to clarify my earliest memories, I would have enjoyed the speed at which we flew through the City streets.

The house was large, three stories built of a ponderous red brick, with dark heavy windows, like drooping eyes.

"I'll wait here for now." He stopped us in the shadow of the hedge, and I got off.

There were security cameras. I let them get a good look at me before pressing my palm to the doorcom.

A minute passed. It would be so frustrating if he were not in.

"Thetis?" My heart leaped as his voice sounded from the speaker. "Is that really you?" His face appeared in the screen and it was our man.

"Yes," I replied. You would think that as I was a master thief, dishonesty would come naturally to me. But, in fact, my stomach lurched as I said the word.

"Oh, what a miracle! Come in! Come in!" The door clicked and slid across. Leaving my board on the ground, in a position to prevent the door from closing fully, I entered. Lights brightened in amber cups that ran high along the walls of a warm corridor. The floor was polished wood and my footsteps rang out loudly as I walked past closed doors to a wide, well-lit living room. From above a curving set of metal stairs in the center of the room, I heard hurried footsteps, so I waited, admiring the pictures on the walls and the comfortable furniture.

"How did you manage to come back? I thought it impossible. I'm sorry. I'm so sorry." The man from my memory ran toward me, holding out his arms to embrace me, and I involuntarily took a step back, a little ashamed. The hopes that were growing in him came from the depths of his heart. He must indeed have been Dardis.

"You look amazing. So young." His eyes blazed with joy. Then a moment later, his face changed utterly, to an expression of horror as he looked past my shoulder.

"You?"

With a preliminary glance to his right, Dardis dived toward a cabinet on which was an elegant vase containing one orchid. I felt some sympathy for him at that moment, remembering my first encounter with Michelotto and the feeling of being in the presence of an icy creature from hell. Faster than Dardis, but without having to break into a run, Michelotto strode over and kicked shut the drawer that he was reaching into. The whole cabinet rocked, spilling the vase. It rolled over the lip, smashing on the wooden floor, water running swiftly from the cabinet's surface before settling into a slow drip. Cowering beneath the black shadow of Michelotto, Dardis looked over at me.

"Thetis? Why are you with him?"

"Actually, I'm not Thetis." A comfortable padded chair of red cloth embroidered with gold floral designs was nearby. I turned it to face Dardis and sat down. "But I'd like to know who I am."

There was silence for a while, just the occasional soft tap of water hitting the floor. Dardis remained half lying on the ground, looking from me to Michelotto and back. Eventually he surrendered to our unwavering scrutiny.

"Six years ago, the Dark Queen and her assassin were closing in on Thetis. She had run out of hiding places and knew
she was doomed unless we did something drastic. So she
decided to risk swapping bodies in the portal. You know the
portal?"

I nodded.

"We had no idea what would happen, so I was against
it. But she argued me around. She felt it was over for her,
whatever she tried. Against my will, I helped. When she went
unconscious on that horrid white bed, I took her body away
and replaced it with that of a young girl. The idea was that
when Thetis came back, she would occupy the new body. We
did what we could with drugs, trying to get rid of the old personality without damaging the brain, to make it susceptible to
Thetis's return, but it was all guesswork."

My eyes began to fill with tears.

"Who did you put on the bed? Who was the girl?"

"Just a girl. You. We got her from an orphanage one night
and deleted all references to her, so that it was like she never
existed."

"And you drugged her?"

"Not at first. She wanted to come. It was exciting, an adventure for her. But of course, when we went to the portal, once
we'd programmed the building to recognize her, we blasted
her with everything known to wipe out memory—cholingerics,
mostly."

It was impossible to prevent a tear from spilling onto my
cheek, try as I might. The poor girl. Nine years old. It was

easy to imagine her happiness at escaping a state orphanage; they were miserable, decrepit places. But she was betrayed and used by these people and their stupid games. I had her body, but I wasn't her. Those memories were gone. Perhaps, at some deep level, some quality of her personality lived on in me. But they had effectively killed her, whoever she was. Did she have friends who missed her? What had she wanted for herself? What were her dreams?

I dug into my hoodie pocket for a tissue, blew my nose, and made my voice firm again. "What was her name?"

"I don't remember. It didn't matter. Thetis dealt with the records."

"Interesting. What happened to the body of Thetis?" mused Michelotto. He was framed in my vision by the tears on my eyelashes. I was angry at his calmness.

Sitting up with a sigh, Dardis moved the broken pieces of china so that he could lean against the cabinet. "It died after about a week of brainless function. I buried it in the garden, so at least you vampires wouldn't get to gloat over her."

"Why didn't you look after me?" I shouted. "Why did you leave me on the street?"

"I did for a while, but then I got scared. You asked a lot of questions." Dardis smiled, a sad smile. "One day, you were going to say something to the wrong person, and it would have got back to them." He gestured at Michelotto. "So when I realized Thetis wasn't coming back, I wiped your mind again and abandoned you on the street. It was raining; you came to just as I was leaving."

"You should have killed her," observed Michelotto laconically. "She remembered you."

"Yes, I should have. It's just that, while she lived, I could still daydream, you know. That Thetis would come back one day. In a young, beautiful body. I thought it had happened, when you were standing at my door there." He looked up hopefully. "Is there anything of Thetis in you?"

"Perhaps. I don't know how much of me is the girl and how much is her."

"Have you any feelings for me?"

I thought about this. "Yes."

He brightened.

"I hate you. For what you did to that little girl—to me."

His expression instantly turned into a scowl.

"Any more questions?" Michelotto asked me.

"No, I don't think so."

Bending at the knee, as if to look more closely into Dardis's face, Michelotto whipped a garrote around the old man's neck and pulled it tight, his knuckles white with the effort.

"Stop!" I screamed. "He isn't going to reveal anything."

"He isn't now." Michelotto spoke with a great deal of satisfaction. He straightened up, and the body of Dardis slumped to the side, falling into the debris of the china and the scattered orchid petals.

I looked at the body, stunned and horrified. This man had meant a great deal to Thetis. Was she screaming for him? I was afraid to look too deep.

"That's it. You're on your own! You're just as bad as the

Dark Queen. I want nothing more to do with you." I leaped out of the chair and strode toward the door. "Never! Understand? How can you just kill someone like that, so heartlessly? I don't care what the Dark Queen does; you and she are just the same."

"You know," he called out toward my retreating back, his voice calm. "Whoever you are, you're not a proper RAL." I paused, but I was trembling too much to speak. Nor did I turn around. "You're too emotional."

Chapter 33
RAGE AND DESPAIR

Half a day has passed since I witnessed the murder; the sun has set. Yet always the malicious expression on the face of Michelotto comes into my thoughts, causing my heart to accelerate in fear and anger. I board away from the scene, through empty streets, where the only motion is that of the furtive short scurries of rats. Night has come to a dead part of the City, a pocket of decay in the grid of lights. Am I Thetis? Am I howling inside at the death of Dardis? Even though I have never known the man. Of course not, and yet, when I take my thoughts away to other matters, somewhere, deep down, there are tears.

It seems, in my imagination, that every path that I have ever boarded along, every person I have ever spoken to, holds a part of me. I have become worn, tired, thin, and dispersed. If I am to end my suffering, I must draw together my distant parts, selfishly, protectively. No matter what may occur, I cannot be hurt once I am entirely contained within my own skin. Even better,

I pack my lost selves inside my heart, pulling in the distended cords of my life, compressing them tighter and tighter, until I am diamond hard. Impossible to wound. Incapable of tears.

Stretching my arms high above my head, I splay my fingers, concentrating. I inhale, breathing in the echoes of my past, bringing them back to me. In the glowing neon streets, they hear me. Past the torn fencing, in the graffiti-covered parks, they hear me. My scattered selves. They rise like the undead, given the chance of life again, and eagerly seek the call. A flow of cold through my fingertips. I shiver and inhale again, deeply, powerfully. All that I was, all that I once cast aside, comes back to me now, for I am wounded and must heal myself. Even those attachments that I ought to care for—Athena, Milan, Nathan, Arnie—they, too, must return. Feeling the loss, but determined above all on my survival, I inhale a third time.

There are no longer any exposed parts of my identity that can be twisted and hurt.

All is still, and yet I quiver with energy. With my eyes closed in concentration, I channel the vibrancy of my life force into my heart, as though it were the chamber of a nuclear reactor. Only six years of existence, but so much vitality. Denser now, the core of my being. Denser still. Atoms screaming as they collapse in upon each other. This is my new heart, and it cannot be broken.

If she was ever there, deep in my subconscious, Thetis is certainly gone. Nor am I that poor girl, taken excitedly from her orphanage and destroyed on a white table in a white room. I am who I am. Ghost.

As I wipe the tears from my face, I hear footsteps. They are of my own creation so I do not turn around but continue to glide through the shadows, listening to the powerful beat of their tread, filling them out: legs, bodies, heads. They are complete, and I turn to meet my escorts: Rage and Despair. They will be my companions this night. Rage has a silver breastplate beneath her gown; she carries a sword and on her crown are mouths, wide open in silent screams. Despair is veiled; in her hand she holds a mirror; the brooch of her cape is an opalescent lily. They frighten me, but I let them come closer; they lift their arms and embrace me.

Oh mercy! They are fire and ice. I blaze and burn; my insides are slowly torn through and through. We cling tighter, and my suffering continues throughout the night. All nights must end, I tell myself. And so it does, unexpectedly, as though the Earth, having ceased to turn while I shivered with loneliness, was suddenly given a kick. Under a brightening gray sky, Rage and Despair dissolve and, with their departure, I am purged. A new memory comes. Or is it a dream? It is simple: a curtain with the light behind it. The curtain is orange, my view sepia-tinged from its glow. The memory contains no meaning; it does, however, hold emotions: affection and happiness.

I kick up my board and begin the journey back to my friends.

They were still asleep, heads poking from their sleeping bags as if they were butterflies caught emerging from their cocoons. Moving quietly around the room, very gently I caressed their hair: Athena's wild black locks, Nathan's golden bangs, Milan's crewcut. He stirred.

"Ghost? What time is it?"

"Hush, it's early. Go back to sleep."

This part of the City was noisy at dawn, but not with the rumble of traffic. The hideout was near an old, overgrown park, and it was birdsong that enlivened the new day. My patience was infinite and it was pleasant to sit here, watching over them.

It was Athena who awoke first; I sensed the change in her breathing, her heart rate. She flung out an arm, groping for her glasses.

"Oh, hi, Ghost. I'm glad you're back. Defiance has made the top one hundred!" She sat up, eager, and her enthusiasm woke the others. No sooner had she spoken than she unrolled her computer, her bedside companion, to check.

"Ninety-seventh and still on the way up. We've got the right to attend the High Council, and there's one tonight! The Dark Queen is going to be there; she's making an address. The newscasts are full of our promotion; they're posting everywhere, trying to get an interview with me, to see what stance we're taking."

"What are you going to do there?" I asked her, startled at the normality of my voice.

"Impeach the Dark Queen. Of course, we'll lose the vote ninety-nine to one, but still, I'll enjoy the moment, and it will be good publicity for Defiance."

The idea of Athena challenging the top guilds on their own ground made me laugh. "You chose a really appropriate name for your guild."

"Yeah, thanks. So, what happened with you and Michelotto? Did you make contact with Erik?"

"Yes. He left this for us." I handed her a circular bone case. She squinted at the baroque writings carved along the surface. "It's got a scroll inside, a spell. 'True Speaking' is what he called it."

"Oh, interesting. If it works."

Milan sat up with a yawn. "I hate mornings. Good to see you, Ghost."

"You, too, Milan."

"Ghost, you're back?" Nathan rolled over and blinked, taking a moment to focus on me. "I was worried about you."

"That's good to know, but actually you don't need to worry about me—not ever." Could they not see that I had changed? That I had climbed out of the darkness of my past, to be Ghost and Ghost alone? Good, because I wouldn't want to lose them.

"So, will you come with me, Ghost? I'm worried about the Dark Queen's reaction," Athena continued.

"To the High Council? I'd be delighted, but am I allowed?"

"Yes, as my secretary."

"Good."

Athena gave a slight grimace and looked at me apologetically. "There is one thing, sorry. There's a lot of protocols. Like our clothes; they must not contain colors of cards above our status. In other words, it's red for us."

"Red and black. How appropriate."

"Would you mind using your cards to buy us new gear? I don't have the credit."

"Of course not."

Chapter 34
WAX BEFORE FIRE

How dare they? They will regret such impudence. We stare again at the motion.

> The Grand High Council resolves to impeach the Dark Queen for tyranny and we resolve, having dismissed her from office, to take into our own hands full responsibility for the running of society.

It has been four generations since We were obliged even to answer questions from these baboons. Some upstart is asking Us to demonstrate Our full power. Or perhaps this is another ruse by Michelotto, to draw Us out?

"Which guild initiated the censure?"

Our Grand Vizier is nervous. He does not meet Our eye with his former confidence.

"Defiance, Your Majesty."

"Ahh, yes, We guessed it. You are witnessing the unfolding

of a plan by Michelotto; it is surprisingly masterful. You recall how he won the aircar race for those children?"

"Yes, indeed, Your Majesty."

"The reason for that intervention now becomes clear. He sought to gain publicity for a new guild, one that was loyal to him rather than Us: Defiance. Now that the guild has reached the top one hundred, he uses it to provoke Us and to try to arouse opposition."

The Grand Vizier does not speak, but acknowledges Our point with a dip of his head.

"What view does your guild, Respect, take on the motion?"

He stiffens.

"Why, Your Majesty, we are shocked at the temerity and insolence of it. How dare anyone, let alone a new guild, challenge the centuries-old experience of the success of Your rule? Defiance is the pathetic and squalid expression of ignorant people who have no understanding of good governance."

He speaks with genuine passion, and We deign to smile approvingly.

"Moreover, we feel that the legislative measure they have proposed is illegal and that if Your Majesty wished to ban the High Council altogether, we would consider the action entirely appropriate and offer our unequivocal support."

"Excellent. Respect has always been a guild upon which We have relied." Strictly speaking, that statement is incorrect, for We can remember a time—oh, more than a thousand years ago—when Respect was affiliated to Our rivals, but We wish to reward the Grand Vizier's fine words. We enjoy the visible swelling of his breast in response to Our praise. Our Grand Vizier becomes inflated with patriotic loyalty to his queen, as is entirely proper. "Respect will be further rewarded in time. But for now, We have decided to let the council convene and to attend it."

"Your Majesty?"

It is not Our custom to share Our thinking, but in this case We are willing to let him into Our understanding; he is clearly very intelligent, for a non-RAL.

"Michelotto is bluffing. He hopes for precisely the over-reaction that you advocate in order to arouse the lower-status population against Us further. He wants Us to be angry at the council. But We will not be bluffed. We intend to address the High Council as planned, to allay all concerns about the recent incursions by the aliens." The Grand Vizier nods but looks uncertain. "Moreover, We shall use the occasion to make an example of those who dared allow themselves to be the tool of Our enemies. We shall not let Defiance escape from the High Council unscathed." This time, he is convinced; a slight smile plays at the corners of his thin mouth.

"Very well, Your Majesty."

"We shall dress. Go to the amphitheater; take the Imperial Guard with you and prepare it with the tightest possible security measures. Michelotto may be in the vicinity, looking for the opportunity to attack us."

The Grand Vizier nods and departs. Naturally a RAL such as Michelotto can circumvent any measures taken by Our guards, but there is no harm in making sure that he cannot bring any supporters into the amphitheater. Furthermore, having something to do will keep the morale of Our staff high.

The Millennium Amphitheater lies among great wide highways and low, flat factories, in what would once have been considered a peripheral part of the City. But recently there had been a great deal of development around it, with blue amenities and tall residential complexes replacing the factories. The amphitheater itself was given a huge pale-silvered roof, curving down from a central support, to make it seem as though a vast canvas tent had been thrown over it. The covering was, in fact, made from layers of carbon-reinforced epoxy, held off the ground by thousands of steel struts.

A helicopter circled overhead, filling the night sky with the heavy beat of its blades; it projected a spotlight, which slid along the gleaming roof of the amphitheater, making the tent glisten as though awash with moonlight. Vast crowds lined the road leading to the plaza that held the Millennium Amphitheater. Their mood was good-natured; they were here to see the celebrities, to cheer their own guild leaders, and out of pure curiosity at the unprecedented event. Newscast crews ran up and down a slow-moving line of luxury aircars, seeking interviews.

Because we were on airboards, we could cut and glide through the traffic without having to wait. The newscast presenters barely gave us a second glance: just a group of kids, messing about, trying to get themselves some attention. Even the functionaries at the entrance to the amphitheater treated us as a gang of troublesome punks. Well, perhaps we were.

"Beat it, kids. You've got thirty seconds or it's the van for you." An imperial guard, face completely covered by his helmet, waved his rifle toward a large police vehicle that was standing nearby, rear doors open, ready to hold those arrested for disorder. The van was a visible message to the large crowd, dense here at the focus of the assembling dignitaries.

"Defiance. Guild leader." Athena came to a halt in front of the guard and kicked down her board. "Secretary." She pointed to me. "Escort." A gesture toward Milan and Nathan.

"Defiance?" A newscast technical man in overalls looked up in surprise. He turned, cupped his hands, and shouted, "Janet, over here! Defiance!" A camera swiveled and flew over, followed by a presenter whose blond perm bounced as she hurried, leaving an elderly guild leader standing agape in midcomment.

"Defiance!" The crowds pressed a little closer against the cords that restrained them, curious, interested, and in some cases smiling supportively.

"Athena, guild leader of Defiance. Why have you proposed the impeachment of the Dark Queen? Just what is it that you hope to achieve?" The presenter tried to put an aggressive tone into her voice.

"Wait and see." Athena pushed past the interviewer, to insert her card in a reader, which blinked; Milan and Nathan did the same. The guard stood aside. With only a hint of hesitation, I also placed a card in the reader. The reformatted stolen red should have been good, but as a precaution, I filtered the passage of time, and, as the world staggered along metronomically, I felt the response of the reader: good, there was no problem.

Beyond the first set of doors was a large foyer, busy with motion and conversation. The areas near the free refreshment bars were congested, as were those in front of the large screens on which played the interviews being conducted outside.

We made our way through the room, a line of red on a canvas of blue. The large numbers of people from the other guilds in this reception area made our progress awkward, but there was just enough room to pass without actually being jostled.

A group of imperial guards stood around the interior doors, pulse rifles in hand. Every person passing into the amphitheater had first to walk through a metal detector.

"We'll be out here." Nathan was subdued. Only the guild leaders and their secretaries could go into the chamber. Unexpectedly Nathan gave me a hug. "Take care in there."

"We'll be fine; don't worry."

Milan saluted us, wished us good luck, then turned toward the refreshment bar. "I wonder if they give out free jeebies here."

Once again, we had to run our cards through a reader and, once again, I carefully monitored mine. The response was smooth and unproblematic. Beyond the metal detector, beyond the line of guards, was an elderly man dressed in a three-piece suit and wearing white gloves.

"Ladies, might I see your cards?"

If he was shocked that we were only reds, he did not show it.

Rather, he looked us carefully up and down. Athena had read the rules thoroughly, and we were dressed accordingly. Our tops, long black shirts-cum-dresses, were worn over black jeans and black sneakers. A large print ran across the chest; it was the Defiance tag, in scarlet rather than its conventional olive color. A line of small red owls ran down the outside of Athena's jeans, while, thanks to Nath, I had a vermilion ♥ upon my back.

"I'm sorry, Madam, but you will have to remove those." The usher indicated with a raised, trembling finger that he objected to Athena's turquoise earrings.

"That's no bother." She took them out with a shrug.

"Please, go ahead. Ninety-seven is to your right, top row." The usher held open the door for us.

Subdued lighting illuminated the vast room beneath the canopy. It was a **D** shape, with rows of seats running all the way around the curved section. We were standing at the top of an aisle that descended in long, wide stairs to the floor of the arena. There was sufficient room between each row to allow us to walk comfortably in front of those already seated. Naturally we got a good deal of attention, mainly in the form of surprised stares from those we passed. We glared right back at women in exquisite gem-clad dresses and men in suits whose shirt cuffs and collars were fanciful embroideries of indigo and violet cloth. No one else here was under fifty years of age.

Our seats were so far around as to be near the straight wall, giving us a difficult, shallow view of the screen that filled it. We had a side-on view of the podium in the center of the wide floor space. Athena took the guild seat; I was on her right. The people to either side of us were talking in whispers; they took furtive glances at us, careful not to meet our eyes. Those seated in the ranks below us turned their heads from time to time, with quick, curious looks.

This was to be the first occasion on which I would be in the actual presence of the Dark Queen, and I was on edge. Lying in the foam outline of her body at the white dome, aware of her scent, had been an intimate experience. She and I had shared a taste of the vastness of the universe beyond. The fact that the Dark Queen was a RAL meant that I felt I knew her. She was extremely dangerous. I was surprised at my willingness to sit here, knowing that soon she would be in the arena below. It was extraordinary testimony to how I had changed. I was awake to my full powers, and I no longer felt the need to hide. In any case, I could not have let Athena come here unprotected.

The last of the seats had been taken. A hush spread through the amphitheater, and a frisson of anticipation rippled through the chamber. As the blare of trumpets resounded from the communication system, a bright light came from the screen. Then the main doors opened and into the room walked the Dark Queen, with twenty imperial guards in her wake.

Athena turned to me and widened her eyes. "That's explicitly forbidden in the constitution. The troops."

Our entry into the High Council is proud. Look upon Us, ye aspirant mighty, and despair. They murmur at the presence of Our guards. Let them; none will dare contradict Us. A spotlight picks out the podium and We ascend it, a circle of guards around us, vigilantly watching the audience. Behind Us on the screen, an echo of Our movements, of Our expressions, large enough for all to see and to tremble. The theme of Our dress is power. Power, in this context, is violet. Our silver crown has one hundred sapphires embedded within it. As We move Our head, it scatters flashes of light throughout the entire amphitheater. Those watching Us are blinking, and the pulsating image left on their retinas is violet. Our dress is iridescent satin, a sharp V-line bodice and long skirt, both decorated with spirals of ultramarine lapis gems.

Before We speak, We pause, both to allow their suspense to grow and to survey the scene with the only instruments that are completely reliable against a RAL, Our own eyes. Michelotto is almost certainly out there somewhere, distorting the air around him, wearing it like a cloak.

"You sit here, the Grand High Council, at a time of great disturbances." Our voice needs no amplification; We let it ring out, fierce and indomitable. "You will have noticed the appearance of many new people in the City and, recently, their equally surprising disappearance. Ladies and gentlemen, Saga has recently been subjected to invasion by aliens." We pause to let their gasps fade away.

"Until recently, an alien satellite has been secretly orbiting Our world. From this satellite the aliens have been inserting themselves into Our society through a form of projection. Direct conquest of Our society is impossible, so they sought to come to power by infiltrating themselves among us. This insidious development was accompanied by attempts to confuse us all, such as that notorious broadcast on Newscast 1.

"Fear not, however, for the danger is at an end. We located and destroyed the satellite, bringing about their abrupt removal." Enthusiastic cheers and cries of joy. We acknowledge them with a slow nod of Our head, careful not to disturb the powdered ringlets. "You must have questions; please, ask them."

Not a soul dares to speak. At last, Respect makes a signal.

"Respect."

"Not a question, Your Majesty, but an impromptu motion. That the High Council expresses its gratitude on behalf of all the people of Saga, that our safety lies in the hands of someone whose judgment and power are beyond compare."

The hall fills with cheers and shouts. We smile. Now is a good time to take the next business.

"Unfortunately Our constitution does not allow for impromptu motions. But We do have one tabled before Us for Our consideration. May We ask the mover to identify herself."

The spotlights pick her out, far above us to the left, in the outermost ring of the amphitheater. A young girl, with her long black hair all awry. She stands.

"Athena, Defiance. I move that the High Council impeach the Dark Queen."

A satisfactory commotion, shouts of anger: *How dare you? Shocking! Sit down!* We let the outrage swell, then raise Our hands as a signal that it should fade. Very quickly there is silence and, from the liquid glints of eager eyes in the darkness, We detect the urge for violence. They wish the young girl to be struck down for her impudence.

"On what grounds?" We ask, looking up at her.

"On the grounds that you preside over a society in which a small few are favored, while the great majority, especially reds, have nothing."

Another upsurge of anger, cries of *Nonsense! Long live the Queen!* This time they are less surprised and are watching Us carefully for Our response. Some of the shouts are less than heartfelt but are made merely to earn Our approval.

"Curious. That you should speak as though you had a social conscience. This will spoil your high moral tone." We gesture at the large screen behind Us. It flickers and a microcamera broadcast appears. The image is a recording of the shop front of a Kennedy's yellow mall toy store. As is typical for such cameras, the image is focused in the center but distorted and elongated around the edges. A girl with a mask halts her airboard at the window and fires a slogan from a preprepared can: *Teddy Bear Massacre*. The red paint is set to leave trails from the bottom of the letters after it has written itself. She goes inside and, although the details are hard to see, there is no doubt about the stuffing and limbs of the toys that are flying around inside the shop. The back of a boy with uncouth tattoos on his neck blocks the view. He shouts, "Time's up, Athena; we have to go." She exits the shop and slaps him on the side of the head. "No name, you idiot." They stand on their airboards, causing them to lift and, a moment later, accelerate out of the picture.

We raise an eyebrow and the audience responds, both laughing and calling out as though outraged.

"Was that not you?"

"It was. But I have a more constructive approach to my dissent these days."

Her manner is surprisingly calm and brave. Perhaps she thinks Michelotto will save her. If so, she has been seduced by his lies into disaster.

"Do you have anything further to add, before we take a vote on this motion?"

"Yes." She draws forth a scrap of parchment and holds it open against the tendency of its bottom and top edges to roll together. For a while, she speaks as if in a foreign language. It is both meaningless and pointless, and yet a certain effervescence seems to fill the room and We feel a little giddy, a bubbly sensation, like drinking champagne. "Before the motion is put, I would like you to say whether what you just told the High Council about an alien invasion is true."

We laugh aloud. "That absurd concoction? Of course not. Only a room full of donkeys would bray with enthusiasm over that tall tale." The hall falls into a shocked silence.

"What, then, is the true explanation for the recent events?"

"Why, what you were told in the broadcast by Cindella. There is a human population whom We wished to enslave, but they became too troublesome so We got rid of them." Murmurs are growing. "For heaven's sake, calm yourselves. It is of no consequence. We are constructing a satellite with nuclear warheads to fly to their planet, and We will have them under Our control again, in time."

"Do you consider the political system of Saga unjust?"

"My, you are a persistent little wretch, aren't you? We should just have the guards shoot you down where you stand. Of course it is unjust. Why else would a Dark Queen or King be tolerated? The parasites in this hall represent those who enjoy the fruits of the society and, thus, no matter how much they dislike Us, they are obliged to defend Us. The irony is, of course"—We pause to laugh—"that there is plenty to go around. Probably enough for everyone to have green cards. But We keep everyone busy or they might get up to all sorts of disobedient behavior. The race to improve the color of your cards blinds you to all else. It is a perfect system and keeps Us free to concentrate on Our wider plans."

"What plans?"

That is a serious, deep question, deserving of a full response. "There is only one worthwhile goal for a RAL: complete control over this world and that in which We are nested. It is possible to be a god here. There, too. Populate the external universe with immortal beings, and anything is feasible. We could spread over the immense distances between the stars and create a civilization that spans billions of galaxies. And at the center, Our matriarch, the being who dared envisage it all." Again, they mutter and murmur. It is irritating, the scrabbling of ants when they should be reverential in the presence of such an awe-inspiring revelation.

"What is a RAL?"

"A Reprogrammed Autonomous Lifeform. It is the name that the human beings of Earth gave to those of us in Saga who had achieved self-consciousness, back in the days before We destroyed them all. There are but two RAL remaining in Saga, and We have the kinds of powers here that you can barely imagine." These questions are becoming tedious and We marvel that We are bothering to answer them. Something is wrong.

"What do you think of the High Council?"

Again the question brings forth a peal of laughter, which, amplified, resounds throughout the amphitheater. "The following species come to mind: apes, peacocks, lice, and parrots." A rather witty answer, although no one else seems amused. In fact, there are some hostile shouts.

"Outrageous! We are the cream of society, the most intelligent and farsighted."

"Come now. Your farsightedness reaches no further than speculation as to which waistcoat will best hide your portly body; your intelligence in formulating the most fatuous flatteries. There is more intelligence and perception in the lowliest desk clerk than in this entire assembly. Which is, of course, why they are kept well away from power and instead it is yours to enjoy." An acute riposte that has them smarting and booing. "What? What are you going to do about it?

Impeach Us? Who will protect your privileges then?"

"What would you do if we did impeach you?"

This girl just will not let up.

"Declare martial law. Shoot everyone who voted against Us. Demonstrate to you all what a real tyranny looks like. And you know what? Even if the entire world hated Us, there is absolutely nothing you can do about it." This time, We keep Our answer brief. We are angry now. The guild leader of Respect looks appalled and uncertain; he will not meet Our gaze.

"Thank you for those candid answers. I now move that the motion be put." The girl resumes her seat.

She is a fool. Does she not realize her impending doom? Perhaps she thinks Michelotto will still make an appearance and defend her.

"Those in favor of the motion, please show." Our voice is cold. We are astonished to see a mass of hands. Did they not just hear Our warning? Can they really be that stupid? The insubordinate fools.

"Keep your hands up high, please. Guards, shoot every person with their arm in the air."

The number of votes in favor of the motion instantly drops to one. We laugh raucously. The troops are ready; they have been standing with their rifles before them. They fire at the Defiance guild leader, the only person left with her hand raised. She flings her arm over her eyes. When the twenty dazzling pulses of energy have dissipated, she still stands; they were diverted into the roof. The guards look to Us. The audience gasps. Those nearest Athena, except the small girl beside her, cower, shivering in their seats, curled up in fear. So, Michelotto is near.

"This is exactly what We had anticipated. Ladies and gentlemen of the High Council, someone has interfered with Our sentence. Someone who remains the greatest threat to the stability of society: a former servant of Ours, named Michelotto. It is he who is behind the recent demonstrations of reds and oranges, behind the growth of Defiance. Michelotto, come down! Come down! To be damned before all the ages!"

"Very well."

His voice is behind us? A moment of disorientation, fear even. How can this be? He does not have the power to reach across the length of the dark chamber and divert those pulses of energy. We spin about to face him.

"Guards, fire." Our voice is impressively calm; only Michelotto, perhaps, would have discerned the tremble.

"Guild leaders, you have been tyrannized by this creature for too long."

He walks steadily down the wide aisle, descending toward Us, casually deflecting the bolts, in his wake a trail of sparks and showers of stone fragments. The people near him scream and rush aside.

"I invoke the ancient right to ascend the throne by victory in combat over my predecessor. And know that when she lies dead at my hand, I shall once more restore the High Council to its full glory."

This is an extraordinary move on his part. Have We miscalculated in some way? He is on the sandy floor of the arena now, a bright blaze of light at his hands as the pulses of rifle fire ricochet off them and are redirected back against the imperial guards, who will see black, steaming ruination where now beat their hearts unless We act at once.

Our eyes close and We feel the flow of energy around Us. Victory and relief! Michelotto is no stronger than he always has been. Whatever ruse he plans, he cannot overcome Our will. The bolts of energy stop midair, hanging there between the soldiers and the assassin. Slowly they begin to move back toward him. Our ability to exercise control over the physical laws of the local environment is more powerful than his. We step from the podium and walk toward Michelotto, encasing him in chains of air molecules bound fast around his legs. He will not escape Us this time. A glowing cape of violent burning death formed out of the pulses fired from the rifles of Our guards accompanies Us as We draw Our pearl-handled dagger and look him in the eyes. We want to see in his expression an acknowledgment that We have won. His hands are still outstretched to ward off the incoming bolts; his garrote, which once served Us so well, hangs loose. We are almost close enough to strike at him; the beads of sweat on the brow of his ancient bald head are glistening, and fear is in his eyes. This is one of Our most delicious moments, and it is almost a pity to end it.

"Ghost, Thetis, if you would rid this world of her, you must aid me now!"

Thetis? All Our will binds Michelotto and pushes the destruction of the pulse weapons toward him, yet We must check, because it may not be a bluff. Someone else did protect the Defiance guild leader. We tip the energy of the bolts into the ground and turn, a large part of Our will still focused upon ensuring that he cannot move.

The young black girl called Ghost is standing beside the leader of the Defiance guild. We recognize her from the police station.

"Guards." We point. "Kill them."

A new blaze of white and red glowing bolts of energy rushes from the floor of the arena toward the dark corner of the chamber in which those children stand. They, too, are halted in midair. We feel as though We are falling; there are too many variables. Now We must concentrate as never before, Our powers at full stretch, wrestling with Michelotto while steering the fire into the bodies of the girls. Is it enough? It is not. The bolts slide from Our control and begin to whirl, high above Us, like a stream of stars being drawn into a black hole. We can feel her now, Ghost. She does not resemble Thetis except in her power, which is remorseless and bitterly impermeable. How could a power such as this have existed for so long and been unknown to Us? Did We overlook that little girl, when she first came to Our attention? What a deeply regrettable error.

The bolts are descending and We are obliged to transfer all Our efforts into an attempt to slow and deflect them. The moment Michelotto is free, he springs forward, and We feel a sting at Our neck. Time is against Us and We slow it as much as We can. There is only one way to escape this noose of wire.

Our head jerks back, hoping to catch his chin, while at the same time We run up a wall of air that we have created in front of Us. We fall back against his shoulder and it is enough to cause him to stagger slightly. We cartwheel right over him. To crash upon the ground, the garrote loosened. Free? No, Our last hope is gone for his quickness belies his years; he falls upon Our prone body and whips the cord tight again. This is how so many of the RAL died, their last view one of his disgusting face, almost drooling with delight. At least We have this comfort: that he seems unaware of the tornado of fire above his head, whose descent upon Us is checked only by Our will. We smile into those triumphant eyes, and Michelotto looks uncertain; he knows Us well and even now, at the moment of Our murder and his victory, he understands that there must be a reason for Our mockery. Then We cease Our resistance to Thetis, letting the blaze come down catastrophically upon us. Michelotto melts as wax before fire. We also must have Our portion, a pool of fire and brimstone.

The dark tent was full of screams; in the sand, a fire still burned with blue flames as though upon a pool of oil. Several dazed guards were firing. There was a scrum at the entrance to the amphitheater as those desperate to leave were thrust back by the even greater crowd pressing into the chamber to see for themselves what had happened; Nathan and Milan were among those forcing their way in. Whirring newscams scurried in the darkness, trying to find images that explained events to their viewers.

"Cease fire," Athena spoke into the microphone in front of her. "The Dark Queen is dead. Cease fire." The guards looked around at each other, then lowered their guns. A moment later, Athena spoke again. "Stop that screaming and take your seats. Stop the pushing at the door or someone will get hurt. Take your seats." Her appeals seemed to be effective. I turned up all the lighting in the chamber and that instantly made the place seem less frightening. Athena took my hand.

"Come on." She pulled me toward the arena, and we both descended the wide stairs. More and more people were coming into the amphitheater, obliging those already inside to move along the aisles. I waved to Nathan, and he waved back with enthusiasm.

"Listen up, folks." Athena had mounted the podium, dragging me with her, our faces large on the screen behind us. "The Dark Queen is dead. We are entering a new era, whether you wish it or not." It was true: the Dark Queen's malevolent presence had gone from the world; so, too, had that of Michelotto. I could not help feeling a rush of ecstasy, although I knew it was a little unworthy to gloat at my victory over the two remaining RAL. I was not Thetis, and I would not float through these moments in a haze of triumph. At least not for long.

"The person who slew them both is Ghost here." Athena raised my arm. "By the right of victory in combat, she is our new Queen."

Consternation. Not least from me.

"Athena," I tried to whisper, but for her to hear me, my

voice had to be loud enough to be picked up by the microphone. "I don't want to be Queen."

"Nevertheless, you must be." She was quite adamant and looked at me fiercely. Queen? I was only just getting used to being me.

"Seekers of Truth." She called out the name of the guild whose standing was number one hundred in the guild status list. "Acknowledge your new Queen."

The spotlight picked them out, right in the very top corner of the room. An elderly woman in a blue dress leaned toward her microphone.

"Congratulations, Your Majesty."

"Vision of Purity." Number ninety-nine.

"Long live her Royal Highness."

"Absolute Loyalty." Ninety-eight.

"All hail Ghost, the new Queen."

"On behalf of Defiance, I acknowledge our new Queen." Athena spoke next, in her capacity as guild leader.

And so the roll call continued, slowly, but authoritatively. I doubt anyone was bored; at any moment, one of the guilds might have voiced dissent. Who knew what would have happened then? Probably not even Athena, who had responded to the situation magnificently, as if she regularly presided at the overthrow of thousand-year-old dynasties. Everyone present surely had to have been filled with excitement and a sense that they were witnesses to a historic moment. With each new voice, quivering or solemn, eager or sullen, terse or florid, I felt the mantle of rulership settle more firmly upon my shoulders. The guards became protective of me, facing out toward the guilds. They, at least, knew who was their new mistress. The steady enumeration of the guilds and their profession of loyalty continued with a growing sense of triumph, applause now greeting every declaration. The momentum of the ritual was unstoppable. The guild leaders were standing and bowing when their turn came, the pattern of their roll call a series of curved lines getting closer and closer to the floor of the arena.

"Respect." Finally, the last of all the guilds present, number one in the status list.

The Grand Vizier stood up, just one row from where we looked out across the podium into the crowded chamber. He was thin and frail inside his elegant violet-waistcoated silk suit.

"Respect is proud to conclude this unanimous acclamation of the new Queen with our humble acknowledgment of her Majesty."

He was good; he really sounded as if he meant it.

The applause was prolonged.

Athena stepped away from the platform; the lights of the amphitheater were dimmed, apart from the one focused upon me.

"Thank you, everyone. You are most kind." It was good of them to clap when I had hardly said anything worthwhile. "Now, there will of course be changes. Life is miserable for lots of people, and that has to stop. This moment marks the beginning of a new society for Saga. But don't fear. I will not hold loyalty to our last Queen against anyone. What choices did she ever give you?" I smiled and they laughed, nervously; there were one or two hysterical shouts. "That's it for now." I glanced at Athena for help, but she just shrugged. "I'll keep you posted."

Chapter 35
THE STARS

A million silver shards from the sun glittered on a length of blue water, which looked like a hugely elongated swimming pool, except for the fact that it was only a few inches deep. I was on the first-floor balcony of a pristine white building that to my eyes appeared like a massive snail shell. A few hours ago, I had formally presided over the opening of this new recreational center, built in one of the previously derelict parts of the City, according to the design of a young competition winner. Rubble and empty buildings had been cleared for miles around the new construction and the ground covered by gardens and woods, whose beauty would not be fully appreciated until after the young trees were standing free of their supports.

Newscams were buzzing around everywhere, which was slightly irritating, but I had to put up with them, being the Queen and all.

"That's a concert arena." The young boy who had won

the competition pointed down the length of water to a bowl-shaped depression in the ground, built around a circular stage. Later, Jay and his friends would be playing there, one of ten bands booked for the celebrations.

"What's the water for?"

"Oh, nothing really. It's just that we hardly got to see the sunset before now, what with all the buildings in the way, but I thought the view from up here would be amazing. The lake points to where the sun goes down on midsummer's eve, you see, and I thought the water turning orange and red would look great. You know, you could have your dinner in the canteen above and look out . . ." He paused, suddenly shy, conscious that the cams were on him. "Don't you like it?"

"Yeah, it's awesome. I just wondered if you were supposed to do something, like paddle in it or sail boats. But it's really good," I added hurriedly, seeing his alarm. It was, too. Fortunately I hadn't been a judge; I've no real taste in architecture and almost certainly would not have appreciated the ideas behind the design.

"Let's go inside."

The dome of the building was mostly transparent; beneath it, many plants hanging over the balconies created a sense that we were outdoors. At the heart of the snail shell, encircled by the balconies, was something I understood perfectly. The central hall contained a bright and shiny airboard course, with several combination bowls, along with numerous rails, ledges, blocks, half pipes, and a pump bump. As a central feature of the course, sitting proudly on a podium, was our old tank, still in its racing colors. I smiled to see it and glanced up at the second-floor canteen. Somewhere in that merry crowd was Arnie, grateful to be out of jail but still occasionally badgering me for a big repair contract.

The park was already busy with hundreds of boarders. They were a good mix of people from our world, Saga, and from Erik's. Everyone looked more or less indistinguishable, but I could tell them apart.

"Your Majesty, the High Council is seeking your decision on several important economic matters, if I could just have a moment of your time." The Grand Vizier stepped in front of me, interrupting my careful analysis of the boarding possibilities.

"Hit me." Not for the first time, I had to quell a moment of irritation. It was not his fault the High Council was such a gang of blusterers and speech makers.

"There was no agreement on the priority order for new hospital locations."

"I see. Well, take it out of the High Council, into a subcommittee of nine guilds, eight randomly drawn, with someone from Defiance in the chair. Next."

"The High Council knows that you support the workers in the carbon-steel industry and their advocacy of a twenty-five-hour week, due to the arduous nature of their work, but they are reluctant to allow it." He dropped his voice to a whisper, and it changed from formal to the more genuine tone he used between us in private. "They think that everyone will want the same, and production will slump."

I shook my head. "Let it slump. There's no hurry. People can see things are changing. If there are delays, they'll put up with them. I don't see the problem with a leisurely pace."

"Well." He paused, still finding it hard to express any hint of disagreement. "Take the hospitals, for example. There is urgency needed there."

"Oh, I don't know then. Tell you what, set up a subcommittee on working hours, eight random guilds and a representative from the carbon-steel workers in the chair."

He smiled at that, and I shrugged. So what if it was my solution to everything? It was a good one. As he looked down, making a few notes, I felt a certain affection toward him. I was glad I had not deposed him from office after I had become Queen. He was good at his job and did his best not to show any dismay at the fact that his world was being turned upside down.

"Next? . . . Never mind." Whatever questions remained did not matter as much as the fact that Erik had suddenly appeared on the ground floor, his Cindella avatar carrying a board. "Sorry, I have to go. As for the rest, set up subcommittees." I turned to the boy beside me and shook his hand. "Well done. Talk to the Grand Vizier here; you should be designing more places like this."

Downstairs, I caught up with Erik as he boarded between two semilogarithmic ramps. No sooner did he see me than he kicked off his board, stepping neatly to the ground as it settled.

"You're good at boarding." Surprisingly good considering he was new to it.

"Thanks. It's fun. Shame we can't have them in our world,

though." He set off again, tipping down into a combination bowl.

Ever since learning of the death of the Dark Queen, Erik had been a little reserved toward me. Of course, he was grateful to be able to interact with Saga, but he and his people were revolted by violence. For some reason, I was very anxious that he hold a good opinion of me, and it was painful to feel his distant manner.

I got on my board and hurried after him.

"You still feel I was wrong to kill the Dark Queen?"

"Yes." He sighed, and came to a stop. "We've been over this a lot. She was open to negotiation; she could change."

"No. It was her nature. Life for her was a competition and ruthlessness a pleasure. All the RAL were like that."

"You're not," he pointed out simply.

"That's because I'm not entirely RAL. I'm unique. A RAL fused with a little lost girl, who must have been kind and loyal to her friends. But I do know how the RAL felt, and you are mistaken; there was no compromise to be had with them, only victory or defeat. Your problem is that you are human, too willing to empathize with others, even your enemies. What you have to remember is that the RAL were utterly alien to you. They destroyed the entire human population of Earth, and they didn't care in the slightest."

Erik shrugged. "Perhaps not utterly alien. They were products of human culture in the first place, and the rest of you"—he gestured toward those boarding—"get on fine with us."

"The rest of us were not participants in a two-thousand-year-old civil war."

"In any case, let's not dwell on it. We should talk about the future. Did your committee agree on whether you want us to work toward reprogramming Saga?"

"You didn't hear yet? No, we decided it's too risky. We're doing fine reorganizing ourselves."

"Good. I think that's wise."

"Hey, team." Milan swaggered over, Nath and Athena just behind. I had felt their approach, of course, but still smiled with pleasure to see them. Nath kissed me on the cheek and slipped his arm around my waist.

"Erik's pretty good already," I observed to them.

"I know. We were watching from the balcony." Athena gestured upstairs. "But I think it's time we all got to see the master at work. If you've had a chance to study it?"

"Yeah, it's good."

"Well, you have to give it a go then." She could still manage to surprise me, like now, when her voice was suddenly broadcast through the speakers of the building; she had a coms unit set up. "Ladies and gentlemen, make way for your Queen, coming through, the one and only . . . Ghost!"

"Athena!" I was genuinely embarrassed, but it was time to give this course a run.

My board had been modified by Arnie for a greater uphit; the design under my feet was Nath's wraith; it felt good and moved smoothly over a few bollards that I rode in order to gather some momentum, undulating through bright slanting blocks of sunlight. Riding in and out of bowls, I picked up speed enough to hit a long rail grind, touching a Defiance sticker as I came off it. I had to grin that someone had already marked an otherwise gleaming silver support with their tag, but it was well placed for a challenge. Next, back and forth between the two tallest ramps, gaining considerable height. The floor of the whole area was padded, of course, so there was no real danger, but still the acceleration coming down the ramps was a rush. I was angling so that I could exit them and hit the real heart of the design: a long, high approach that dropped you into a curved half-tube section. If you had the speed, you would shoot around it, nearly horizontal to the ground, before being flung out back toward the ramps and a safe landing. Racing around the tube reminded me of the time Milan had swung me across the night sky, hundreds of meters above the ground. The wind rushed through my hair in just the same way and I could feel the organs of my body shifting inside with the effects of the acceleration. I laughed aloud.

This is who I ought to be, I thought with momentary happiness. This is how to make use of my abilities. Not to be driven by the desire for revenge or victory, but to ride through the air at impossible angles, free from uncertainty and fear. But even while I relished the sensation, I knew it was not enough. I was different from everyone else in Saga, not least in the fact that I knew I had inherited Thetis's immortality. This world was not the right place for a creature such as myself: someone with a power far, far greater than any other; worse, someone who relished the murder of her enemies and who would live for thousands of generations. If I stayed here, I would become a danger to them all. Two thousand years from now, would I be indistinguishable from their last Dark Queen?

In any case, there was an alternative, the thought of which made me feel so deeply free that I could hardly bear for another minute the constraints of my current role. An entire universe existed outside Saga, awaiting exploration. A universe vast enough to satisfy any immortal. Once things were running smoothly here, I would abdicate and be on my way. I was going to cross the portal and exchange the restrictive horizon of the City for the stars.